**Eleanor Webster** loves high heels and sun—which is ironic, as she lives in northern Canada, the land of snow hills and unflattering footwear. Various crafting experiences—including a nasty glue gun episode—have proved that her creative soul is best expressed through the written word. Eleanor has a Masters Degree in Education and is a school psychologist. She also holds an undergraduate degree in history, and loves to use her writing to explore her fascination with the past.

**Also by Eleanor Webster**

*No Conventional Miss*
*Married for His Convenience*

Discover more at millsandboon.co.uk.

# HER CONVENIENT HUSBAND'S RETURN

Eleanor Webster

MILLS & BOON

First published in Great Britain 2018
by Mills & Boon, an imprint of HarperCollins*Publishers*
1 London Bridge Street, London, SE1 9GF

Large Print edition 2018

© 2018 Eleanor Webster

ISBN: 978-0-263-07511-3

MIX
Paper from
responsible sources
FSC® C007454

Printed and bound in Great Britain
by CPI Group (UK) Ltd, Croydon, CR0 4YY

To all those who choose to follow their hearts and refuse to be limited by society's norms, their own fears or physical and emotional challenges.

To my husband, who encouraged me when the struggle to get published overwhelmed.

To my father-in-law, for his ongoing interest and his insistence that the villain receives suitable retribution for heinous crimes committed.

To my father, who inspires with his love of life and his continued joy and interest in the world—not to mention a daily diary spanning 78 years!

# *Prologue*

Her fingers touched the pins which impaled each fragile butterfly. She felt the cold hardness, contrasting with the spread-eagled insect wings, delicate as gossamer.

The air smelled of dust, laden with a cloying sweetness. Despite her lack of sight, Beth could feel the Duke's gaze on her. Goose pimples prickled on her neck and she shivered even though the chamber was warm from the crackling fire.

'Ren?' she called.

'Your friend is in the other room, looking at the tiger I shot. An artistic boy, it would seem?'

He stepped closer. 'So, do you like the butterflies?'

She could smell his breath, a mix of alcohol, tobacco and that odd sweetness.

'I find them sad.'

'That is because you cannot see,' the Duke said. 'If you could see, you would admire their beauty. I pin them when they are still alive. The colour of their wings stays so much brighter, I find.'

She swallowed. Her throat felt dry. Her tongue stuck to the roof of her mouth as if swollen, making words difficult to form.

'You are yourself very beautiful,' he said. 'An unusual beauty, a perfection that is so seldom seen in nature. Your face, your features have a perfect symmetry. That is why I like the butterflies.'

She withdrew her hands from the display case, shifting abruptly and instinctively away. Stumbling, she felt a sharp corner strike her thigh.

'Do be careful.' The Duke's hand touched her arm.

She felt the pressure of his fingers and the smell of his breath. She pulled her arms back, hugging them tight to her body.

'Ren!' she called again.

'The walls are very thick here. It is nice to know that one's residence is well built, don't you think?'

She felt her breath quicken as sweat dampened her palms.

'Beth?'

Relief bubbled up in a weird mix of euphoria and panic as she heard Ren's familiar step.

'That stuffed tiger is fantastic,' he said. 'I'd love to see one alive. Did you want to feel it?' He paused. She heard him step to her. 'Beth, are you sick?'

She nodded and he grasped her hand, his touch warm and familiar.

'I—would—like—to—go—home.' She forced the words out in a staccato rhythm, each syllable punctuated with a harsh gasp.

'Do return, any time you would like,' the Duke said.

She held tight to Ren's hand as they exited the room and stepped down the stairs. They said nothing as they traversed the drive and then took the shortcut through the woods and back to the familiarity of Graham Hill.

It was only as they sat in their favourite spot, leaning against the oak's stout trunk with her hands touching the damp velvet moss, that her breathing slowed.

'Don't let's go there again,' she said. 'Ever.'

'What happened?'

'Nothing.' This was true and yet she had felt more fearful than she ever had before. More fearful than the time she had fallen off the fence into the bull's paddock. Or when she had got lost in the woods. Or when her horse had got spooked.

'He looks at you strangely.'

'Yes, I feel it.'

'We won't go back,' Ren agreed. 'I thought he would have more animals. One tiger isn't much.'

'And butterflies.'

Ren stood. He could never stay still for long, unless he was painting. 'Let's forget about that creepy old place. We'll not return, not for a hundred tigers. What should we do now—fishing, or should we see if Mrs Bridges has baked?'

Beth sniffed. 'I think I can smell fresh scones.'

'Your brother would say that is a scientific impossibility,' Ren laughed.

'And yours would say we should check it out anyway.'

He took her hand and she stood. Together they scrambled across the field towards Ren's home. In the warm sunshine and with the promise of Mrs Bridges's fresh baking, Beth forgot about the Duke and his butterflies.

# Chapter One

*Ten years later*

'You should marry me.'

'What? Why?' Beth gripped the couch's worn velvet arms as though to ground herself in a world gone mad. Or perhaps she had misheard Ren's stark statement.

'It is the best solution.'

'To what exactly? That you've been suffering from unrequited love during the ten years of your absence?'

'Of course not,' Ren said, with typical bluntness.

Beth felt almost reassured. At least he had not entirely taken leave of his senses.

'If it is because of Father's death, you need not do so. Jamie and I will fare well enough.'

'Not if you marry the Duke, you won't,' Ren said.

'You heard?' Beth felt her energy sap, her spine bending. Her breath was released in a muted exhalation.

'Bad news travels fast.'

'I have not... He asked me to marry him, but it would be the very last resort. If I could think of no other option.'

'It would be a catastrophe.'

Did he think she did not know this? Even now, her stomach was a tight, hard knot of dread and too often she lay awake at night, clammy with sweat and fear.

'It would be better than debtors' prison,' she said tartly. 'Anyhow, I hope to merely sell him the land.'

'I'd take prison. Besides, he'll never buy the land. He wants the land *and* you.'

'I cannot see why Ayrebourne would want to marry a woman like me.'

She heard Ren's sharp intake of breath.

'As always you underestimate yourself,' he muttered. 'The Duke is a collector. He likes beautiful things. You are exquisitely beautiful.'

'I—' She touched her hands to her face. People had always told her that she had an ephemeral, other-worldly beauty. Indeed, she had traced and retraced her features, pressing her fingers along her jawbone and the outline of her cheeks to find some difference between her own and the faces of others.

She dropped her hands. 'How did you learn about this anyway?'

'Jamie.'

'Jamie? You have seen Jamie already?'

'Not here. In London. Gambling.' Ren spoke in a flat, even tone.

'Jamie gambling?' Her hand tightened, reflexively balling the cloth of her dress in her fist. 'I mean—he can't—he hardly even socialises.'

'I found him at a gambling house. I removed him, of course, before much harm was done.'

'He hates London. When was he even in London?'

'Last weekend.'

'He said he was going to sell two horses at Horbury Mews.'

'Apparently, he took a less-than-direct route,' Ren said.

Beth's thoughts whirled, bouncing around her mind, quick and panicked. It did not make sense.

Jamie was so…so entirely different than Father. Where Father had been glib, Jamie spoke either in monosyllables or else was mired in pedantic detail and scientific hypothesis.

'But why? Why would he do that? He knows only too well the harm gambling can do.'

'I presume he hopes his facility with numbers will enable him to be more successful than your father.'

'Except his inability with people will make him more disastrous.'

For a moment she was silent. Then she stood, rousing herself with a conscious effort, keeping her hand on the back of her chair to orientate herself. This was not Ren's problem. She had not seen him for years and he had no need to make some heroic sacrifice for her or her family.

'Thank you for telling me about Jamie. I will speak to him,' she said stiffly.

'Logic seldom wins against desperation.'

'He has no reason to be desperate.'

'He loves you and he loves this land. He'd hate to see you married to the Duke and he'd hate to sell as much as a blade of grass. He was cataloguing seeds when he was three.'

'Seven,' she corrected. 'He was cataloguing seeds when he was seven. But I will determine another solution.'

'I have presented you with another solution.'

'Marriage? To you?'

'I am not the devil incarnate, only a close relative.'

She released the chair, taking the four steps to the window, as though physical distance might serve to clear her thoughts. She could feel his presence. Even without sight, she was aware of his height, the deep timbre of his voice, the smell of hay and soap, now tinged with tobacco. There was a disorienting mix of familiarity and new strangeness. He was both the boy she had once known and this stranger who had just now bounded back into her life.

Beth wished she could touch his face. She wanted to read his features, as she would have done once without thought, an action as natural as breathing.

'You do not come here for ten years and now turn up with a—a marriage proposal. How would marriage even help? It would not enable us to pay off Father's debt. I already suggested to your brother that he buy the land, but he is as poor as we are.'

Ren laughed in a manner devoid of humour. 'In contrast to my brother, I am a veritable Croesus. And you need not fear, I know you require independence and dislike the concept of marriage. This will be a marriage in name only.'

'But why?' she asked, then flushed, turning. 'I did not mean—I mean, why marry me? Could you not just buy the land or loan us the money if you are so rich and eager to save us?'

She heard the rustle of cloth as though Ren had shrugged and could almost feel his lips curl in a derisive smile. 'It would provide you with a guardian.'

'I do not need a guardian.'

'You are not yet twenty-one.'

'I have Jamie.'

'He is not yet twenty. Besides, he is no match for Ayrebourne. Marriage to me would make any marriage to the Duke impossible.' He paused. 'You were my best friend, you know.'

Beth rubbed her fingers against the smooth finish of the painted sill, while leaning her forehead against the pane. Her eyes stung with the flood of memories: long afternoons beside the brook, winter walks with the snow crisply crunching under their feet and long tramps through whistling windy days in fall.

'Childhood friendship does not require this level of sacrifice. You and I haven't spoken in years.'

For a moment he did not respond, but when he did, something in his voice sent a nervous tingling through her body making her breath uneven.

'You know with us that doesn't matter.'

She felt it, that intangible connection, that closeness that was rooted in childhood, but it had also changed. She heard him shift. She heard his breath quicken.

She bit her lip. 'Why didn't you write or come back or visit?'

There was a pause. She heard his discomfort, the intake of his breath and the movement of his clothes.

'I couldn't.'

'It doesn't take much. You inhale and speak. You pick up a pen or...or hire a horse.'

'You'll just have to believe me.'

'And now you expect me to marry you after all these years?'

'I expect nothing. I am merely offering a preferable alternative to the Duke,' he said, his voice now hard and clipped.

She shivered. Few things frightened her, but the Duke was one of them. Marriage to him would destroy her. Even if she avoided that and he agreed to buy the land, it was an unpleasant concept and would give him even more reason to linger in the village or woods. She rubbed her arms. Goose pimples prickled the skin. She hated the thought of him owning the land on her own doorstep. Already, she felt watched. And sometimes, as she walked through the woods, she'd smell that odd sweet fragrance that seemed to emanate from him.

The Duke would use everything against her: her sex, her youth, her poverty, her sightless eyes, her wonderfully odd brother.

Ren stepped closer to her. She felt his breath on her neck, his tall presence behind her and his hand on her own. Warmth filled her, which was both comfortable and uncomfortable. The urge for distance and separation lessened so that, for an impulsive, crazy moment, she wanted only to lean against him and to feel his strength.

Ren was her friend. He had guided her over rivers and up steep hillsides.

His hand stilled the nervous movement of her fingers against the sill. 'You can trust me.'

She nodded.

'Let me honour our childhood friendship.'

'We were good friends.'

His grip tightened and she felt the warmth grow, a tingling energy snaking through her.

'The best. Don't put yourself in that man's power. Let me help,' he said in a voice now oddly soft. 'Don't marry him.'

'I don't have the option to be selective,' she muttered.

'You do now.'

# Chapter Two

Eighteen months later

Beth strode towards the stable. As always, she counted her steps, tapping the path with her cane. She lifted her face to the sky, enjoying the warmth of the sun's rays and the soft whisper of breeze. She enjoyed spring. She liked the smell of grass and earth. She liked the rustle of fresh leaves, so different from the dry, crisp wintery crack of bare branches. She liked that giddy, happy sense of renewal.

Even better, she welcomed the ease of movement which came with drier weather. Country life at Allington was dreadfully dull.

Worse than dull, it was lonely. Her beloved sister-in-law was dead. Jamie seldom conversed.

Edmund had left. Ren never came. Her maid chattered of ribbons.

For a fleeting second, she remembered childhood winters: walks with Ren, afternoons by the fire's crackling heat in a room rich with the aroma of cinnamon toast. Sometimes Edmund would read while Ren painted and Jamie pored over a botanical thesis.

Beth pushed the past away, recognising her brother's footsteps on the rutted path. She lifted her hand in greeting.

'Field's ready for planting,' Jamie said without preamble, satisfaction lacing his tones.

'You are trying new crops this year?'

'New variety of beans. They will be hardier.'

'In Edmund's fields as well as our own?'

Jamie grunted assent. 'As I doubt your husband plans to do so.'

'He's in London,' she said flatly. 'Besides, Edmund left a manager in charge.'

Edmund, or rather Lord Graham, was Ren's brother. Her husband's brother...husband. Even after eighteen months her mind stumbled over the word—it wasn't surprising since she had likely conversed more with the village blacksmith, a man of guttural grunts and limited vocabulary, than her spouse.

'I am also trying a new variety of peas,' Jamie said.

She nodded. 'By the way, do we have any surplus supplies? I went to the Duke's estate yesterday. The people are starving so I asked Arnold to take grain.'

She heard Jamie's quick intake of breath. 'You should not go there.'

'Arnold was with me. Besides, the Duke is away. He hasn't visited me since I turned down his proposal.'

'One good thing about your marriage. But he has been at his estate on occasion. I also saw him on our own grounds once. Said his hound had strayed.'

Beth felt a shiver of apprehension. Dampness prickled her palms and her lungs felt tight as if unable to properly inhale the air. She pushed the feeling away. 'The important thing is to get his people food.'

'It is that bad?'

'Yes.' Beth's fingers tightened on her cane. Her jaw clenched at the thought of yesterday's visit.

She remembered a mother's desperate effort to soothe her hungry child. She'd held his hands and felt the thin boniness of his tiny fingers pressed into her palm like twigs devoid of flesh. 'The Duke's treatment of his tenants has worsened. I worry that it is a form of punishment.'

'Punishment?'

'Yes, for avoiding marriage to him.'

'The tenants were hardly responsible and I see no evidence for such an assumption.'

Beth nodded. Jamie's world was so wonderfully black and white. 'Sometimes human nature defies science.'

She felt his confusion and could imagine his skin creasing into a pucker between his eyes.

'I'll send some root vegetables as well,' he said. 'Are you going there now?'

'No, but Arnold will later.'

'We will send what we can,' Jaime said, in his steady way.

That was Jamie all over. Steady, scientific, kind but without sentiment.

In contrast, Ren had married her in a wild, crazy, heroic gesture, disappearing after their wedding into the capital's giddy whirl of brandy and women.

She tried to ignore that quick, predictable flicker of pain and anger. Obviously, she had not expected anything close to a regular marriage, but to be so abandoned and ignored was painful to her. For some ludicrous reason, as she had stood beside him in the still air of the tiny church, she'd imagined that they might become friends again.

Instead, they had ridden back to Graham Hall in an uncomfortable silence broken only by the rattle of carriage wheels and a discussion about the weather. Within half a day, Ren's carriage had been loaded and he had disappeared as though he could no longer bear his childhood home or those associated with it.

Still, she had no reason to complain. He had paid off her father's debts, Allington was profitable and the Duke remained largely in London. Thank goodness. She still shivered when she remembered their last interview.

'I must go,' she said to Jamie, diverting her thoughts. 'I promised Edmund I would look in on a few of his tenants during his absence.'

She sighed. Mere weeks ago, Edmund had gone

to war. She wished desperately he had not done so and knew he had been driven more by grief than patriotism. His father, his wife and their unborn child... Too many losses crammed into too few years.

'A sight more than his brother will do,' Jamie said.

'His life is in London,' she said. 'We always knew that.'

The road to Graham Hill was a winding, meandering path through shaded woods and across open pasture. She had brought Arnold today, but even without her groom Beth knew her way. She could easily differentiate between sounds—the muted clip-clop of hooves on an earthy path was so different from the sharper noise of a horse's shoe against a cobbled drive.

In some ways, her father had lacked moral fibre. In others, he had been remarkable. He'd helped her to see with her hands, to learn from sounds and scents and textures.

But it was her mother who had taught her independence and, more importantly, how swiftly such independence could be lost.

Lil, short for Lilliputian due to her small stature, slowed when the drive ended. Beth leaned forward, stroking the mare's neck, warm and damp with sweat. Arnold swung off his mount to open the gate. She heard its creak as it swung forward and, more through habit than need, counted the twenty-one steps across the courtyard.

Lil stopped and Beth dismounted. She paused, leaning against the animal, her hand stretched against Lil's warm round barrel of a ribcage. She heard the horse's breath. She heard the movement of her tail, its swish, and Arnold's footsteps as he took Lil from her, the reins jangling.

Except... She frowned, discomfort snaking through her. There was a wrongness, a silence, an emptiness about the place. No one had greeted her; no groom or footman had come. She could hear nothing except the retreating tap of Lil's hooves as Arnold led her to the stable.

The unease grew. Dobson should be here opening the door, ushering her inwards, offering refreshment. Beth walked to the entrance. The door was closed. She laid her palm flat against its smooth surface, reaching upward to ring the bell.

It echoed hollowly.

Goose pimples prickled despite the spring sunshine. Pushing open the door, she stepped inside.

'Dobson?' Her voice sounded small, swallowed in the emptiness. 'Dobson?' she repeated.

This time she was rewarded by the butler's familiar step.

'Ma'am,' he said. 'I am sorry no one was there to meet you.'

'It's fine. But is anything wrong? Has something happened?'

'Her ladyship is on her way, ma'am,' he said.

Beth exhaled with relief. 'That is all right then.'

Granted, her mother-in-law was a woman of limited intelligence and considerable hysteria, but her arrival was hardly tragic. Besides, Lady Graham would not stay long; she loathed the country almost as much as Ren and spent most of her time in London.

'No, ma'am that is not it,' Dobson said, pausing as the clatter of carriage wheels sounded outside. 'Excuse me, ma'am,' he said.

After Dobson left, Beth found herself standing disoriented within the hall. She had forgotten to count her steps and reached forward tentatively, feeling for the wall or a piece of furniture which might serve to determine her location. In doing so, she dropped her cane. Stooping, she picked it up, her fingertips fumbling across the cool hard marble. Before she could rise, she heard the approach of rapid footsteps, accompanied by the swish of skirts: her mother-in-law. She recognised her perfume, lily of the valley.

'Lady Graham?' Beth straightened.

'Beth—what are you doing here?' Lady Graham said. Then with a groan, the elder woman stumbled against her in what seemed to be half-embrace and half-faint.

'Lady Graham? What is it? What has happened?'

'My son is dead.'

'Ren?' Beth's heart thundered, pounding against her ears so loudly that its beat obliterated all other sounds. Every part of her body chilled, the blood pooling in her feet like solid ice. Her stomach tightened. The taste of bile rose in her throat so that she feared she might vomit.

'No, Edmund,' Lady Graham said.

'Edmund.'

A mix of relief, sorrow and guilt washed over

her as she clutched at her mother-in-law, conscious of the woman's trembling form beneath her hands. 'I'm so sorry.'

Edmund was Ren's brother. He was a friend. He was a country gentleman. He loved the land, his people, science and innovation.

'He was a good man,' she said inadequately.

Then, above the thudding of her heart, Beth heard the approach of quick footsteps. With another sob, Lady Graham released Beth's arm and Beth heard her maid's comforting tones and the duet of their steps cross the floor and ascend the stairs.

Again disoriented, Beth stepped to the wall, but stumbled over her cane, almost falling. The wall saved her and, thankfully, she leaned against it. Her thoughts had slowed and merged into a single refrain: *not Ren, not Ren, not Ren.* Her breath came in pants as though she had been running. She felt dizzy and pushed her spine and palms against the wall as though its cool hardness might serve as an anchor.

That moment when she'd thought…when she'd thought Ren had died shuddered through her, sharper and more intense than the pain she now felt for Edmund.

And yet, Edmund had been her friend. Good God, she had spent more time in his company than that of her husband. Ren was but a name on a marriage certificate—a boy who had been her friend, a man who had married her and left—

'Beth?'

Ren's voice. Beth's knees shook and tears prickled, spilling over and tracking down her cheeks. Impulsively she stretched out her hands. For a moment she felt only emptiness and then she touched the solid, reassuring bulk of his arm. Her hand tightened. She could feel the fine wool under her fingertips. She could feel the hard strength of his muscles tensing under the cloth and recognised the smell of him: part-cologne, part-fresh hay and part his own scent.

'You're here?'

His presence seemed like a miracle, all the more precious because, for a moment, she had thought him dead.

Impulsively, she tightened her hold on him, leaning into him, placing her face on his chest, conscious of the cloth against her cheek and, beneath it, the steady, constant thumping of his heart.

Her hair smelled of soap. The years disappeared. They were chums again. He was Rendell Graham once more. He belonged. His hold tightened as he felt her strength, her comfort, her essential goodness. Strands of her hair tickled his chin. He had forgotten its vibrancy. He had forgotten its luminosity. He had forgotten how she seemed to impart her own light, so that she more closely resembled angels in a church window than flesh and blood.

And he had forgotten also how she made his senses swim, how he wanted both to protect her above all things and yet also to hold her, to press her to him, to take that which he did not deserve, breaking his word—

'Excuse me, my lord.' Dobson entered the hall, clearing his throat.

Ren stiffened, stepping back abruptly. 'Don't!' he said. 'That is my brother's name.'

'I am—um—sorry—my—Master Rendell, sir.'

Ren exhaled. It was not this man's fault that he had called him by a name he did not merit. 'Yes?'

'There are a number of matters we must discuss,' Dobson said.

'Very well, I will see you in the study shortly.'

Dobson left. Ren glanced at this slight woman... his wife. She was as beautiful as he remembered—more so since her body had rounded slightly so that she looked less waif and more woman. Her skin was flushed, but still resembled fine porcelain and she held herself with a calm grace and composure.

He'd tried to paint her once. It had not worked. He had not been able to get that skin tone, that luminosity. Of course, that was back when he still painted.

'I am sorry,' Beth said, angling her head and looking at him with eyes that couldn't see yet saw too much. 'Is there anything I can do to help you or your mother?'

'No,' Ren said, briskly. 'No. You should not be wasting your time with us. Jamie will need you. He was as much Edmund's brother as I.'

Despite the four-year age difference, Edmund and Jamie had shared a common interest in the scientific and a devotion to the land.

Worry and shock flickered across her features.

'You're right,' she said. 'I must tell him. I don't want him to find out from someone else. Except I don't even know yet what happened. Edmund could not have even reached the Continent.'

'Cholera outbreak on board the ship.'

Ren still couldn't fathom how he'd managed to survive duels, crazy horse races, boxing matches and drunken gallops while Edmund had succumbed within days of leaving home.

'He didn't even see battle?'

'No. Would it have made it better if he had? If he'd died for King and country?' Ren asked, with bitter anger.

'I don't know. It wouldn't change that he is gone.'

She was honest at least. Most women of his acquaintance seemed to glamorise such sacrifice.

'Will there be a—a funeral?' she asked.

'We do not have a body.' He spoke harshly, wanting to inflict pain although on whom he did not know.

'A service, at least? I want—I need to say goodbye. The tenants, too.'

'It is not customary for ladies to attend funerals,' he said. The need for distance became greater. He must not grow used to her company. He must not seek her advice or her comfort. He must not rely on her. Beth had never wanted marriage to anyone. She valued her independence. Moreover, she belonged here in the country. Indeed, familiarity with her environment was an integral part of her independence.

And Graham Hill was the one place he could not live.

'You know I have never been bound by custom.'

That much was true. If custom were to prevail she should be housebound, dependent on servants. Instead, she rode about her estate on that tiny horse and ran Jamie's house and even aspects of the estate with admirable efficiency.

He forced his mind to shift. He was not here to analyse the woman who was his wife in name only, but to bury his brother 'in name only.' Efficiency was essential. He must take whatever steps were needed to cut his ties with the estate. To stay here was torture. Graham Hill was everything he had loved, everything he had taken for granted as his birth right and everything which had been ripped from him.

For a moment, he let his gaze wander over the

familiar hall with the huge stone fireplace and dark beams criss-crossing the high arched ceiling. He had been back maybe five times since he had learned the truth, since he had learned that he was not really Rendell Graham, the legitimate child of Marcus Graham.

Instead, he was the bastard offspring of a mediocre portrait painter.

Abruptly, he turned back to Beth. 'I will let you and Jamie know the time for the service,' he said brusquely.

'Thank you.'

For a moment she did not move. Her mouth opened slightly. She bit her lower lip. Her hand reached up to him. She ran her fingers across his cheek as she used to do. The touch was both familiar, but infinitely different. The moment stilled.

'You do not always have to be strong and brave,' she said.

His lips twisted. He thought of his life in London, of the stupid bets and nights obliterated by alcohol.

'I'm not,' he said.

# Chapter Three

Beth sat beside the fire. It crackled, the snap of the flames tangling with the rhythmic tick of the mantel clock. She rubbed her hands with a dry chafing sound. She felt chilled, despite the spring season.

Jamie would be home soon. He would come in and talk crops and science in his single-minded manner.

And she would tell him about Edmund.

In many ways, Edmund had been his only friend; they had shared a fascination with science. Granted, Edmund had been older and more interested in mechanised invention than seeds, but there had been similarities in their minds and intellects.

And now, she must tell him about Edmund's death. Strange how someone remains alive until one is told otherwise. Edmund was still alive to Jamie and would remain alive until she told him he was not. In many ways it made her the executioner.

Beth stood, too restless to be contained within the easy chair. She paced the seven steps to the window. She thought of Ren. He and Edmund had been inseparable as children—although he had spent little enough time here since. Her heart hurt for him, but she also felt anger. Why had he turned so resolutely against Graham Hill? How had London's lure become so strong for the boy she used to know?

She remembered the four of them scrambling across the countryside. Well, Jamie and Edmund would scramble. She would often sit while Ren painted. She'd hear the movement of his brush strokes across the canvas, mixed with myriad woodland sounds; water, birds, bees, leaves... And Ren would describe everything: puffy clouds resembling sheep before shearing, streams dancing with the tinkling of harpsichords and tiny snowdrops hidden under the bushes like shy maidens.

Yet now Ren was at the big house with a mother he did not like.

Alone.

He no longer painted. He no longer liked the country. If gossip was true, his life in London was dissolute.

'Arnold said you needed to speak to me.'

She startled at Jamie's voice, wheeling from the window.

'Yes. I need to tell—'

'I know about Edmund,' he said.

'You do?' She exhaled, both relieved that she need not tell him and guilty that she had not been the one to do so.

'Lady Graham's maid told the whole staff. Should not have enlisted. Tried to talk sense into him.'

She heard the wheeze of cushioning as her brother threw himself heavily into his chair.

'He never was the same after Mirabelle died,' she said.

'Still had the land.'

Beth permitted herself a sad half-smile. For Jamie, the land, the scientific pursuit of hardy crops and livestock would always be sufficient. There was an invulnerability about him that she envied.

'So Ren is Lord Graham now,' Jamie said.

'Yes.'

He made a grumbling sound. 'I hope he intends to take his responsibilities seriously. No more capering about. He'll have to spend more time here.'

'I guess—' she said jerkily.

His words startled her. She had not thought of this and felt that quick mix of emotion too tangled to properly discern: a jumble of breathless disorientation; anticipation and apprehension.

'He may not want to,' she said.

'Must. His responsibility now,' Jamie said. 'Wonder what he knows about seeds?'

'Not much. London isn't big on seeds.' She gave a half-smile that felt more like a stifled sob.

'Guess I could teach him.'

Beth nodded. The young boy she had known would have needed no convincing. He had loved the estate from its every aspect. He'd loved the tenants, the fields, the animals.

But the man—her husband—did not.

The morning of the memorial dawned clear. Beth could feel the sun's warmth through the window pane. She was glad it was sunny. Edmund had liked the sun.

She'd visited Graham Hill the previous day, but neither Ren nor his mother had been available, so she had returned with the nebulous feeling that she ought to do something more.

That was the thing about this marriage: it had brought them no closer. There had been no return of their former friendship, no occasional visits, no notes from London, laughter or pleasant strolls.

With Mirabelle's death, she'd taken on more duties on the Graham estate but with a confused uncertainty, unsure if she was a family member helping out or a neighbour overstepping.

Now she wondered if she should go to Graham Hill prior to the service? Or merely join Ren at the church? Likely he'd prefer to ignore her or have her sit like a stranger. But the tenants would not.

Fortunately, the arrival of a curt missive from Graham Hill settled this dilemma. Jamie read the abrupt note which stated only that the Graham carriage would collect them so that she could attend the service with her husband.

'Indeed, that is only logical. It would be foolish to bring out both carriages to go to the same location,' he concluded in his blunt sensible manner as though practicality was the only issue at stake.

*Husband.* It had been so much easier to cope with a husband when he remained unseen in London. Then she had been able to think of that quick ceremony as a dream or an episode from a past life with little impact on her present. Indeed, he had felt less absent miles away than now when she knew they were within half a mile of each other, shared a common grief, but were as remote as two islands separated by an ocean.

Of course, his instant removal the day of the marriage service had hurt. She remembered listening to the fast trot of his fashionable curricle down the drive at Allington with a confused mix of pain, relief, embarrassment.

But truthfully, relief had overshadowed all other emotion. Allington had not been sold. Her father's gambling debt to the Duke had been paid. She was safe from Ayrebourne. Indeed, she'd not been in that unpleasant man's presence since she had politely declined *his* proposal, although she still felt an uneasy prickle of goose pimples when she remembered that interview.

Even now, close to two years later, the tightness returned to her stomach whenever she remembered the day. The chill cold silence of the library had felt so absolute. She'd wished that she had ordered a fire lit. She'd felt so enclosed, so isolated alone with this man.

'You have an answer for me?' he'd asked, taking her hand in his.

His fingers had been cold—not a dry, crisp cold, but clammy.

She'd said the right things, the pretty phrases of refusal. Of course, she hadn't been able to see his expression, but she'd felt his anger. His hand had tightened on her own, his fingers digging into her flesh so that for days after it had felt bruised.

'You are refusing?'

'Yes, with gratitude for—for the honour, of course.'

'And this other suitor? He will be able to pay off your father's debts. They are substantial.'

'Yes,' she'd said.

For a moment, Ayrebourne had made no reply. Then he'd leaned closer. She'd heard his movement, the rustle of his clothes and felt a slow, growing dread, as though time had been oddly slowed or elongated. With careful movements, he'd lifted his hand and touched her face with one single finger. 'A shame.'

Nauseous distaste had risen, like bile, into her throat. Twisting fear had made her tongue dry and swell, becoming bulbous as if grown too big for her mouth.

She had not been able to make a response and had remained still as though paralysed. Very slowly, his finger had traced her cheek, a slow, slithering touch. Then he'd pressed close to her ear, so that she could feel his warm moist breath and the damp touch of his lips.

'But we are still neighbours so likely I will see you from time to time. In fact, I will make sure of it.'

His lips had touched again the tip of her ear.

'I would enjoy that,' he'd said.


'Shall I be helping you with your hair this morning—ma'am—my lady?'

Beth jumped at her maid's words. 'Yes.'

'Gracious, you're white as a ghost. Are you well?' Allie entered, bringing with her the sweet smell of hot chocolate.

Beth nodded. 'Yes, I was just thinking—

unpleasant thoughts. But I am glad of the distraction.'

'And your hair?'

'Best see what you can do.'

Usually Beth paid little attention to her appearance, but today she'd make an effort. It would show respect. Besides, she didn't want to give Lady Graham reason to criticise. Lady Graham had never approved of the marriage. Who would want a blind country miss as one's son's wife—even a second son?

She startled, the movement so abrupt that Allie made a *tsk*ing, chastising noise.

'He's going to be Lord Graham,' she said.

'Yes, my lady.'

Of course, Beth had known that since she'd first heard of Edmund's death and yet it seemed as though she only now recognised its full import. It changed everything. She could not believe that she had not recognised this earlier. Ren was no longer just the family black sheep. He was Lord Graham. He had duties, social responsibilities, a seat in the House of Lords.

Most importantly, he'd need an heir.

That single thought thundered through her. She

clasped her hands so tightly together she could feel her nails sharp against the skin.

She'd known, since childhood, she would not—must not—have children.

Her thoughts circled and bounced. They would have to get an annulment. That was the only option. But was it possible? Would they qualify? Good Lord, 'qualify'? It sounded as though she was seeking entrance into an exclusive club or scientific society. Or would they have to get a divorce? And what were the rules about divorce?

When should she talk to Ren about this? His brother's funeral hardly seemed suitable. Was there a good time? A protocol for the dissolution of marriage? Would he agree?

Ally made another tut-tutting sound behind her. 'Please stay still, my lady. You are that wriggly! Worse than a dog with fleas, if I may say so. I'm thinking I'll trim your fringe, too, while I'm about it and really you don't want to be wriggly when I do that or goodness knows how we'll end up.'

'Yes,' Beth said, dully.

She made her breathing slow, as she used to do whenever she became lost or panicked. Their farce of a marriage would be annulled. But tomorrow was soon enough to worry. Today, she would show respect and support. She would bid farewell to Edmund.

After finishing Beth's hair, Allie helped Beth put on her black bombazine. The cool, stiff cloth brushed over her skin, sliding into place. It was the same dress she'd worn while mourning Edmund's wife Mirabelle. That had hurt also, but not like this. This loss of a childhood friend hurt in a gut-wrenching way.

Beth had intended to wait for the carriage in the front room, but didn't. It felt too enclosed and she found herself drawn outside. Without sight, an empty room could be a chill place, bereft of sound or movement. In the outer world, the air stirred. She could discern the comforting and familiar sounds of life, the distant jangle of cow bells or the mewling of the stable cat.

The rattle of carriage wheels caught her attention and she stepped forward as soon the noise eased, wheels and hooves silenced. The door opened and Ren got out. She knew it was him. It was in the firmness of his step. It was in his smell, that mix of scents: cologne, hay, soap. Even more striking, it was her reaction to him, a feeling which was both of comfort and discomfort.

'You were in the stable,' she said.

'And you are still eerily accurate.'

He took her hand, helping her into the carriage. It was a common enough courtesy and yet her reaction was not usual. Her breathing quickened but she felt, conversely, as though she had insufficient air.

She sank into the cushioning, so much more comfortable than that in her own more economic vehicle. He sat beside her. She could feel his body's warmth, but also the tension, as though his every nerve and muscle was as tight as the strings on the violin Mirabelle used to play.

Impulsively, she reached for his hand. She wanted to touch him as she used to do, to break through the darkness which was her world and to communicate the feelings which could not be put into words. He jolted at her touch. Disconcerted, she withdrew her hand, clasping her fingers together as though to ensure restraint.

The silence was broken as Jamie entered also, his movements slow and heavy. The cushioning creaked as he sat opposite.

The carriage door closed.

'You're here,' Jamie said.

'Your observation is also eerily accurate,' Ren said, but with that snide note to his voice he never used to have.

'Hope you're planning to spend some time here, now you're Lord Graham.'

Ren became, if possible, more rigid. She felt the stiffening of his limbs and straightened back. 'Shall we focus on my dead brother and not my itinerary?' he said.

The silence was almost physical now, a heavy weight as the carriage moved. It closed in on them, the quiet punctuated only by the rattling of wheels and the creaking of springs.

She swallowed, aware of a stinging in her eyes and a terrible sadness—for Edmund and also that his three best friends should sit so wordlessly.

'Thank you for collecting us,' she said at last when she could bear the stillness no more.

'The villagers would not want us to arrive separately,' he said.

'We would not wish to risk upsetting them.' She spoke tightly.

His words hurt. She was not certain why. She

did not need him to think of her as a wife. She knew he did not. She knew she did not want that. Yet, conversely, she needed him to think of her, to acknowledge her, to recognise that it was only right that she and Jamie and Ren bid farewell to Edmund together. They had been a band, a group, a fellowship.

'Your mother is not coming?' she asked.

'She is more bound by custom than yourself. Besides, she has been unable to rise since our arrival.'

'That was four days ago.'

'Yes.'

'She has been in bed since then?' she asked.

'Yes.'

'You have been alone in the big house? With no one to talk to?'

'Mrs Bridges loves to discuss the menus.' He spoke in crisp tight syllables, like twigs snapping.

She was cruel, that woman. Selfish. Lady Graham, not the cook.

Without conscious thought, Beth reached again for him, taking his hand within her own. She felt its size and breadth. She felt the small calluses.

This time he did not jolt away. Instead, with a soft sigh, he allowed his grip to fold into hers.

Ren wanted only to leave, to spring astride the nearest horse and ride and ride and ride until everyone and everything were but tiny pinpoints, minutiae on a distant horizon.

The carriage halted in front of the country church. The building was as familiar as his own face, its walls a patchwork of slate-grey stone criss-crossed with verdant moss. His glance was drawn to the graveyard, a place he and Edmund had tiptoed past, scaring each other with wonderful stories of disturbed ancestors, ghosts, spooks and clanking chains.

Now Edmund would join their number.

Ren looked also to the grassy enclosure with its clutter of uneven tombstones, clustered about the family mausoleum.

Edmund's family.

The church was full. The villagers had placed vases of yellow daffodils at the end of every pew. Their blossoms formed bright dabs of colour against the darkness of the polished wood.

Sunlight flickered through the stained-glass windows, splashing rainbows across the slate floor. Particles of dust danced lazily, flecks suspended and golden within the light. The atmosphere was heavy with hushed whispers, perfume, flowers and the shuffle of people trying too hard to be quiet.

Ren went to the Graham family pew where he'd sat as a child. The organ played. He could feel its vibration through the wooden seat. Beth loved that feeling. She used to say that she didn't even miss her sight when she could both hear and feel each note.

The villagers looked at him, covert glances from across the aisle. He wondered how many of the farmers and tenants knew or suspected his questionable paternity? Did they despise him? Hate him? Pity him? Did he even have a right to mourn?

His gaze slid to Beth. Black suited her, the dark cloth dramatic against her pale skin and golden hair. Not that she would know, or even care. Beside her, Jamie sat solid and silent.

Ren did not know if their presence comforted or hurt. They reminded him of a time before loss, a time of childhood happiness, a time when his identify, his belonging had been without question.

His mother's secret had shattered everything. Even his art no longer brought joy. Indeed, his talent was nothing but a lasting reminder of the cheap portrait painter who had seduced his mother and sired a bastard.

The vicar stood. He cleared his throat, the quiet noise effectively silencing the congregation's muted whispering. He had changed little from the days when they'd attended as children, though he was perhaps balder. The long tassels of his moustache drooped lower, framing the beginnings of a double chin. Thank God for the moustache. It kept sentiment at bay.

The organ swelled, off key and yet moving.

They'd been here for their wedding. No spectators, of course. Just Beth and Jamie and the vicar with his moustache.

Ren swallowed. He could not wait to be gone from here. He wanted to escape to London with its distractions of women, wine and gambling.

In London, he was a real person—not a pleasant or a nice person—but real none the less. Here he was a pretender, acting a part.

In London, he could forget about Graham Hill and a life that was no longer his.

Slaughtered in a single truth.

Finally, as with all things, the service ended. Everyone rose simultaneously like obedient puppets.

Beth stood also, touching his arm, the gesture caring. Except he did not deserve her care. Or want it.

'Best get this done with,' he muttered. 'You don't need to stand with me at the door, you know.'

She tensed. He felt her body stiffen and her jaw tighten, thrusting forward. 'I do,' she said.

He shrugged. He would not debate the issue in the middle of the church. 'Fine.'

They stood at the church entrance beside the vicar. Ren felt both the fresh breeze, combined with the warm, stuffy, perfume-laden air from the church's interior. It felt thick with its long centuries of candle wax and humanity.

The tenants came in a straggling line. They gave their condolences, paid their respects with bobbing curtsies and bows. Strange how he rec-

ognised each face, but knew also a shocked confusion at the changes wrought by time.

And strange, too, how difficult it was to focus
as though forming simple sentences involved
mental capabilities beyond him. The vicar seemed
to have an endless supply of small talk, caring
questions and platitudes as though he stored them
within his robes like a squirrel stores nuts.

Surprisingly, Beth also appeared aware of each
tenant's issues: births, deaths and crops. Her
knowledge of such minutiae made him realise
the level of her involvement. He had not fully
recognised this before.

At last, when they had spoken to everyone and
the steps had cleared, he turned to Beth, touching her arm.

'I can't go into the carriage yet,' he said. 'I
need—'

He stopped. He didn't know what he needed—
a break from these people with their condolences
who thought he mourned when he had no right
to. Escape from the pain which clamped about
his ribcage so that he could breathe only in harsh,
intermittent gulps.

'We used to go to service here every Sunday.

The family and the servants. I remember Mrs Cridge, Nanny, would see us all around back to "get rid of them fidgets".'

'We can do that now, if you want?'

He nodded. He could not go into that carriage with its memories, echoes of their childish giggles. She placed her hand on his arm and allowed him to guide her as they stepped around to the other side of the church which overlooked the valley and winding stream.

'I can hear it,' Beth said, cocking her head. 'The brook. Once you said it was as though the bells of a hundred fairy churches rang.'

'Good Lord, what utter nonsense I used to spout.'

'I liked it. You made me see in a way Jamie and Edmund could not. I suppose it is because you are a painter.'

'Was.'

'You don't paint at all now?'

'No,' he said.

For long seconds, Ren stared at the expanse of green, the grass sloping into the twisting brook. The weather had worsened, the clouds thickening and dimming the light, muting the greens and making the landscape grey.

Beth placed her hand on his arm. He glanced down. Even in gloves, her hands looked delicate, the fingers thin.

'Ren?' She spoke with unusual hesitation. She bit her lip and he felt her grip tighten. 'How long will you stay here?'

'We can go to the carriage now if you are cold.'

'No, I mean at Graham Hill before leaving for London. I want—I would like to talk to you some time.'

'I will leave as soon as possible,' he said. 'Tomorrow most likely.'

This was a fact, a given, in a world turned upside down. Everything felt worse here. He was more conscious of Edmund's absence. He was more conscious of the wrongness that Edmund should predecease him and that he belonged nowhere.

'Tomorrow? But you can't. I mean, will you come back soon?'

'No.'

'But the tenants need you.'

'Then they will have to make do without.'

He watched her frown, pursing her lips and straightening her shoulders, an expression of familiar obstinacy flickering across her features.

'The tenants look to the big house for support at times like this. They need to know that they will be all right. That there is a continuity of leadership that transcends the individual. If they are too worried, they can't grieve properly.'

'A continuity—heavens, you sound like a vicar or a politician. Is there a subject on which you don't have an opinion?'

'Icebergs,' she said with a faint half-smile.

'Pardon?'

'I don't have an opinion on icebergs.'

For a brief moment, he felt his lips twist into a grin, the feeling both pleasant and unfamiliar. 'We don't even get icebergs in Britain.'

'Probably why I don't have an opinion on them,' she said.

For a moment, he longed to pull her to him, to bury his face into the soft gold of her hair and feel that he was not a solitary creature.

Except he was a solitary creature, a bastard. Moreover, even if his birth hadn't made him unworthy of her, his more recent behaviour had.

He stepped away, squaring his shoulders. 'My life is in London. The tenants will have to grieve as best they can without me. Therefore, if you need to speak to me, I suggest you do so now.'

She inhaled, brows drawing together. 'But...' She paused. 'Very well, this is not really the best time, but we are alone and I do not know when I will next have the opportunity.'

'Yes?' he prompted.

'It is just that, as Lord Graham, it is important for you to have a suitable wife and heir. When— when you married me, this was not the case. We thought Edmund and Mirabelle— Anyway, Allington is prosperous, our debts paid. The Duke is seldom here. And I...um... I thank you so much for your protection, but...but you must wish for your freedom. Likely that would be the best course of...of action, given the circumstances.' She finished in a hurried garbled, stammering rush.

'An annulment? You're asking for an annulment?' The effort to remain without expression was greater than that exerted in a thousand poker games.

'Yes—an annulment—I suppose.'

The pain was physical. The word slammed into him, so that he felt himself winded. *Annulment...* It was a battering ram, beating into his eardrums, punching at his stomach. Fury, anger, hurt twisted and exploded. He clenched his fists so tightly the muscles hurt.

'You choose to mention this now?' he said when he could trust his voice.

Her face flushed. 'I did not want to, but you gave me little option. Besides, I have never beaten about the bush. You have a new role and you need a proper wife. Anyway, it is not as though we have a real marriage. I mean, we have hardly spoken in eighteen months. You have not visited—'

'I have no need of either wife or heir,' he snapped, cutting through her words.

'As Lord Graham, it is your duty—'

'Stop!' he shouted, losing any semblance of his hard-won self-control. 'Stop calling me that ludicrous name.'

'It is your name.'

'A name I do not merit and do not wish to assume.'

'You don't have a choice.'

'I may have to assume the title,' he ground out.

'But I can certainly choose to dispose of the estate, thus alleviating your unreasonable worry that I might require an heir.'

'Dispose of?' She twisted, angling herself to face him as though sighted and able to discern his expression. 'How?'

'The Duke of Ayrebourne will have the estate.'

He did not know why he felt compelled to speak the words. It was as though everything was hurting and he was driven to hurt also. Or perhaps he needed to voice his intent to make his decision real.

There was a pause. An expression of disbelief flickered across her features. 'The Duke? How? Why?'

'I intend to give it to him.'

'What?' Her hands reached for his face, her fingers skimming across his skin to discern expression. He startled as she traced his jaw and cheek.

'You are serious,' she whispered. 'I thought it was a foul joke.'

'I am serious.'

'But why?' Her hands dropped from his face, reaching for him and clutching the cloth of his sleeve. 'The Duke of Ayrebourne? Your cousin?

He is despicable. You always said so. That is the reason we married. You can't—do that.'

'I believe I can. I have confirmed it with the solicitor,' he said.

'Your solicitor? It isn't entailed?'

'No.'

She shifted, her grip still tight. 'If you are in straitened circumstances, we can help. Jamie has made Allington prosperous. He will help you with Graham Hill. He is surprisingly clever with agriculture.'

'I am not in straitened circumstances.'

'He is blackmailing you?'

Ren laughed. 'One has to care about the opinion of others to be susceptible to blackmail.'

'Then why sell?'

'Give.'

'Give?' Her face had flushed, a mottled mix of red and white marking her neck. 'Have you taken leave of your senses? Your family has owned this land for generations. Ayrebourne cares nothing for the people or the animals or the land.'

'Then we have much in common,' Ren said.

'But you are not cruel.'

He shrugged. 'People change.'

She shook her head, the movement so violent that her black bonnet slid to one side, giving her a peculiar appearance and making him want to straighten it. The odd impulse cut through his anger. His eyes stung. He wished—

'Not like this,' she said. 'Something has happened. Something has changed you.'

'My bro—' He stopped himself. 'Edmund died, if you recall. That is not enough?'

'No. Something else. It happened long before Edmund left.'

For a moment, he was tempted to tell her everything. To tell her that Lord Graham was not his father, that Rendell Graham did not exist, had never existed. Why not? So many suspected anyway.

Then he straightened, moving from her.

She had always seen the best in him. She had run her fingers over his artwork and found beauty. She had touched his scrawny boyish arms and discerned muscle. He could not tell her. Not now. Not today. Not yet.

'We should go to the carriage,' he said.

'And that's it? You throw out this...this...

ludicrous, awful proposal and then suggest we go home for tea.'

'I will be having something considerably stronger, but you may stick to tea if you prefer.'

'You're doing it again.'

'Yes?' He raised a brow.

'The drawl. It makes you sound not yourself.'

He smiled. 'Perhaps because I am not myself,' he said.

## Chapter Four

Beth told Jamie after dinner that Ren intended to dispose of the estate. She had delayed, fearing it would distress him. Besides, she needed the time to mull over the news, to ensure that she was capable of speaking the words without smashing plates or throwing cutlery.

She heard Jamie's angry movement. He stood and the dining room chair clattered, crashing into the wall behind him. 'What? Why? Why sell?'

'He is not selling. He intends to give it away.'

'Give it away?' Jamie paced. 'Even more ludicrous. You have to stop him.'

'Me?'

'You are his wife.'

'Not really. And he certainly will not listen to me.'

'Who will he give it to?' Jamie asked.

'The Duke.'

'The Duke?' Jamie's movements stopped, his stunned disbelief echoed her own. 'Why? Good Lord, Ayrebourne turns his fields into park land so his rich friends can hunt. Starves his tenants. Why? Why the Duke?'

'I don't know,' Beth said. 'I mean, Ren knows that his cousin is loathsome. That is why he married me. It makes no sense that he would choose that man out of all humanity!'

'His cousin...' Jamie spoke softly. She heard him return to his chair and sit. His fingers drummed on the table.

'You've thought of something? It matters that the Duke is his cousin?'

'Yes.'

'Why?'

'I—' She heard Jamie's movement from the creaking of the chair. 'Can't.'

Jamie had never been able to speak when distressed. Words were never easy for him, particularly if the topic digressed from agricultural matters.

'But you know something that makes this understandable, or at least more so?'

He grunted.

'And you can't tell me?'

'No.' Jamie pushed his chair back. It banged against the wall. She heard him rise. She heard the quick, rapid movement of his footsteps across the room. 'Don't *know* anything anyway. Rumour. Best ask your husband.'

With this curt statement, he left. The door swung shut, muting the rapid clatter of his brisk footsteps as he proceeded down the passageway.

'Bother.' Beth spoke to the empty room. Jamie would drive a saint to distraction, she was sure of it. His knowledge was usually limited to seedlings and now, when he actually knew something useful, he refused to speak of it.

She half-rose, intent on pressing him further, but that would accomplish nothing. He was right, she supposed. She should talk to Ren. He was her husband, at least in name, and she deserved some form of explanation. Besides, she thought, with a characteristic surge of optimism, the fact that a logical reason existed, however warped the logic, was hopeful. One could argue against a plan rooted in reason and while she lacked any number of skills, fluency in words or argument was not one of them.

Beth stood with sudden purpose. She was not of the personality to give up. She would talk to Ren. She would make him tell her why he was so driven to give away his birthright. She would remind him that, whatever he felt now, he had once loved this land and its people—

That was it!

For a second, she felt transported. The plan flashed across her mind, fully formed and brilliant. She could almost feel those heady, optimistic days of childhood: the sun's warmth, the splash of water, the smell of moss and dirt mixed with a tang of turpentine and paint.

Grasping her cane, she hurried, counting her steps between her chair and the door and then took the twenty paces along the passageway to the stairs. Of course, she hadn't been to the nursery in eons, but everything was familiar: the smooth wood of the banister rail, the creak of the third stair under her foot and the whine of the door handle. Everything was reminiscent of childhood. Layered under the dusty scent of a closed room, she even detected a hint of cinnamon left over from long-ago nursery teas.

Beth crossed the hardwood flooring until her cane struck the cupboard. She knelt, swinging open the door and reaching inwards. Papers rustled under her fingertips. She could feel the cool dustiness of chalk, the hardness of the slate boards and the smooth leather covers of books, soft from use.

Then her fingers found the artist's palette with its hard ovals of dried paint and, beside it, the spiky bristles of brushes. She stretched her fingers from them and, to her delight, felt the dry, smooth texture of rolled canvas. She grinned, pulling eagerly so that the canvasses tumbled on to the floor with a rustling thud.

Squatting lower, she unrolled them, bending close as though proximity might help her see. Carefully, she ran her fingers across each one, focusing as Ren had taught her to do. She felt the dusty residue of chalk, the ridged texture of oils and the smooth flatness of water paints.

She saw, as her fingers roamed the images. Memories flooded her. She felt close to him here, yet also distant. This was the person she had known. This was the person who had captured beauty and who had joked and laughed as they walked for miles, dragging with them the clattering easel.

The bottom canvas fascinated her most. It was a landscape. She could feel the tiny delicate strokes which formed the tufts of grass mixed with the strong, bold lines of fence posts and trees.

Likely she'd been with him when he'd painted this, lying with the sun hot on her face and the grass cool against her back. Ren had said that the grass was green and she'd decided that green must smell of mint and that it would feel damp like spring mist. In autumn she'd touch the dry stubble in the hay field and he'd say it was yellow and she would decide that yellow was like the sun's heat.

In those days, he had loved every inch of this land.

And then everything had changed.

The next morning, Ren glared at the neat columns of figures written on the ledger in front of him. The estate was in excellent shape. The tenants seemed content and the crops prosperous. Sad to give it to a man such as the Duke.

He shifted back in his seat, glancing at the paintings on the study wall left over from his grandfather's time: a hunting scene and a poorly executed depiction of a black stallion in profile.

He felt more an imposter here than anywhere else on the sprawling estate. In fact, he had been in the study only twice since the return of the cheap portrait painter—the before and after of his life. He'd been summoned that day. Lord Graham had been sitting behind his desk, his face set in harsh lines and his skin so grey it was as though he had aged a lifetime within twenty-four hours. He'd stood immediately upon Ren's entry, picking up the birch switch.

And then his usually kindly father had whipped him. And he hadn't even known why.

He had been summoned one other time, after completing school. There had been no violence. Instead, Lord Graham had sat behind this desk, his eyes shuttered and without emotion. He'd spoken in measured tones, stating only that an allowance would be paid, provided Ren stayed away from Graham Hill and kept his silence. Ren had taken the stipend for three months before profitable investments had allowed him to return it and refuse any further payment.

Now, in an ironic twist of fate, Graham Hill could be his. Ren looked instinctively to the window and the park outside. The branches were still largely bare, but touched with miniscule green leaves, unfurling in the pale sunshine. Patches of moss dotted the lawn, bright and verdant beside grass still yellowed from winter.

It hurt to give it up, just as it had hurt to leave it.

A movement caught his attention and he saw a female figure approach. She held a cane in one hand and a basket in the other. His wife. She was counting her steps. He could see it in the tap and swing of her cane and the slight movement of her lips. She moved with care, but also with that ease which he had so often admired. Good Lord, if he were deprived of sight he would be paralysed, unable to move for fear of falling into an abyss.

He watched as she progressed briskly, disappearing about the side of the house. He supposed she had returned to berate him. Or else she wanted to again demand an annulment.

Anger tightened his gut. He'd kept his word.

She'd had freedom, autonomy and yet she'd thrown it back at him—

'My lord, Miss...um, your...her ladyship is in the parlour,' Dobson announced.

He stood at the study door, his elderly face solemn and lugubrious.

Poor Dobson—he'd found the marriage difficult enough. Not that Dobson disliked Beth, he simply disliked the unconventional.

Beth entered immediately. Naturally, she had not remained in the parlour, as instructed. She never had been good with directions. He watched her approach and knew both a confused desire as well as a reluctance to see her. Even after years spent amidst London's most glamorous women, he found her beauty arresting. She was not stunning, exactly. Her clothes were elegant, but in no way ostentatious or even fashionable. Yet there was something about her—she had a delicacy of feature, a luminosity which made her oddly not of this world, as though she were a fairy creature from a magic realm—

'Ren!' Beth interrupted his thoughts in that blunt way of hers. She approached, counting her steps to his desk, and now stood before him. With a thud, she put down the large wicker basket. 'You must see these!'

He dismissed Dobson and watched as Beth opened the carrier.

Then his breath caught. A stabbing pain shot just below his ribcage. His hands tightened into balled fists as she pulled out the rolled canvasses, laying them flat on the mahogany desktop.

'Where did you find those?' He forcibly pushed out the words, his throat so tight he feared he'd choke.

He stared at the images: the barn, its grey planks splitting with age, his old horse, the mosaic of autumnal colours, orange leaves and grass yellowed into straw from summer heat.

They were childishly executed, but with such care…such love.

For a moment, he felt that eager enthusiasm to paint. It was a tingling within his fingers, a salivation, a need, an all-consuming drive to create and capture beauty, if only for a moment.

'Why did you bring these here?' he asked in a staccato rhythm.

He felt his face twist into bitter lines—not that Beth could see them. It should have made him feel less vulnerable, that she could not discern his expression, but oddly it did not. He'd always felt as though Beth saw more, as though she was better able to discern human frailty, despite her lack of sight.

'To remind you.'

'I do not need reminding.'

He ran his fingers across the dry dustiness of the paint. It had been late August. The weather had been hot, a perfect weekend of cloudless skies and air still redolent with summer scent as though fate had conspired to give him that one, final, beautiful weekend.

'I wanted you to remember how you felt,' Beth said.

Of course he remembered! How could he forget? He'd felt as though, within a single instant, everything he had known, everything he had loved, everything he had believed had been erased, disappearing within a yawning hole, a cess pit.

The pain, the darkness—worse—the hopelessness had grown, twisting through him, debilitating even now. He closed his eyes, squeezing them tight as a child might to block out nightmares.

He pushed the canvasses away. They fell to the floor, taking with them the brass paperweight and a candle stick, the crash huge.

'Ren?'

'Take them!'

'But why? You loved to paint. You loved this land.'

'You need to go.' He forced himself to keep his voice low and his hands tight to his sides because he wanted to punch the wall and hurl objects against windows in a mad chaos of destruction.

'Nonsense! I'm not going anywhere until I understand the reason behind your decision. There is a reason. Jamie said so.'

'Jamie? Jamie?' Did even Jamie know his secret—a man who seldom spoke except about seedlings? 'What did he say?'

'Nothing. He went silent. But I need to know, to understand. I thought these would remind you. I thought you might enjoy them.'

'You were wrong.'

'Why?'

'I—' Words usually came so glibly, fluidly. Now they stuck in his throat. 'You need to go,' he repeated.

'Why?'

'Because I am angry and I do not want to frighten you.'

The woman laughed—not harsh laughter, but gentle. 'Ren, you could never frighten me. You could not frighten me in a million years.'

Of course not! He might frighten grown men in duels. He might race his horse so fast that his groom paled or punch so hard his knuckles bled, but this tiny woman laughed in the face of his rage.

'Perhaps I should explain to you what my life-style has become. Even the fringes of polite society avoid me.'

'Which is too bad as you can be excellent company. However, I do not frighten easily. Jamie used to have some terrible tantrums,' she added.

And now he was being likened to an angry child. It made him want to laugh.

'Right.' He stepped around to the front of the desk, bending to scoop up the fallen canvasses, candlestick and paperweight with businesslike swiftness. 'You are right. I could never hurt or even frighten you. And really it doesn't matter whether you stay or go because I could stare at these childish chicken scratches for ever and my decision would remain unchanged.'

'But why? I want to know. Doesn't even a wife in name only deserve that much?'

Her tone seemed laced with distaste and derision as she said the words 'name only.' My God, he could have made her more than a wife in name only. He could have dragged her to London or to the marriage bed if he hadn't respected her so damned much, if he hadn't known about her aversion to marriage and her need for independence.

'And why Ayrebourne?' she persisted.

'Graham Hill is his birthright.' He ground out the words between clenched jaws.

She shook her head. 'What utter tosh. It is your birthright.'

'Not so much.'

'I don't understand.'

'Likely because it is none of your business.'

Two bright crimson spots highlighted her cheeks and her breathing quickened. They stood quite close now, in front of his huge oak desk. She shifted so that she was square to him, her hands tightened into fists, her chin out-thrust.

'That is where you are wrong. You can marry

me and then ignore me, but this *is* my business. I have been here. While you were in London, I was here. I helped Edmund after Mirabelle's death. I organised village events, teas and fairs. I cooed over babies I could not see. I advised on how best to treat a bee sting and a—a boil which was on a place I cannot mention. Mirabelle was dead. Edmund was mourning. Jamie was Jamie. Your mother never came. You never came. I made this estate my business. I made the people my business. I helped Jensen run the place. I kept things going. I am sorry Edmund is dead, but if you are going to absolve yourself of this responsibility, I deserve to know why. You are Lord Graham's second son. You are the heir.'

Out of breath, she fell silent. After the flow of words, the stillness felt intense. He heard a clock chime from the library and a gardener or stable hand shout something outside.

'Actually, I'm not,' he said.

'Not what?'

'Lord Graham's son—second or otherwise.'

## Chapter Five

'Lord Graham was not my father.'

'That is not possible.' Her face blanched, the hectic red of anger now mottled.

'Given my mother's personality, it is,' he said.

'But…but who?'

'A portrait painter. He came to paint my parents' portraits in the year prior to my birth. Apparently his activities were not limited to capturing my mother's likeness.'

'He fell in love with your mother?'

'Something like that,' Ren said, although he doubted love had had anything to do with it. In fact, he rather doubted love's existence.

'But Lord Graham loved you so—' She stopped. 'He didn't know?'

'Not until the untimely return of the portrait

painter. We rather resemble each other, you see. Me and the painter. Most unfortunate.'

'Oh.' She placed her hand on the top of his desk as if needing its support.

She would despise him now, he supposed. He waited, unconsciously bracing himself as though for physical assault. But her face showed only a dawning comprehension and compassion.

'So that's why everything changed,' she said softly. 'You must have been so sad and…shocked when you learned.'

'Not so much. I was more intent on not drowning.'

'Lord Graham tried to drown you?'

'No.'

Lord Graham had flogged him. Ren hadn't known why until Jason Barnes had blurted it out while the other boys had held his head under the water pump that the school used for the horses.

He remembered the boys' faces, their mockery, the jeers and hard words. It had hurt and yet had also brought peculiar relief. At least he knew the reason for his father's sudden hatred.

'Who?'

'The boys at school.'

'I'm so sorry,' she repeated. Tears shimmered in her sightless sky-blue eyes.

Where he had expected...rejection, he saw only sympathy. He reached forward, touching a tear's glistening trail as it spilled down her cheek. Her skin was soft and smooth.

'It's ancient history. Not worth your tears.'

'When Lord Graham found out, he sent you to school early? That is why you left so suddenly and why you don't paint?'

'Yes.'

'And never came back for holidays?'

'Lord Graham did not want me.'

Another tear brimmed over. 'I'm so sorry. I did not think he could be so cruel.'

'I do not blame him. What man would want his wife's bastard?'

Her brows drew together at his words. She straightened, her cheeks an even brighter crimson. 'Well, I do. Cruelty is never warranted. I blame your mother. I blame the painter. But not you. You are blameless. You were a child.'

He shrugged. 'Opinions may differ on that score, but now you see why I must give the land to the Duke.'

Surprisingly, she shook her head. 'No. He is still vile.'

'Agreed. But he is my father's nearest blood relative.'

'It cannot be right or honourable to give the land, and therefore the tenants also, to a man who is dishonourable.'

'It certainly is not honourable to keep property to which I have no right. I am not the true heir. You cannot argue with that.'

'Jamie says I can argue about almost anything,' she said, her lips twisting into a wry grin. 'Did Lord Graham ever disinherit you? Did Edmund?'

'Lord Graham died before Edmund's wife died. He had every reason to expect that Edmund would have many children and live to a ripe old age.'

'But Edmund? He knew before he went to war that he might not come back.'

'Edmund was one of the few people who did not know the truth,' Ren said.

'You said the resemblance was obvious.'

'He was at school when the painter came and then went to Oxford the next term. His attitude towards me never changed.'

'But you said the students knew at school?'

'I suppose they kept it to themselves. They liked Edmund.'

Edmund was the sort of boy who had fit in well at boarding school. They had understood him: strong, sizeable, not overly bright but good at sports and fishing and hunting.

In contrast, Ren was not. He had been an undersized runt, too bright, poor at sports and fishing and hunting.

A misfit.

Beth paced Ren's study. Her thoughts whirled, a confused mix of comprehension, anger, pity and myriad other emotions. Her fingers trailed across the top of the desk, touching the familiar objects, the smooth metal of the paperweight which Ren had picked up from the floor, the leather portfolio, the edges of the inkstand and pen.

Then she turned, shaking her head. 'It still is not right to give the land to the Duke. There is more than one kind of honour. I know Edmund would not want Ayrebourne to have it. He loved this land, almost like Jamie loves the land. He cared for the tenants.'

'The Duke has a right to the land,' Ren repeated in dull tones, like a child reciting lines.

'And the tenants?'

'I am sorry about them, but I cannot change facts. The tenants have no rights. They do not own the land.'

'They have lived here for generations, for centuries. That doesn't give them rights?'

'No.'

'It should.'

'So now you plan to change society?'

She shrugged. 'Why not? If I had acted the way people said I should, I would not be walking about this land. I would not be independent—'

'Beth—for goodness sake—this is not about you. It is totally different. We all know you are independent and have done things no one else could do. But this is not the same.'

'I—' His tone hurt. 'I haven't.'

'No? You have always been on a crusade. You always wanted to demonstrate that you were not inferior, that you are independent. You never wanted to marry because of that very independence. Likely you want an annulment for the same reason. Well, we're agreed, you are the equal to any woman. But that doesn't change the fact that this land is not morally or honourably mine. I must give it to Edmund's closest relative. I am honour bound.'

'Then it is a peculiarly cruel breed of honour.'

'You can have that opinion, but my decision must stand. Anyhow Allington is completely independent and profitable so this should have a limited impact on the running of your affairs.'

'What?' Anger exploded like scalding water, pulsing through her veins, unpleasantly tangled with the fear she always felt when she considered the Duke.

She turned on Ren, hands tightened into fists. 'Weren't you even listening to me? These people, your tenants, are my friends. They will be kicked off land they've farmed for centuries. Or they will pay exorbitant rents so that they're unable to feed their own children. I will feel gaunt faces, arms like sticks and the bellies of bloated babies. And I will know that the man who was once my friend and *sort of* husband is to blame.'

'I am your friend and what *sort of* husband would you have me be?'

'One that is not so—so self-righteous and honourable. You want to punish yourself because you are illegitimate. Fine, drink yourself into an early grave. Gamble yourself into oblivion, but don't punish people far weaker than you and call it honour.'

Perhaps it was that cool disdain lacing the words she spat out as though they were noxious. Perhaps, for once, his anger could not be contained behind trite words and calm façade. Or maybe it was none of this but merely an impulsive, instinctive surge of lust.

His hands reached for her. He gripped her shoulders, pulling her tight, needing to feel her, to feel something. She stiffened, her shock palpable. Her hands pushed against his shoulders, ineffective like fluttering birds.

He didn't care. Her futile movements fuelled the angry molten heat.

Her head moved, angling away as she twisted from him. He caught her lips, kissing her with a hard, punishing kiss.

Her fury met his own, her balled fists pushing him away.

Briefly, it was all fire and heat and rage. Then

something changed. She no longer pushed against him; instead, her fists opened, her hands reaching upwards to grip his shoulders, pulling him closer. Her clenched jaw relaxed, her lips parting as anger eased, morphing into something equally strong. His kiss gentled. Her fingers stretched across his back, winding into his hair. He held her tight to him, hands at the small of her back.

The anger, the pain, the hurt drained away, pushed aside by a growing, pulsing need. He had wanted this woman for ever—long before he had known about want or lust or need. And she was here now, warm, willing, pliable and giving beneath him. He explored the sweetness of her mouth, shifting her backwards, pushing her against the edge of his desk. He stroked the column of her neck, the smooth line of her spine, the curved roundness of her bottom under the soft muslin gown.

He wanted—he needed—to fill her, to find forgetfulness in physical release, to make her his own. He wanted her to cling to him, to need him and desire him and to forget that annulment was even a word.

One hand pushed at her neckline, forcing the

cloth off her shoulder so that his fingers could feel her skin and the fullness of her breast. With growing urgency, his other hand pushed up at the fabric of her skirt, his hands feeling and stroking the stockings she wore over shapely legs.

She said his name.

Something fell.

He stilled. He stared down at her flushed cheeks, tousled hair and bodice half-undone.

Disgust rolled over him.

What, in the name of all that was good and holy, was he doing? He moved from her so suddenly that she almost lost her balance, striking the lamp.

It fell, splintering against the hearth.

'Ren?'

Self-loathing mixed with frustrated need. She was not one of his doxies. She was not one of the women who populated his London life. Moreover, she had made it quite clear she wanted to end their pseudo-marriage, which could hardly be construed as an invitation to consummate their union.

'It would seem indeed that, after all, my sense of honour is somewhat impaired,' he said.

## Chapter Six

Beth's confused mix of anger, embarrassment and a new, unexpected yearning was such that she could hardly focus to count her steps to her carriage or later traverse the gravel path to Jamie's small office attached to the stable. The numbers swam in her head, mixed and mired with darting thoughts and seesawing emotions. It felt as though her heart still beat as loud as thunder. An unusual restless energy filled her body, combined with a hunger which was new to her.

The very contrariness of her reactions irritated her. It was not only that she was shocked by his actions. Rather, she was shocked by her own reactions and by that crazy, contrary part of her that had not wanted him to stop, that feared she would not have stopped him.

She was not a creature of emotion. Her mother

and Jamie valued rational thought above all things. It was in no way rational to consummate this marriage. Indeed, had they done so, an annulment might not be possible. Even worse, she might have been with child.

Apprehension snaked through her. She knew she must not have children. She had known that since Jamie had arrived with that prize bull from across the county.

*Strength begets strength*, he'd said.

So why had she been prepared to put sense and reason aside? From the first moment of her marriage she had been contrary. She should have been thankful, relieved, when he'd disappeared so swiftly back to his London life. Right now, she should be offended by that kiss and furious at his liberty.

She wasn't. Rather, she was angry that he had dropped her like a hot potato at a children's game. He'd practically bolted to the door, bellowing for Dobson and sending her with all possible haste back to Allington—

A sudden noxious stench stopped her in her tracks. She gripped the railing which Jamie had installed, wrinkling her nose. It smelled of manure and rotting vegetation.

'Jamie?' she called out.

She pushed open the door to his office and heard the rustle of paper from the direction of the desk. She crossed the five steps towards it, placing her hands on the polished wood of its top.

'It smells quite dreadful outside.'

'It's supposed to,' he said.

'What?'

'Edmund and I were experimenting.'

His words brought her attention back to the matter at hand. 'I doubt you will do much more experimenting on the Graham estate. Ren thinks he is illegitimate and remains determined to give the estate to the Duke,' she said without preamble.

'He told you?' Jamie's chair creaked as though he had leaned back.

'So you did know.'

'People talk,' he said.

She sat. Her jaw slackened. She was briefly dumbstruck that her brother, who cared nothing for human drama, could be privy to this information while she was not.

'You didn't tell me?'

'Didn't think of it.'

'You didn't think of it?' she spluttered. 'He is my husband.'

'Yes,' Jamie acknowledged.

'And you didn't think to tell me?'

There was a silence. Of course, Jamie had not thought to tell her.

'You didn't ask,' he said at last.

'I didn't—' She drummed her fingers on the desk. 'Of course, I didn't— No matter. You must talk to him now.'

'What? What about?' Jamie asked, fear rippling through his voice so that she almost wanted to laugh.

'Not about being illegitimate. Just about the estate and how Edmund loved it. And what it is like for the Duke's tenants. And how the Duke charges them an exorbitant rent and never returns any money to the estate. And how Edmund would not want the Duke to take over Graham Hill.'

'But Edmund and I only spoke about seeds and cattle.'

'Good gracious, there is more to life than seeds and cattle. Surely you could tell Ren that Edmond would not want a man like the Duke taking over.'

'But he did not say so.'

'He did not say so! What? Would he need to spell it out?'

But of course for Jamie, he would. Any amusement fled and, with a quick, almost violent, movement, Beth stood, grabbed her cane and walked the five paces back towards the door.

'Where are you going?' her brother asked.

'I don't know.'

He was silent. Sometimes she could almost feel his confusion. He would in no way understand how someone could start to go somewhere without any knowledge of their destination. She paused, hand resting on the door knob, again aware of the smell from outside. An idea flickered.

'You said Edmund was involved in the experiment?' She turned back to him. 'I thought his interest lay more in mechanical invention.'

'Yes, but we wanted to see if manure, combined with gypsum, caused greater crop growth than manure alone.'

'And Edmund was involved?'

'Yes, he wanted to increase the crop's yield.'

'Why?' she asked.

'To provide more food for the tenants, of course.' His tone suggested he doubted her intelligence.

'Exactly!' She grinned, the hopeful bubble growing. She clapped her hands. 'Look, see if you can find any letters or notes from Edmund and give them to me.'

'Really? You are interested? I have the data. I can read it to you. I have kept meticulous notes. I always do, you know.'

'No,' she interrupted. 'No, it is Edmund's letters I need. Look for them while I am away.'

'Where are you going?' he asked again.

'To see Ren.'

Beth was met by Dobson at the door.

'His lordship has left already,' he said.

'No matter, I'll wait. When will he be back?'

'He won't. He's gone to London, my lady.'

'London,' she spoke flatly.

Beth had dreaded seeing Ren again. Yet now that she knew he'd left without even giving her that opportunity, she felt a heaviness in her stomach as though she had eaten too much of Mrs Bridges's raw dough.

Her husband had returned to London and not

even told her. She had spoken to him mere hours ago. He had kissed her. He had upturned her world…shaken it…changed it and yet she had not even warranted a goodbye, a note, or any form of communication.

She blinked. Her eyes stung. He had kissed her. Her lips still felt bruised.

'Would you care to see her ladyship? She is still here,' Dobson offered.

'I—' Beth was about to refuse and turn away. 'Yes,' she said instead.

As was her habit, she placed her hand on Dobson's arm and allowed him to lead her into the small salon.

'I will inform her ladyship.'

'Thank you.' Beth sat on a low sofa, her fingers rubbing the watered silk, the scratch-scratch of her movement loud in the still chamber. She seldom came to this room. As a child, they had not been allowed. Instead, they had spent time in the nursery or the kitchen where Mrs Bridges might give them cakes or let them lick a mixing spoon.

Lady Graham's entrance was announced by a swish of skirts and the creak of the door opening.

'Beth, it is nice of you to visit,' her mother-in-law said.

'I wanted to talk to you and—and see how you were faring,' Beth said awkwardly.

'I will survive. And yourself, you are managing?'

The words were not offensive, but Lady Graham's tone rankled. It was as though she expected her to fall apart and her failure to do so was both disappointing and a sign of bad breeding.

Beth again rubbed at the silk settee, then stilled her hand, unwilling to give her mother-in-law cause to think her nervous. 'Lady Graham—I wanted to talk to you,' she repeated.

'So you mentioned.'

There was a pause punctuated only by the clock's tick.

'I know,' Beth said.

The pause lengthened, the tick-tock-tick rhythmic.

'You will have to elucidate on the exact content of this knowledge,' her ladyship said.

'I know that Lord Graham was not Ren's father.' Beth pushed the words out, her hands tight fists about the folds of her dress.

She heard Lady Graham's sharp intake of breath. 'Good gracious, Beth, I knew you were blind, but I didn't know that madness also ran in your family.'

'Ren told me.'

'Grief has obviously affected his mind, poor boy.'

'No,' Beth said. Now that the words were out, she felt a growing strength. 'It makes sense. I think it is true.'

'I— Even if it were true, I do not see why you concern yourself with this.'

'Because Ren is my husband, in case you have forgotten.'

'A youthful mistake which I am certain he regrets.'

Beth felt herself flinch. She had not fully understood the elder woman's hostility. 'Perhaps,' she replied. 'But I am also his friend and your lies are impacting him dreadfully.'

'I think you forget to whom you are speaking.'

'I am speaking to my husband's mother, the person who should be most interested in his well-being.'

'You are suggesting I am not?'

'I—' Beth paused. She felt out of her depth and conscious that her words were making things worse. 'I am suggesting that he is making a mistake. I am worried about him and I thought that you might be able to talk to him.'

The silence lengthened, again punctuated by that ever-rhythmic clock.

'About what?' her mother-in-law asked at last.

'Ren thinks he has no right to this estate.'

'Nonsense. It is his.'

'Legally, perhaps. But he doesn't believe it would be honourable to inherit. He is considering other options.'

She heard Lady Graham stand. The scent of lily of the valley wafted towards her with the movement.

'What other options?' Lady Graham asked.

'I fear he might give it away to—to a near relative.'

'The Duke?'

'Yes.'

'I had not considered that.' The footsteps paused as though Lady Graham was standing to better contemplate her next words.

'It would be so bad for the tenants,' Beth said.

'And what would you have me do?'

'Talk to him.'

Her ladyship gave a short mirthless laugh. 'Good Lord, girl, Ren and I have said only ten words to each other in the last five years and most of those were in this last sennight. He would no more listen to me than fly in the air. Besides, it may not be a bad idea. My son is hardly known for his responsible lifestyle. The Duke is businesslike. He could well improve the estate.'

'What?' Beth felt her hand reach out as though in supplication. 'Businesslike? Have you seen the tenants on his estate? The rents are so high that people starve.'

'Do not indulge in such melodrama. My husband and Edmund pandered too much to the whims of the tenants.'

'They made certain people had food. They reinvested in the land and in roads. The Duke does none of these things. He charges rent merely to support his own extravagance.'

'Good Lord child, you sound positively revolutionary. You cannot change the world.'

The words were said in that mocking tone which had always made Beth feel much younger than her years and foolish, as though both her youth and lack of sight conspired to make her witless.

Anger and frustration flared. She rose, grasping her cane, her palms sweaty against the wood.

'No, but I can try,' she said.

By habit, Beth detoured to the kitchen. She always felt more at home there anyway. Kitchens had such lovely comforting smells, as if cinnamon infused its very foundation of solid beam and brick. She'd always liked places with a smell. Scents, even the unpleasant, gave information and served to orientate her.

Mrs Bridges's kitchen smelled wonderful, a mix of yeast, fresh bread, onions and beef roast. In childhood, it had been filled with a busy bustling: the clatter of pans, the rhythmic beat of a spoon in batter and the movement of many feet and hands. Now the staff was small, just Mrs Bridges and a scullery maid.

'You always did have a knack of showing up exactly when the bread was fresh from the oven,' Mrs Bridges stated, upon her entry. 'Although by rights, I didn't have the heart to bake, what with Master Edmund being gone, but then we need to eat. Besides, it was that nice to have Master Ren back. I was hoping he'd stay a while. I was thinking it would be nice if he'd pop down to poor Mrs Cridge. She'll be feeling Master Edmund's loss something terrible.'

'Yes,' Beth said. 'I had forgotten her. I'll go.'

Mrs Cridge had been the Grahams' nanny. She'd seemed old even in their childhood.

'Will you? You always were a brave one. She can be mighty irascible.'

'Her bark is worse than her bite. I go quite often,' Beth said.

'Do you? Me, I prefer my pots and pans. They are considerably more obliging.'

'But not half so interesting.'

Mrs Cridge's cottage was in the north-east corner of the estate, bordered by fields and a small brook cutting across the left corner. Mrs Cridge had been on the Graham estate for ever and knew more about the family than anyone. She had come first as nanny to Ren's father, remaining to look after both Ren and Edmund. Retired now, she seldom left her cottage, limited by poor eyesight and goutarthritis.

Beth left Arnold with the horses and stepped carefully up the uneven path. The door was off the latch and, after knocking, she stepped inside. The interior smelled of old age; the scent was of coal fires, mothballs and damp.

'My lady?' Mrs Cridge said immediately, her voice croaky from either disuse or age. She sounded even frailer than she had at the memorial. Beth took her hand, conscious of the elder woman's weakened grip.

'I brought some bread,' Beth said, unclasping the elder woman's hand and giving her the loaf.

'Fresh, I hope. I don't want Mrs Bridges's day-olds.'

'Fresh, I am sure.'

'Good, then I will put the kettle on.'

Beth sat as the older woman got up, her breath heavy with exertion. She set about making tea, her shuffling movement, accompanied by the splash of water and the clang of the kettle being placed above the fire. Would the Duke let her stay? She had heard that at Ayrebourne he removed anyone unable to labour on the land.

Surely Ren would not let that happen. She wished he had not left for London. If he had remained she would have dragged him here. Surely Mrs Cridge could have talked sense into him.

'There now,' Mrs Cridge said. 'I've put your cup on the table to your left, just by your hand. And then you'd best be telling me what's the matter. The face on you is enough to turn the milk sour.'

It was typical that Mrs Cridge wasted no time on pleasantries.

'So what's he done now, your man?' she asked. 'Other than up sticks and leave.'

'He's not my man,' Beth said, irritably.

'You're married to him.'

'Yes, but it isn't... I mean...'

Mrs Cridge made a tutting sound and Beth fell silent. 'Right now you're the only wife he has, so he's yours for all intents and purposes. Besides, I have a feeling he needs someone or else he'll make a big mistake.'

'What? How do you know?'

'I don't *know* anything exactly, only that he is sad and has left this estate when he should be here.'

'He doesn't want it—the estate, I mean. He's going to give it to the Duke,' Beth said.

'That would be mighty foolish.'

'I know, and wrong, too. The tenants would suffer. I know neither Edmund nor his father would have wanted that.'

'It would seem that you'll need to convince him of that,' Mrs Cridge said.

'Me?'

'Like I said, you're the only wife he has.'

'But I can't. I was going to try. But he's already left. Besides I spoke to him yesterday and it did no good,' Beth said.

'What did you say? Sounds like you didn't use the right words.'

'Me? I didn't?' she said stung. 'I tried. I even took the time to unearth his paintings'

'That was foolish. It likely only served to remind him of his parentage.'

'I know. At the time, I hadn't heard—how did you know?' In her shock, Beth miscalculated the distance to the table so her tea spilled, the liquid hot on her hand.

'There's not much I don't know about my lads,' Mrs Cridge said.

'Obviously,' Beth muttered with some irritation, dabbing ineffectively at the spill with her handkerchief. 'Well, unlike the rest of the world,

I didn't know that Lord Graham wasn't Ren's father. If I'd known anything about the portrait painter, I might not have brought out the paintings. I just wanted to remind Ren of the love he had for this estate. When did you find out? About his father?'

'I've always known.'

'Always? You mean before Lord Graham even knew.'

'From day one.'

'Apparently, Edmund and I are the only people who did not know,' Beth said.

'Edmund knew.' Mrs Cridge spoke in flat tones, as though stating an established fact.

'He did?' Beth leaned forward with sudden eagerness.

'Yes.'

'You know this for a certainty?'

'Yes. We spoke of it.'

'But Ren thought he didn't know,' Beth said.

'He knew.'

'And he didn't care?'

'He loved Ren,' Mrs Cridge said. 'That did not change. That could never change.'

'And he wanted Ren to inherit?'

'He certainly would not have wanted the Duke to do so,' Mrs Cridge said.

Beth reached towards the older woman and grasped her hand within her own. Mrs Cridge's fingers were crooked and the joints swollen, the painful knots and bulges discernible under thin, dry skin. 'You must tell him. You must go to London and tell him.'

'Good Lord, child. Look at me. I can barely move around this cottage. I could not travel to London. Any carriage would rattle every joint loose. My legs would not stand it.'

'But someone has to,' Beth said.

'Indeed.'

'I could ask Jamie.'

'Your brother could not convince anyone out of anything—or into anything for that matter. Likely he would merely find a new variation of seed or some such nonsense. Besides, it's not his responsibility,' Mrs Cridge added.

'You think it's mine?'

'You married the man.'

'But—I… I mean it's not a real marriage.'

'It's real enough when you act lady of the manor with the tenants.'

Beth dropped the elder woman's hand, stung. 'I don't act. I help.'

'Then best help now. The tenants need it and so does Ren.'

'He doesn't. At least, not my help.'

Mrs Cridge made no answer. Beth reached forward to touch the elder woman's face. Her skin felt soft, despite its crinkles and folds, her expression serious.

Beth dropped her hands. 'You think he does?'

'He is unhappy.'

Beth shifted in her seat, tension twisting through her stomach. Her palms felt damp with sweat. 'I can't go to London.'

She had only considered going once and that had been with Mirabelle. And now Mirabelle was dead. The thought of travelling, of going into that busy, bustling city with its noise and smells frightened her, had always frightened her. She rubbed her palms against the cloth of her gown, swallowing nervously.

'I see no reason why not. You have a carriage, horses and your health.'

'But where would I stay?'

'You also have a husband and a house. Or you could make arrangements with a relative.'

'But—' Beth shivered. She felt nervous on so many levels. It was about the physical act of travelling, of going to London, of tracking Ren down and turning up on his door step. It was about his reaction when she tracked him down.

And her own reaction. Unconsciously, she touched her lips as though they were still imprinted with his kiss.

'I can't,' she said.

'And I remember a little girl who didn't know the meaning of that word,' Mrs Cridge said.

Beth *had* said that. She *had* believed it. Her mother had believed it. But her mother had been thrown from a horse and her belief in the impossible broken as surely as her back.

Again, Beth rubbed her palms on her dress so that the fabric rustled. She shivered despite the fire's crackling warmth.

'Sometimes you have to fight for what is right.' The silence stretched between them, the words seeming to reverberate. 'And you have to try because at least then you will know that you have done everything.'

The fire crackled. A twig brushed against the cottage window with a soft rata-tat-tat.

'He saved you from the Duke,' Mrs Cridge said.

'Yes.'

'Perhaps you should return the favour.'

'He doesn't need saving.'

'You're certain about that?'

Brooks's was as familiar to Ren as his own rooms or Celeste's sumptuous quarters. Indeed, he had stopped at his mistress's place, but his restlessness had been too great. Despite Celeste's attributes, so admirably displayed, he had found himself lacking interest and his mind wandering.

Grief, most like. The fact that his mind so often circled to Beth was because she was so intricately linked with his family. It was not so much about her but about what she represented.

A load of claptrap, he knew.

So, seeking diversion, he had driven briskly to Brooks's and now strode through the Great Subscription Room. Several acquaintances lounged in low sofas close to the huge blazing fires and he nodded to them, pausing by Lord Amherst, a flushed and amiable gentleman, lolling within a comfortable armchair, his leg propped on a foot stool.

'Graham, care to bet?' Amherst asked, raising his glass in Ren's direction.

'Not today,' he said.

'Betting on snails. Going to find two snails and see which will travel a foot in the shortest time.'

'Do we have anything to measure the foot?' another gentleman enquired from a seat on the other side of the hearth, his words slurred.

'Don't know. I suppose we could use a flagstone.' Amherst grunted, removing his foot from the stool and pulling himself into a seated position. He glanced towards the huge windows across the room. 'Bit cold out there, though, to look for snails crossing flagstones.'

'We could bet on who finds a snail first,' the other gentleman suggested, lifting his glass and peering at the amber liquid with apparent fascination.

'Or perhaps we could find an indoor insect. A spider. We can bet on which one of us first finds a spider—'

Ren left them, mounting the stairs. Sometimes he enjoyed such nonsense and had placed any number of ludicrous bets in the past. This evening he had no interest. He felt an unjustified anger that men like Amherst should still live to spend their time betting on snails and spiders while Edmund was dead.

The card room upstairs was much smaller and more crowded than the Subscription room downstairs. The air was warmer and laced with sweat. The golden glow from the heavy chandeliers lit the swirls of blue smoke, which hung, like London fog, just below the ceiling. Several men huddled about the card table, their features reflected and multiplied within the long gilt-framed mirrors lining the walls.

A roar rose as the dice tumbled across the felt. Hazard, a pleasant enough game, but not for today. Ren needed escape. He needed something more than a light game of Hazard. He needed something which would push out all other thoughts and focus all his faculties on the moment.

Several men had turned at his entrance. He felt the change in the room. He felt the stiffening and the flicker of nervous apprehension as though their world had become more dangerous with his presence.

He did not mind.

'Whist?' he suggested. 'But only for those with damn deep pockets.'

He walked over to an empty table and signalled for brandy which he swallowed in a fiery gulp. Several individuals joined him and they formed a group at the far end of the room, away from the more raucous play at the Hazard table.

This table was different. There was less joking and jocularity. Here the men still drank, but there was a quiet intensity to their game. Conversation was limited and under the polite words there was always the knowledge that fortunes were being won and lost with the soft shuffle and thwack of cards.

Ren picked up his hand. He kept his gaze focused, his concentration complete. This was why he liked high stakes—it rooted him in this single moment so that all else dwindled to unimportance.

His facility with cards had served him well. It was likely the only thing which had made his school life tolerable and had served to provide income until several investments in north Yorkshire paid off.

Now it whiled away the long hours and nights when he could not sleep.

Sometimes he won. Sometimes he lost. Tonight he was winning, but he kept his face grim, his expression unreadable. Gradually night turned into day. The candles burned out into puddles of wax as the grey light of dawn flickered through the windows. But time was a meaningless concept, subservient to the soft thwack of the cards.

# *Chapter Seven*

The journey was both never-ending and all too swiftly completed. Beth huddled within the confines of the coach, her body bruised by the continual bumping and bouncing as they clattered along rutted country roads. She felt a peculiar combination of boredom and terror as if suspended in a dark, jostling purgatory.

Allie tried to help. She patted her mistress' hand and Beth focused on her maid's fingers and the roughened calluses dotting the girl's palm. Allie also described the landscape as best she could. She spoke of low stone walls and green fields dotted with sheep and cows.

'And the cows don't look any different than ours at home, my lady.'

'That is a relief. I feared that the cows near London had two heads.'

'Are there such things?'

'No.' She laughed.

Perhaps the best remedy for her nerves was her maid's excitement. It permeated the carriage. Allie, although chatty, was usually of a practical nature and seldom allowed herself to be swayed by emotion. But now Beth could feel the girl's excitement as she wriggled, bouncing on the cushioning, as though a child once more.

'We must be getting close, my lady,' she said. 'I can see more houses and the fields are not half so big.'

'I imagine we will find London filled with houses and nary a field in sight,' Beth said.

They continued for several more minutes, before Allie again twisted towards the window. 'We must be ever so close now. And I've never seen so many people, my lady. Nor so many houses. Lud, but they're squished so tight. Not enough room to swing a cat, as my sainted mother would say. And there are people of all types. Urchins and rough men and women. And garbage and other muck, too.'

'The latter does not sound entirely enticing.'

'Oh, no, my lady. But it is ever so interesting. I wish you could see it.'

'Me, too.'

Eventually, the carriage slowed. From outside, Beth heard shouts, the singsong calls of news-boys, the rattle of other vehicles and the clatter of hooves upon pavement.

'The houses are looking ever so fancy now, my lady,' Allie continued. 'And bigger and the people look smarter, too. And the streets are wider. Ooh—and such a fancy carriage just passed us. His lordship must live in a big house.'

Beth shivered at the reminder of her purpose. That was the moment when the journey seemed too quickly over. Briefly, she wished that, despite the physical discomfort, it would continue.

How would Ren react to her presence? And how would she react to him? She'd spent the major-ity of her marriage reconciling herself that they could not even be friends.

And then he'd kissed her.

And that one kiss had started a flood of emo-tions like spring run-off. Now her fears ran the gamut. She worried that he would try to kiss her again.

And that he wouldn't.

'We're here, my lady,' Allie said as the coach lurched to a stop.

Beth jerked upright. She felt an eager, nervous jumpiness which might be apprehension or anticipation. It was all ludicrous—one kiss did not change an entire relationship. They had been friends. The friendship had dwindled into mere acquaintance until his heroic gesture of this marriage.

Now her duty was clear. She needed to convince him to accept this new role, to be the new Lord Graham, to save the tenants and possibly himself. She would not let her mind dwell on the fact that, by doing so, she made the need for an annulment even greater. She would not allow herself to wish for some other impossible, happy ending—

'Gracious, my lady, it is three storeys high,' said Allie. 'And it has a wrought-iron gate and ever such a fancy entranceway with a brass knocker that looks like a lion.'

Beth smiled at the awe rippling through her maid's voice. She shifted forward on hearing the movement of the carriage door, the creak of its hinges and the whisper of wind. As Arnold helped her out, she stepped on to the pavement, inhaling the damp London air for the first time. It felt moister here than in the country and there was a fascinating layering of smells: an earthy scent, a mix of garbage, sewage and spring growth.

Allie stood beside her and, placing her hand on her maid's arm, Beth walked to the front door. Behind her she could hear the horses' movement, the jangle of reins and the stamp of impatient hooves as Arnold led them away.

The door opened. 'Miss?' a masculine voice said.

'Lady Graham,' she corrected, trying to keep her voice firm.

There was a pause, as though the man was trying to make sense of this new information.

'Of course, my lady,' he said.

The door creaked as it swung wider. She took her cane from Allie, tapping carefully. The flooring sounded like marble. There was a sharp tone unlike the softer, muffled sound of wood and it echoed as though in a big space with high ceilings.

'Do you require assistance, my lady?' the butler asked.

'I would like to see my husband.' No point beating about the proverbial bush.

'He is out, my lady.'

'Do you know when he might return?'

'No, my lady.'

'Very well. Could you find me a suitable room where I might take tea and await my husband's return? Perhaps the cook could provide a simple dinner later.'

'Will you be staying the night, my lady?'

'No, I have made alternate arrangements.'

She almost wanted to giggle. She sounded so fustian and quite unlike herself. It was as though she had put on a mantle of sophistication and was play acting. Still, her tone apparently worked and the butler led her into a comfortable room with a crackling fire.

'Tea will be served directly. Would you like us to send word of your arrival to his lordship?'

A nervous shiver slid, like moth's wings, down her spine.

'It might serve to expedite his return,' she said.

Although whether she wanted this or not she did not know.

\* \* \*

It was, Ren thought, the unexpectedness of her appearance which undid him. When Robbins had said 'Lady Graham,' he had assumed his mother waited for him and not his wife.

Therefore, he was in no way prepared for the sight of Beth with her hair shining like spun gold and her face illuminated by the flicker of flames so that he was again struck by that other-worldly aspect of her beauty.

In that moment, he felt a quick, unexpected, unprecedented flash of joy. The sentiment was all the more dramatic by virtue of the fact that he never felt joy. Indeed, he could not remember the last time he had felt anything akin to that emotion.

Then, chasing after that initial reaction, came the memory of the kiss with its complex mix of confusion, guilt, irritation and desire. He admired self-control above all things. It had, quite literally, been beaten into him at school. One did not show emotion, vulnerability or sentiment. It had been difficult at first, but now it was second nature. Besides, he seldom experienced emotion, at least not one strong enough to cause an impulsivity of action.

So how could Beth, his childhood friend, have caused such a slip? How could he have felt such a flare of anger and desire? How could he have so forgotten himself as to kiss her? And it had been no chaste kiss or romantic gesture. It had been fuelled by something primitive, primal almost.

But she had changed, too, he thought. She was not the little blind girl of childhood memory or even the scared, lost, grieving young woman attempting to avoid marriage to a cruel man while looking after her brother and paying off her father's debts. There was a difference, a sophistication and an aura of capability mixed with that pale, fragile, ephemeral beauty.

'I know perfectly well you are there. And I know you are studying me like you used to before church on Sunday. So, do I pass muster or have I a smudge on my face?' She turned, a slight smile touching her lips.

'How do you always know?'

'I heard your footsteps and they are in no way as deferential as those of your butler. Besides being considerably swifter.'

'Thank goodness, since Robbins is forty years my senior. You should have told me you were coming.'

'The last time I did so you dissuaded me from the enterprise.'

That was true enough—Mirabelle had suggested the visit shortly after their wedding.

'So, you decided to act first and seek permission later?' Which was, he thought, entirely typical.

'I seldom seek permission either early or late.'

That was also true, although few of his acquaintances would have been so bold. Indeed, few of his acquaintances sought to challenge him at all. He frowned, admiration and irritation flickering.

The latter won out. 'So is anything wrong? Jamie is well?' he asked curtly.

'Yes.'

'Is there some problem with the estate?'

'Only if you have already given it to the Duke.'

So that was it. Likely she still hoped to dissuade him. The bloody woman was like a dog with a bone.

His frown deepened. He stepped to the fireplace, drumming his fingers on the mantel. 'I haven't,' he said. 'But you won't deter me. I am seldom deterred once a decision is made. In fact, it was foolish to undertake the journey.'

'Only the weak will not change their minds when faced with a logical alternative and I do not see why I should not travel. People do so all the time.'

His hand tightened at her words and the underlying belligerence of her tone, but he spoke calmly. 'Unaccompanied females do not. Did Jamie come?'

'No, but Allie and Arnold did.'

'You came with only two servants. This journey will cause comment.'

'I am married and live apart from my husband. Therefore, I am rather inured to comment,' she retorted.

'Spending time without one's husband is seldom cause for comment. Women do it all the time. However, travelling pell-mell up to London only accompanied by servants is different.'

'I doubt Arnold has ever driven anywhere pell-mell. And they are good company once you chat with them.'

'I do not intend to chat...' He paused, exhaling.

'That is beside the point. I only ask that you behave in a way which does not make us the subject of comment. I do not like to invoke gossip.'

'Really? Perhaps you should have thought of that before securing any number of mistresses, as well as a wife.'

Shame, anger and myriad other emotions flashed and flared through him. His shoulders knotted. Heat washed into his face and he felt his jaw clench.

'What? Who told you this?' he ground out, turning from the mantel. 'You should not even know of such things.'

'Fiddlesticks.'

'Excuse me?' He spoke jerkily, startled out of both his anger and sophistication. No one disagreed with him and certainly not with the word 'fiddlesticks.'

She shrugged. 'Your affairs are entirely your own concern, but it is foolish to think I should not know of such things, particularly as you apparently flaunt them openly enough when you are in town. According to Allie, they are frequently remarked upon in the servants' hall at Graham Hill and Allington.'

'I— You— Allie should not discuss such things.'

'I fail to see why. It would seem to be pertinent given that I am married to you. Talking of which, I think we should clear the air about—about— well—the elephant.'

He stared at her. She appeared composed. The black silk suited her, a stark contrast to the blonde-gold of her hair. But her conversation struck him as odder than usual. 'The elephant?'

'My mother had a Russian nurse when she was little. This individual always called something that no one wished to discuss the elephant in the museum. I think it was based on a Russian folk story. In our case I was thinking of the kiss.'

The word dropped, loud as cannon fire at dawn. Its impact seemed all the greater mixed as it was with folk stories and museums.

His breath left him.

'Likely,' she continued airily, 'you are feeling that I may have been shocked or discomfited and I wished to assure you that I am neither. Indeed, I am not likely to expire in a fit of vapours just because of a kiss.'

'I—' His smooth, glib words had left him. He

felt his hand clench and consciously stretched out his fingers in response. Diverse, complex emotions flooded him. How could she so quickly dismiss a kiss which had somehow shifted his world?

In that moment, he realised that simple truth. A single kiss had in some indefinable way changed something... He was a man of debauched tastes and concubines. Celeste had draped herself all over the pillows last night and he had felt a bored indifference, his mind circling to this woman.

'I have given the kiss little—th-thought,' he said stiffly.

'You're lying.'

'What?'

'You always hesitate over the first consonant of a word when attempting to obscure a fact.'

'I do not and I am not attempting to obscure anything. And you have gone bright pink, by the way,' he added. 'A suggestion that you also might be lying.'

'And there I thought sophisticated London gentlemen did not make personal comments.'

'I don't—' He stopped, realising that they were sounding more like adolescents trading insults than grown adults. 'Look, we don't need to discuss the kiss. It was an aberration. I only ask that you behave with decorum and not dash off to London on a whim and talk of elephants.'

'Likely I can avoid discussing elephants, but I think it unfair that you should expect me to remain at Allington.'

'But you like Allington. You said that was why you never wanted to marry. Your mother said it would be too hard for you to gain independence in a new environment. Must you argue about everything?'

'My mother suggested that it was one of my abilities.'

'And mine said it was one you should curb, if you hoped to succeed in society.'

'Which I don't.' Beth grinned, giving one of her spontaneous giggles. 'Besides, Father said I was likely gifted with great oratory to make up for my lack of sight. Indeed, as I recall, he said my tongue was hung in the middle and clacked at both ends.'

It was exactly the sort of thing she might have said years earlier and the comment brought with it memories of childhood summers. His tension eased.

'He also said you should learn decorum.'

'Decorum is overrated. Remember how we used to steal the cream puffs from Mrs Bridges?'

'And she always blamed me.'

'Ah,' she said, grinning with remembered smugness. 'That is the thing with blindness or any disability. It makes people assume one's innocence and good character.'

He gave a reluctant chuckle. 'Indeed, as I recall, you put that to good use. Well, try to practise decorum here or you are quite likely to give some ancient dowager the vapours.'

'I will attempt not to cause any medical incidents.'

There was a pause. He had forgotten how much he liked talking to her and missed her quick wit. He watched the movement of her thumb on the handle of her cane and the delicate sweep of her lashes, casting lacy shadows against her cheek.

'You find travelling easier now? It used to upset you.'

'It still does,' she said somewhat ruefully.

She was pale, he realised.

'Then it was brave of you to come.'

Impulsively, he sat in the seat opposite, reaching forward and touching her hand as it rested on the cane, stilling her nervous movement. He felt a jolt at the touch and was conscious of her smooth skin beneath his palm and of her quick exhalation as though she had felt it, too. He removed his hand with equal impulsivity.

'Except it can do no good. I cannot change my mind, you know,' he said.

'But you can. You see, I have to tell you something. I have to tell you that Edmund would want you to keep the estate. That is why I came.'

'You do not know what Edmund would want,' he said, sharpening his tone.

'I do,' she said.

'You are communicating with ghosts now?'

'I spoke to Mrs Cridge. She says that Edmund knew about your birth and possible parentage and it didn't matter to him.

'What?'

He sat suddenly, the movement heavy, as though physically depleted of strength and energy. He swallowed, feeling young again as though he was that lad in school. 'He said that?'

'Yes, to Mrs Cridge. And if he had not wanted you to have the estate he would have made some form of legal change. I know he would. Edmund was thorough with paperwork. He would not have left for war without doing so, if that was his intent.'

'You are sure of this?'

'Yes. And I am sure he would not want a man such as the Duke to have the estate. He was working with Jamie to increase crop yields. Actually, Jamie is likely still hunting out those letters. He will give us a full scientific review of the experiment, no doubt, although really it doesn't matter what they were investigating or their conclusions. It matters that Edmund was so involved. He wanted to ensure that the tenants had sufficient crops. He wanted to be a good farmer. And I know Edmund would have made some form of arrangement if he had not wanted you to inherit.'

Ren stood again, unable to remain still. He placed his hands against the flat ledge of the window sill, staring into the dull grey of the London street. 'I wish he'd told me. I wish he'd told me that he knew that Lord Graham wasn't my father.

I always thought I should tell him that I was not his true brother. I felt like such a fraud.'

An act of cowardice, he supposed.

'You didn't want to hurt him. You didn't want him to know that his mother was not faithful. It was an act of love.'

'Or weakness.'

'Love,' she said, in that firm way of hers.

'I'm sorry to interrupt, your lordship. There seems to have been a mishap.' Robbins made this announcement from the doorway, pausing after the statement as though for dramatic effect.

'Well,' Ren said irritably, 'will you tell us the details or is this to be a guessing game?'

'It is her ladyship's groom. He has hurt himself.'

'What?' Beth startled upright. 'Arnold? Where is he? Can I help?'

'He thought you might wish to do so, but assured me that there is nothing you can do. He has had a fall, but nothing is broken.'

'Where did he fall?'

'Down the stairs, my lady. He is currently resting within the servants' quarters, but wondered if you might—er—remain here for the—er—night, at least?'

'I—'

'Of course she will stay here. She should be staying here anyway. Tell Mrs Crofton to get a room ready,' Ren directed.

'But I am staying with Mirabelle's aunt. I wrote ahead.'

'Nonsense. We are married. You will stay here. I will send a note to Mirabelle's aunt, whoever that might be.'

'Lady Mortley.' Beth frowned, obviously not liking his tone.

'It would cause comment not to stay here and it would be unkind to disturb your groom.'

'He could remain and Allie could come with me.'

'A ludicrous suggestion. Please make the necessary arrangements,' he directed Robbins. 'Oh, and best get in the doctor to ensure that this groom has not sustained a more serious injury.'

'Yes, my lord,' Robbins said and left.

'You are both insulting and bossy,' Beth told Ren the second the door closed.

He allowed himself a brief, somewhat mirthless

laugh. 'That is hardly news. Moreover, it seems somewhat hypocritical given that the entire purpose of your trip is to tell me what I should do with Graham Hill.'

'Not at all,' she said, her chin jutting characteristically upward, her ramrod-straight back at odds with that delicate, almost ephemeral quality. 'I have helped to run the estate and have earned the right to an opinion. You have seen me twice in as many years and have no such right.'

'The law might think otherwise.'

'The law is a product of men and therefore equally fallible,' she said.

'You don't mince words.'

'I never have.'

It was almost refreshing after the platitudes of courtesans and servants.

'You do realise that most of my acquaintance do not argue with me or answer back,' he said.

'Really? What very dull conversations you must have.'

He thought of Celeste, with her impeccable taste, her pleasant smiling countenance, her well-stocked wine cellar and soothing tones.

'They are somewhat.'

'It is either because they fear you or seek to flatter you. Neither of which are the attributes of true friends.'

'I suppose not.' He wondered if he even had true friends? People feared him. He had fought two duels. People respected him. His ability with cards, pistols, and even his fists at Jackson's was never questioned. Some might even admire his daredevil ways, the curricle races and steeple-chasing, but was that friendship?

'By the way, I have already asked Robbins to prepare a light repast,' she added, jolting him from his reverie.

'You are certain? I can send you over in my carriage to see Mirabelle's aunt if you really wish it,' he offered.

'She is having a dinner party,' Beth said flatly.

He saw her hand again move nervously against her gown and he was reminded of the shy girl who had never enjoyed formal dining for fear she would knock something over and cause a mess.

'Then I will enjoy your company,' he said. 'As long as we talk of the weather and not of Graham Hill.'

She smiled, really more a grin than a smile,

and surprisingly infectious. 'Very well. Although English weather is such a boring topic. Perhaps it might be more entertaining if we lived in a place with blizzards or tornados.'

'We do get the occasional heavy fog, will that do?'

She laughed. 'Much too damp. But you could tell me about London, the places to go and all that is exciting about it.'

'Exciting?' He raised a brow.

'Yes, like Hyde Park or St James's?' She leaned forward, enthusiasm rippling through her voice.

His lips quirked. 'I hadn't actually thought of them as exciting. They are fine, I suppose.'

He could not remember the last time he had gone to either, although likely Celeste had dragged him there on some occasion.

'Fine?' Beth frowned as though not entirely liking his answer. 'And the theatre?'

'Pleasant enough.'

'The ballet?'

'Adequate.'

'Good gracious, you are hardly a fount of information.'

'I had not realised that an in-depth knowledge of London's diversions would be required,' he said.

'But you must like something?'

He liked racing down Rotten Row. He liked the release in physical exhaustion and the joy in the wild tumultuous drumming of hooves. He liked going to Jackson's. He enjoyed the skill of boxing, the weaving, the ducking and the quick hard strikes.

'I will ask Robbins to procure a guidebook so I can endeavour to describe London's many pleasurable pastimes prior to our repast,' he said.

But despite his bland tones, he felt an usual humour and a warmth under his chest. He realised that, for the first time in years, he was almost looking forward to something.

# Chapter Eight

'Mr Robbins promises good weather tomorrow,' Beth said.

She was sitting at the dining table and had heard him enter. She always liked to be at the table first, to orientate herself to the silverware, the crystal, the location of bowls and plates.

'My butler has taken up forecasting the weather?' Ren asked, seating himself with rattle of the chair.

'Indeed, he is able to do so on account of his ankles.'

'His ankles?'

'They ache when it is going to rain.'

'And they are not aching currently?' he asked.

'No.'

'Of course, I am thankful to be kept apprised of any meteorological trends, but as I recall you suggested that English weather was somewhat boring. Is the weather now of particular interest to you?'

'Yes. I have decided we are going on a picnic.'

'You what?' She heard a hard metallic clunk as though he had struck a fork or knife. 'It is only April.'

'It is going to be unseasonably warm tomorrow.'

'Robbins again? His wrists discern temperature?'

'No, it was warm today and he thinks the weather pattern likely to continue,' she said.

'And where are we going to have this picnic?'

'Robbins suggests St George's.'

'My butler appears to be having a much greater impact on my life than usual. And why this sudden interest in outdoor living?'

Beth bit her lip, feeling an unusual nervous fluttering about her midsection. She had struck upon the idea as she had rested on her bed before dressing for dinner. At the time, it had seemed inspired. Now she was less certain.

Indeed, she recognised an unusual reticence. She didn't want to spoil the mood by suggesting something he might not like. Their banter was pleasant—more than pleasant, it created a peculiar tingling awareness about her person, a sharpening of her senses and a feeling that everything about her, every sound, every scent and every texture, was heightened. The sensation felt pleasant, but also new and different from anything she had experienced.

There was also a sense of fragility about it. She remembered how she had once balanced on a low tree stump. For a split second, she had remained upright, perfectly poised, before tumbling into the grass below.

She stretched her fingers on the fine linen table cloth, rubbing the tips against the fabric. He was waiting for an answer, she realised, and would not want prevarication.

'When I asked you about Hyde Park, you said it was fine. When I asked you about the theatre you said it was pleasant and when I asked you about the dancing you said it was adequate,' she said.

'There is something wrong with things being pleasant, fine and adequate?'

'Yes, when there is nothing that is fabulous.'

'And the picnic will be fabulous?' he asked.

'I don't know, but I hope it might be. I remember when you found things fabulous. I remember when I envied you your world of colour and beauty and drama. In those days, you didn't speak in a drawl and you were interested in everything.'

She heard his intake of breath and felt the moment shatter, as though she had gone tumbling face first into the grass.

'That person no longer exists,' he said. 'You cannot chase a ghost.'

He did not drawl, but spoke in hard clipped syllables, like a smith striking a shoe. She swallowed, her hand once more moving against the table linen. She touched her fork, pressing the prongs into her skin, focusing on the pricks of discomfort.

'But I would like to experience London, at least parts of it. Not the busy parts, but the park, the houses or even the shops. And really only you can help. You describe things better than anyone.'

'Describe?'

'Yes, like you used to do.'

'I don't paint,' he said.

'And I am not asking you to do so. But this is my first and possibly my only trip to London and I am left with Allie's descriptions of squished houses and fancy streets. I want you to describe London to me, the way you used talk about Graham Hill and Allington.'

'And if I have something else planned for the day?'

'Your butler does not know of any other engagements.'

'Good Lord, Robbins again. I do not keep my butler apprised of my every move.'

'But you will come?'

There was a pause and Beth again felt that peculiar heightened awareness. She could feel her own pent-up breath and the rhythmic whisper of fabric as he breathed in and out. Almost, she could feel his gaze on her.

'Yes,' he said. 'But you will not change my mind about the estate by force feeding me cream puffs.'

'Actually, I do not intend to discuss the estate. I thought we could have a holiday?'

'A what?' Ren laughed, not that harsh, abrupt bark, but something softer.

'A holiday,' she repeated.

'And what would this holiday consist of?'

'Nothing—that is the joy of a holiday. I thought

we could forget about Allington and Jamie and Graham Hill. And even the Duke. I thought perhaps we could laugh a little, eat a little, talk and forget that we are old, stodgy adults.'

'Talk?'

'Yes, there are very few people with whom I can converse. I don't have many friends. I mean, there is Jamie and I love him, but he really doesn't talk, except to plants.'

'And you are lonely?' he said, as though discovering something unexpected.

'A little. And I thought you might be, too.'

He said nothing for a moment and she wondered both at her temerity and stupidity. The man, after all, was known for having a string of mistresses and doubtless belonged to every gentleman's club in London. Loneliness hardly seemed a likely predicament.

'And how long is this holiday to be?' he asked at length.

She felt uncertain. 'I don't know. Long enough to forget I am a grown-up.'

'You don't want to be grown up?' He gave a slight chuckle, but there was a silky timbre to his voice which made her feel oddly breathless, even though she was not exercising or exerting herself in any manner.

'Don't,' she muttered. 'It makes me—think of elephants.'

He laughed, a full warm sound. 'So, there will be no elephants on this picnic?'

'Definitely no elephants,' she said.

Mr Robbins's ankles proved accurate. The day dawned clear and surprisingly warm for April. Beth had told Ren to be ready shortly before noon and he complied.

'You do realise that I am never out of bed before early afternoon?'

'I hadn't. How peculiar! You require that much sleep?'

'It is not really so much when one doesn't return home until dawn.'

'Gracious. What do you do?'

Two nights ago he had won several thousand at a game of hazard and then there had been last week when he had timed a foot race between two members of the club along a London street. The race hadn't been entirely successful as one gentleman had run into the lamp post and then they had all gone inside to procure steak for his black eye and brandy for his ego. Ren couldn't remember much more about the night, but when he'd come out again it had been well past dawn.

'Anyway,' she added. 'I am quite certain numerous late nights are not healthy. Jamie feels certain that a lack of sleep impacts milk production in cows.'

He raised a quizzical eyebrow. 'A fact that would only interest me if I were a dairy farmer or a cow.'

'Or a gentleman wishing to adopt a healthy lifestyle.'

'Gracious, what a fate.'

Truthfully, Ren had felt no great enthusiasm for the enterprise when forced to get up at the unreasonably early hour. In fact, he was uncertain why he had even agreed and was thinking rather fondly of Celeste who never hatched such harebrained schemes.

Still, as the carriage pulled away he knew a levity of spirit which was quite contrary to his usual lassitude.

He looked at his 'wife' as she sat on the seat opposite. He had schooled himself not to use the term. It was neither accurate nor representative of a lifestyle he desired with Beth or any woman, for that matter.

Yet there was a pleasure in looking at her.

There was, there had always been, a serenity about her. He remembered her ability to sit still while he painted and how she would run her fingers across moss and bark and grass, the concentration evident as she discerned each texture. He remembered that the very act of describing a scene to her had helped his art and somehow stilled that restlessness which was so much a part of his personality. She had made him see things differently. He'd analysed colours, perceiving them not only as one dimensional, but with texture. Of course, he hadn't painted for years. Eleven years, actually.

He'd tried once after he'd finished school. He'd bought the paints and brushes. He'd told himself that his illegitimacy had robbed him of his family, but should not rob him of his art, and he'd stood there, clutching the wooden palette and staring at the blank canvas, until his eyes watered.

And he'd heard the remembered echo of schoolboy laughter. 'But of course he paints, he's a painter's *bastard*.' He remembered also how his mother had never looked at his paintings, averting her gaze and flinching as though in physical pain.

The carriage stopped, jerking his attention back to the present. They were on the crest of a hill in a less popular part of Hyde Park. Ren helped Beth out. The feel of her hand, nestled within his own, sent a ludicrous *frisson* of awareness through him, irrational given the innocuous nature of the touch.

For a moment they stood, the sun warm on their faces. He knew from her expression that she was listening. She had always done that, stayed quite still and catalogued each sound as a detective might discern clues.

'We are near water—a stream or brook.'

'Yes, there is a pond just down the hill. Likely there is a stream feeding it.'

It was a pretty scene; there was no wind and the water was glassy, the reflection broken only by the trailing fronds of the weeping willows and the tiny, infinitesimal ripples of insects skittering across. In that moment, the urge to paint rose again. He felt it in his chest, in a slight quickening of his pulse, a sharp exhalation and a tingling within his fingertips.

'You still feel it?' she said.

'What?'

'You called it the physical ache of beauty. I used to envy you that.'

He remembered the words. He remembered the feeling. 'Good Lord, what a lot of nonsense I spouted,' he said, turning briskly to unload the carriage. 'We'd best take several blankets to sit on or we will get soaked. The ground is still damp.'

'Robbins put one in the basket and a sunshade which might also serve to shield us from the rain if necessary.'

'It appears you have thought of everything.'

'I had help,' she said.

'The omnipotent Robbins.'

Beth insisted that, as they were pretending to be children, they had no need for servants and directed the removal of both the horse and carriage.

'We never had servants following us around at Graham Hill,' she said.

He placed his hand on her elbow. He felt her start and felt his own reaction, as if his fingers had been singed by a spark. He dropped his hand, bending to pick up the basket.

'Good gracious! What on earth have they put in this thing?' he said.

'I am not exactly certain. Sadly, Mrs Crofton said that she couldn't fit in the fishing rod.'

'A fishing rod? You'd have us catch our luncheon?' He glanced towards the small pond. It did not look promising. 'I am glad we have been provided with an additional source of sustenance.'

'Indeed, Mrs Crofton promised all manner of goodies.'

'Hence the basket's weight. Let us hope we find a suitable picnic place soon.'

'I'm sure we will,' Beth inhaled. 'It smells perfect.'

He glanced at their surroundings. Much of the grass was still yellow from winter and muddy from the spring rains. The shrubbery boasted the stark, bare twigs of winter and the pond looked brown.

'It is perfect,' he said.

They walked in silence. She had placed one hand at his elbow while still grasping her cane with the other.

'Describe it to me—' her fingers tightened slightly '—like you used to at home.'

'It is beautiful,' he said, glancing at her.

The sun touched her face. Her lashes formed delicate fans across her cheeks and he became aware of their solitude and wished with startling intensity that things were different. He wished he was not illegitimate, that he was not a rake, that he did not feel this numb, dead ache for a brother who was not a brother, a father who was not a father. He wished that he did not fight duels or have whole nights obliterated by alcohol.

'Tell me.'

'It is grassy with five trees,' he said.

'You are being disobliging.'

'And you are wanting me to be someone I can no longer be. I am not the boy who was your friend. I am not the boy who drew pretty pictures and believed in art and the ache of beauty and other nonsense.'

'But you could still describe it to me,' she said softly. 'Because I still believe in art and the ache of beauty.'

He wanted to say 'more fool you' but couldn't. Instead he stopped, putting down the basket and surveying the scene once more. This time he allowed himself to notice the different shades of green, the bright emerald moss, the verdant jade of willows' unfurled leaves, the dark blue-green of the scattered conifers sombre against the alders' paler shades. He could visualise the palette. He could imagine the delicate mix of yellow and blue.

He felt a heady excitement, like a person gorging on forbidden fruit.

Had he even noticed London's greenery before? He could remember only riding hard and fast, as though punishing himself, immersing himself within London's foggy grey.

He glanced down at her blind, expectant face.

'The grass stretches away from us,' he said. 'It is soft and smooth, like a green carpet. It looks the way the velvet of the curtains at Allington feels. The park is different from the country. It is more open. It is not constrained by fences or hedges. There are no cows or horses and the trees are huge and tall. It's as though they know they are important. They are not crowded, but each owns its space. They are like the women who still wore hooped skirts when we were little.'

She angled her face towards the pond as though his words had truly made it visible. Her smile widened. The breeze had loosened her hair and brightened her cheeks so that they flushed pink.

'I always feel like I can see the colours when you describe them. Pink is sweet like sugar biscuits. And green is mint leaves.'

She touched the bushes beside her as though to illustrate her point. They crackled under her touch. He smiled as they were neither pink nor green, but brown and deadened from winter.

He stepped closer to her, forgetting the basket and stumbled. His movement brought them together as though choreographed in a Sheridan play. He heard her exhalation and felt the soft warmth of her breath as her chest rose.

They stood quite close. The silence magnified and it seemed that everything else had dwarfed to insignificance. Slowly, he touched a glistening strand of gold hair. It wound about his finger, glimmering in the pale spring sunlight.

He felt a contented wholeness, a peacefulness. It was as though some inner darkness, some yawning need, was briefly sated.

* * *

Beth stood within his arms. The sun warmed them. There was a stillness about him that was unusual. She had seen him infrequently since adulthood, but had always been aware of his restlessness, the movement of his arms and legs as though unable to stay still. Even after their wedding day, he had left almost immediately, saying only that he had business in London.

'Thank you,' he said. She felt and heard his voice vibrating through his chest, just as she felt and heard the music at the church. 'For coming to London. For telling me that Edmund knew and still cared. I tried to tell him not to go.'

'I know.'

'I loved him,' Ren said.

'I know.'

They stood entwined, the moment sweet. Then it shifted. Beth became aware not only of the warmth of the sun against her back, but also of the long, lean hardness of him pressing against her. The steady beat of his heart quickened as though in response to the lessening of her own lassitude.

His arms tightened.

Instinctively, she leaned into him. Her breasts, pressed against the lining of her gown, tingled. Sensations—strange, unknown, exciting, complex—surged through her, heating her cheek as she laid it flush to the worsted cloth of his jacket.

She felt him shift away and felt an instant of loss and need. Then his fingers touched her chin, tipping it upwards. His caress left a trail of sparks, igniting something deep into the very heart of her. He was going to kiss her. She wanted him to kiss her. His lips touched hers. The movement was slow, gentle, exploratory. It was not like the kiss in the study which had been fuelled by anger.

His lips touched hers fleetingly, for the merest instant.

The sparks exploded, flooding her with sensation she had not thought possible. Her hand reached into the thickness of his hair, pulling him closer. His lips touched hers again. She felt the intrusion of his tongue—except it did not feel like an intrusion. She pressed closer to him, arching against him, melding her soft curves to his harsh angles.

She was molten, liquid, fused to him. Everything dwarfed to insignificance in contrast to this fiery needfulness.

Ren broke the contact, pulling jerkily away, his breath coming in harsh and ragged gulps.

'Ren?' She reached out with her hands. She felt off balance, confused, as though the earth beneath her feet lacked stability. Her thoughts and emotions swung and circled. She had dropped her cane.

'I'm sorry.' His voice shook.

Her hands found his arm. She grasped it with one hand while reaching up with the other. Stretching her fingers, she explored his features. Slowly, inch by inch, she felt how his face had changed and matured. She felt the strong chin, the familiar cheekbones and aquiline nose. She felt the lines bracketing his mouth which spoke of sadness and also a small scar just above his eyebrow.

'Don't,' he muttered.

'What?'

'That.' He shifted further. The bushes rustled.

'Did I do it wrong?' she asked. 'The kissing?'

'No.' His breath was still uneven and his voice

strained as though his throat had tightened. 'No, you did not do it wrong.'

'But you stopped?'

'I— It— I— Look, I am not— I have always been— You deserve better.'

'Why?' she asked.

'What?'

'Because I am blind?' she asked.

'What? No—'

'Being blind does not make me a saint—that is as limiting as those who think that a lack of sight impacts intelligence. My disability has no impact on my morality, although I suppose it might limit my opportunities for immoral behaviour.'

'Good Lord, what do you know of immoral behaviour?'

'Very little,' she said.

She felt a frisson of regret that she had never felt previously. Those kisses—it felt as though she had glimpsed something, some experience that had been denied to her. It was irrational. It was foolish, but her body felt a need, a yearning—

His free arm moved forward. She heard the rustle of cloth. He touched her chin, tilting it. Time stilled. She heard again his quickened, ragged breath. She felt the slight roughness of his thumb brush her skin.

Then his hand dropped. He stepped back. 'Right,' he said briskly. 'We will aim to keep your knowledge of such behaviour limited.'

'I—' Loss, regret, embarrassment flooded her in a confused disorientating mix. 'Naturally. Absolutely. Certainly.'

She spoke as though the proliferation of words would mitigate the awkwardness and distract her from the confused mix of emotion.

She heard him bend to pick up the basket.

'Shall we find somewhere for this picnic. Sun or shade?'

'Sun,' she said, stiffening both her spine and smile, because in the sun anything seemed possible.

# Chapter Nine

Impatient as always, Beth stepped ahead, tapping out her route with her cane. Her sure-footed ability had always impressed him—how she could feel her way through the world, moving with care but a surprising surety.

They found a spot on a slight hillock overlooking the lake. He laid down the plaid rug and helped her to sit. Then they opened the wicker basket and he was aware again of an almost child-like pleasure, more typical of a child at Christmas than a sophisticated man.

Mrs Crofton had thought of everything: fresh bread, cheese, fruit, chicken, meat pies, wine of an excellent vintage.

Beth leaned over, sniffing with her head slightly cocked and her expression intent.

'You resemble a hunting dog.' He chuckled,

glad of the humour to lessen the tension which still seemed to snap between them.

'Chicken,' she said. 'And that is hardly a flattering comparison.'

'As always, your senses are correct. In addition to the chicken, we have wine, bread, cake and even some strawberries.'

'We cannot possibly have strawberries.'

'But we do.'

'Give me one to prove it,' Beth said.

'What? Dessert before the savoury?'

'Fruit doesn't count. Besides, I like to break the rules.'

'Of course you do.' He passed her a strawberry.

She took it. He watched as she held it between thumb and finger, the juice staining her fingers red. With a whimsical smile, she popped it into her mouth, delicately licking her parted lips. As always, there was a spontaneity in her gesture, a lack of affectedness and an intensity in the way she lived as though all that mattered was the taste of that single fruit.

He wondered when he had last enjoyed a moment like this.

By being unable to see others, she was less cognisant or caring of their opinions. She did not hesitate to show her emotion, be it joy or anger. And she took such pleasure from little things.

Or perhaps this had nothing to do with her blindness, but everything to do with her—Beth.

'A smudge or a strawberry stain?' she asked, interrupting his reverie.

'Pardon?'

'You are staring,' she said, tapping her lips delicately with the napkin.

'How do you always know? I might have been looking at the brook or a bird.'

'There is no brook. At least not one nearby or I would have heard it and currently I can hear no birdsong.'

He smiled. 'No smudge or stain. I was merely thinking that a single strawberry seems to give you much joy.'

She laughed. 'But this is no ordinary strawberry. It is miraculous. You must concede that any strawberry which tastes this good so early in the season is not only fine but fabulous?'

'Likely it was made ripe in a conservatory, which is scientific and not miraculous.'

'Perhaps. But still fabulous.'

'Very well,' he conceded. 'This is—' His gaze lingered on the open parkland and shimmering pond.

'Fabulous?'

'Different from my usual existence,' he said.

They ate the luncheon in a companionable silence. Perhaps, Ren thought, that was the measure of friendship—the ability to spend time with another person without the need to fill in the quiet with words. He did not think he had ever had that with anyone else, certainly no other woman.

Then again, his childhood had been spent worrying about the opinions of others, while in adulthood he had occupied himself proving that he did not care. Indeed, he had made a career of ensuring that the man in no way resembled the lonely, scrawny schoolboy with his palette of paints.

'So,' she said, after they had eaten a good portion of the food. 'The scars on your face—are they from boxing or a duel?'

'Neither.'

Indeed, he'd thought them hardly noticeable. But then, she did not see as others saw.

'Really? How did you get them?'

'A sophisticated lady does not ask personal questions, you know.'

'I have never pretended sophistication.' She licked the tips of her fingers as though to emphasise the point.

'At school,' he said.

'You got them at school?'

'Yes.'

'An accident.'

'Not that accidental,' he said wryly.

It had been in his first year when he had still painted. They'd surrounded him, poking him with sticks that were supposed to be paintbrushes and calling him 'the painter's bastard.'

'Father said boys could be cruel, particularly to people who they perceive as intelligent or different. That is why he didn't send Jamie.'

Ren nodded. 'Your father was wise.'

Jamie would have been mincemeat within the week. Or maybe not. There had always been that singularity of purpose that might make Jamie impervious to schoolboy taunts.

'They were unkind to you?'

'Not for long.'

She was silent and it seemed to him that she

perceived more from his terse three words than he had wanted. He'd survived, thanks to physical growth, a natural ability with his fists and acuity with cards. He'd thrown out his paints and brushes and schooled himself to raise that one eyebrow at their chant. Then he'd hid in the stables and learned to box, striking a hay bale over and over again.

And when he'd felt ready, he had struck the biggest bully of them all. He had heard the boy's nose crack. He had seen the blood, clots of red splattered on to the mix of dirt and snow.

Taking out his handkerchief, he had carefully cleaned his knuckles, raised one brow and turned, walking back into the school.

'You do not wish to talk about it?' Beth angled her face to him.

'Not particularly.'

She bent her head, pulling at a few tufts of grass and rubbing them between her fingers. 'My father was like that. He'd get glum and silent. Mother used to be able to coax him out of his moods. Or sometimes he'd say he needed a break from the quiet of the country and come up here. He loved the museums. I remember he told me that there was a huge stuffed giraffe in one. He'd said if I was brave and wouldn't be afraid of the travelling, he'd bring me.'

'Did you come?'

She shook her head. 'Mother had her accident and he stayed home to look after her. Jamie would never go because he hated crowds, although I suppose he overcame that on at least one occasion.'

'He hasn't gambled since?'

'No. I think you were right. It was desperation.'

He glanced at her. The reminder of that surreal proposal and her suggested annulment caused a flickering tension.

'So was London worth the coach ride?' he asked into the quiet.

Amusement flickered across her face. 'It doesn't seem as though I've missed too much. Although Allie assures me that one can purchase the most exquisite bonnets, some even topped with real fruit or some such nonsense. Likely the country suits me well enough, although it would be pleasant to hear a ballet or the opera.'

The amusement was laced with a hint of wistfulness. He had forgotten how she'd liked music. He remembered her now in church, leaning forward in the pew with an absence of motion that was peculiar to her. She'd stretch her fingers along the pew's wooden back to better 'feel' the music.

'I suppose you have seldom heard an orchestra.'

'Only small quartets when your mother or Mirabelle entertained. Now I must rely on Miss Plimco on the organ. She tries very hard.'

'Goodness! As I recall, she was very trying and her enthusiasm was much greater than her ability.'

'Yes, but there isn't anyone else and I am glad enough for her. In winter we sometimes cannot even get to church.'

'That must be lonely.'

'A little,' she said.

Again he was struck by the solitary nature of her life with only Jamie for company, particularly now that Mirabelle and Edmund were gone.

'Stay here,' he said impulsively.

'In the park?'

'No, I mean London. For an additional night or two. You might as well, now that you have made the journey. The city offers so much: music, the opera, the ballet, plays. Things you've never seen.'

Colour stained her cheeks. 'Jamie—'

'Will fare quite well without you. You know he will. One really is not overly important to Jamie unless one has leaves and roots.'

'He also has a fondness for livestock,' she quipped.

'You'll think about it?'

'I—' She gave a soft gasp, her lips opening, and he found himself watching their soft pinkness and the way she gently bit her bottom lip. 'People would talk.'

'You are my wife. Surely we could go out together.'

Hi mistress Celeste would be irritated, but likely she'd be content enough with a trinket. He was becoming bored anyway. Of course, boredom was his constant companion, interrupted only by grief.

Except—he straightened, an abrupt jerking motion. He hadn't felt that usual ennui at all today. Or even yesterday. And the tight ball of pain that usually woke him at night had lessened a little... mellowed, he might say.

'Why this sudden enthusiasm for my company?

I thought you rather wished to encourage my departure?'

'Perhaps this holiday lifestyle is starting to appeal.'

'I cannot promise not to discuss the estate for ever. That was why I came and it wouldn't feel right not to do so.'

'I know.' Leaning closer, he ran his fingers gently across her cheek. 'But I cannot keep that land.'

She nodded. He saw now that tears shimmered. 'But giving it to the Duke?'

Her words brought back the memory of that first visit. He remembered the stuffed tiger, the cases of butterflies and the way the man's pale eyes had followed Beth.

As a child, he'd not have given the man as much as a stable cat.

'I haven't made a final decision,' he said, almost surprised by his own words.

She smiled, raising sightless eyes, still wet with tears. 'Thank you!'

His finger grazed her chin. She inhaled. He saw her frame contract with her exhalation and could hear the hammer of his own heart. In that moment, this woman, with her blonde hair and pale porcelain skin, made all else inconsequential.

'Come to the opera tonight.'

He saw her confusion; her brows pulled together and her lips parted slightly. Anxiety mixed with temptation flickered across her face. Then she grinned, her face suddenly alight with that vibrant love of life and experience, reminding him of the first time she'd ridden a horse or let him guide her across the brook at Allington.

'Very well,' she said.

Beth sat on her bed, hands clasped tight. She felt like she had on her first full gallop—a wonderful mix of exhilaration, fear and excitement ballooning within.

Except, should she be traipsing off to the opera like a child playing dress up? Her intent when she came to London had not been...this. She shivered, rubbing her arms.

She remembered the morning of her wedding. She had worn a dress of soft silk with pearl beading about the high waist. Mirabelle had insisted that any wedding dress should have some adornment. The beads had felt so tiny and smooth.

Jamie had walked her down the aisle. Miss Plimco had played the organ, enthusiastically discordant. The vicar had sniffed five times and she'd wanted to give him a handkerchief. She remembered being aware of inconsequential details: a buzzing fly, someone raking outside, a horse giving a low whinny.

She'd felt a sense of disbelief, but also a sense of rightness. It felt good to know Ren had come back to them and she had been conscious of their fellowship.

But she had not married a friend. Instead, she had found herself with a stranger—a shadowy, nebulous entity who lived a very different life in London. A man who bore no resemblance to the boy with whom she had once laughed and played, a sophisticated man with mistresses who drank too much, fought too much and gambled too much.

And now, briefly, she had glimpsed the person she had once known. And it felt… Her mind groped for the words. It felt as though she was coming alive again, as though every smell and sound was more intense, more exciting, more exhilarating.

Who was she fooling? She was not going to the opera to discuss the tenants, the village or the Duke. She was going because she wanted to spend time with Ren. She wanted to feel this confused, happy, giddy, teary, prickly somersaulting sensation.

Except...she knew how it would end. Ren was not her childhood friend any more. Yes, perhaps her picnic with its sentimental claptrap had reminded him of childhood and evoked a fleeting shadow of the boy he had been.

But a shadow was not real. Her friend had morphed into a man she did not know. He'd said as much himself.

The door swung open as Allie burst into the room, already talking. 'I heard you were going out. I am that excited! I really didn't think I needed to pack your best dress, but I am so glad that I did! Indeed, my sainted mother always said as how a person should be ready for any eventuality and I am thankful now I listened. Indeed. I've been looking through the fashion magazines and if you'll let me make just a few changes, I'll have you looking quite the thing. As well, I think if we could give your hair a few curls, you know, it would look very well indeed. I am certain I could make you the height of fashion and ever so elegant.'

'I was actually wondering if I should even go,' Beth said.

'What? Of course, you should. It would be rude to do otherwise. Besides, poor Arnold still has a sore leg so really it wouldn't be right to leave London quite yet and if you are going to stay you might as well have some fun while you're at it.'

'I forgot about Arnold. How is he? What did the doctor say?'

'That he was wasted in service and should join the Foreign Legion which seems an odd thing to say. I mean Arnold can't even speak any language other than English and really, he doesn't say that much even then. He's more the strong silent type. Anyhow, we can't possibly leave for Allington at this late time of the day.'

'No, I suppose not,' Beth said. 'But perhaps a quiet evening—'

'You have evenings at Allington with nothing but quiet and well you know it. Right now you have a chance to hear real music which will be a might better than what Marsha Plimco's efforts produce.'

'Very well!' Beth raised her hands in mock surrender. 'You have convinced me.'

'Good. Now the next thing is to do some work with your hair, which is looking somewhat of a haystack, if I may say so.'

Beth feigned reluctance, but recognised an unusual interest in appearing her best. It was, she supposed, natural to wish to look presentable when entering the milieu of the rich and aristocratic. It had nothing, absolutely nothing, to do with any desire to enhance her looks for Ren.

Allie, of course, was thrilled to perfect Beth's style, clapping her hands the second Beth agreed. 'At last! I have been longing to style your hair for eons, but you were so stubborn.'

'I find the cows do not mind.'

'Pardon?'

'At home I am considerably more likely to run into a cow than a person and I find they seldom complain.'

'Well, we are not in the country now and I doubt many cows attend the theatre. No, I will make you look wonderful.'

'Like a princess in a fairy tale,' Beth said, then frowned, reeling back her thoughts. It was all very well to feel like a princess, but she must remember that there would be no happy ending. This was one evening. She could not hope that curls or flounces would make Ren perceive her differently. She was the little blind girl he had married to save her from the big bad Duke. Now that her estate no longer owed money and was prosperous, she had, for all intents and purposes, been saved.

Therefore, annulment was the only sensible course of action. Moreover, it was the only dutiful course of action. It was best for both Ren and for the tenants if he assumed his role as landlord.

And in this role, he must have an heir. Ironically, her duty lay in convincing him to assume a role which would make the dissolution of their marriage the more imperative.

So Allie could work on her curls, her dress, her ribbons and her flounces. She could make Beth look a princess for one night. But it was an act. Beth would enjoy this evening. She would listen to the music and enjoy that spark, that vibrancy that Ren engendered within her. She would store up memories to keep her warm in the cold years ahead.

But she must remember that this was not a fairy tale. She could not remain Ren's wife. She could not construct foolish palaces in her head.

This was one magical night.

Nothing more.

# Chapter Ten

The moment they entered the opera house, Ren heard the lull in the conversation. It was a moment of silence, like the pause between waves lapping on the beach. The hush lasted for the barest moment, quickly followed by increased babble as though a thousand tongues wagged—which likely they did.

'Are they talking about us?' Beth asked.

'Possibly.'

He glanced at her. Her beauty struck him anew. It was ephemeral, but mixed also with a new sophistication.

'Your hair has changed,' he said.

'I let Allie have her way for once.'

'She is a girl of many talents.'

They stepped further into the crowd. He allowed his gaze to flicker across the multicoloured dresses, the gilt trim around the doors and windows, the painted cupids, the heavy sparkling chandeliers, the curious gazes and smiles, half-hidden behind feathered fans.

He felt Beth stiffen, her fingers tightening on his arm as she pressed closer to him. She had paled. Indeed, she was so white that her forehead blended into her blonde hair and he could see that her breathing had quickened.

'I'm sorry. I forgot,' he said.

He remembered how noises and the press of people could overwhelm her. It had happened so infrequently—a weakness she had both feared and despised. Once she had become faint at the village fête and once at a ball organised by his mother. Indeed, she so seldom allowed any aspect of her disability to impede her that he hadn't considered how overwhelming the theatre must be.

'Come,' he said gently. 'It is quieter in my box.' He leaned into her so that she could hear his words over the noise.

'I thought I could be like…a princess for a night.'

'You are.'

Ren,' Beth whispered. 'Ren… I—I can't do this.

I feel I must bolt or that I will be ill and people will talk about us and you.'

'In that case it will be the most innocuous gossip they have had for eons, particularly with me as its subject,' he said drily. 'However, you can do this. I'm here. We will take ten steps up a short staircase. Then we will turn right into my box and it will be quiet and cooler.'

'I—I can't. I feel—'

'You can. Remember, you have always said that bravery is not only action, but action in the face of fear.'

'It is much easier to make such statements when safe in an armchair.'

'You were astride Lil, as I recall.'

She smiled, an infinitesimal upturn of her lips. Perspiration shone on her forehead. He should not have come up with this suggestion, but he had not wanted to spend another evening in his study. Or with Celeste. Or even drinking or gambling. None of these pursuits eased the pain. They only made him feel like an actor taking part in a bad play. Pretending.

But he had wanted to see Beth's face light up when she heard those first strands of music, like when she had touched her lips to that ripe straw-berry. He felt if he could see her joy, it would make his world...better. Purer, somehow.

She couldn't see a damned thing and yet she had the ability to make the world beautiful.

'Come,' he said. 'Ten steps.'

'Are they staring?'

He glanced at the other theatre goers, clustered in groups. They largely ignored him except for furtive sideways glances. His life in London was one which defied convention. Indeed, he cared little for the Dowagers in their fancy clothes, the gentlemen with their discreet mistresses or the mamas who clutched at their offspring as though his very presence would contaminate.

But Beth would care.

'Not at all. We are fast becoming yesterday's news,' he said.

'Describe it to me,' she said. 'It will help.'

He looked about the crowded foyer. 'We are in a huge, beautiful entrance hall. The ceiling is high, as high as a tall tree, and there are chan-deliers which hang down, heavy with candles which glow like dozens of tiny, flickering suns. The people here are beautiful. They look more like exotic birds or flowers with brilliant petals. Indeed, the reds and oranges are so bright they seem to burn like fire and the blues and greens are cool like streams. And they glide or float like the dandelion puffs we used to blow as children.'

Her breathing had slowed from that hurried pant. With a tiny, imperceptible nod, she stepped forward with him. He counted the steps as he had done during childhood whenever they navigated the unfamiliar. Her hand rested on his arm, her grip still firm, but her fingers no longer clenched tight into his arm.

'In three more steps, we will turn left and be at my box,' he continued. 'Then we will be able to hear the orchestra tuning. I remember my mother once had a quartet of string instruments. We listened from the second floor and you said that the violin was talking to the cello.'

She smiled. 'And that the former rather sounded like a nagging spouse.'

'Here is my box.' He led her in and they sat down. He heard her exhale.

'It will be quiet here,' he said. 'Well, except for the orchestra tuning.'

'The quartet is quadrupled like many nagging spouses,' she said, angling her head.

He smiled, listening also to instruments. Many people milled in the pit, but most of the boxes opposite were still empty. She released his arm, her hand dropping to her lap, her fingers long, pale and delicate against the black silk.

A frown flickered, as though more puzzled than distressed. 'I was glad that nobody greeted us, but is that usual in town?'

'It is usual for me.'

'It was not because I looked odd or mad or because I am blind?'

'No,' he said. 'It is because my behaviour is such that the *ton* choose not to recognise me.'

'Good,' she said.

He felt his lips twitch. 'It does save one from dreadful conversations about arthritis and gout.'

'Gout?'

'Yes, gentlemen and ladies past a certain age tend to have one or the other or both and too frequently feel the need to itemise the symptoms.'

'What a fate.'

'To experience the ailment or the conversation?'

'Both,' she said.

He chuckled, appreciating her quick wit and that unusual lightness of spirit that she engendered within him.

'And thank you for keeping me calm and remembering what to do,' she added, after a moment. 'That has not happened for a long time. I thought I was rid of it.'

'Coming to London was an undertaking…' He paused, glancing across the colourful assemblage within the pit and at the boxes opposite now starting to fill. 'I cannot promise it will change my mind, but I do appreciate the effort it took.'

She smiled. 'But I won't concede quite yet. I still hope to persuade you.'

He looked at her. As though strengthened by the inner battle she had just fought and won, her natural optimism shone through. She looked so damned eager and bloody hopeful with her face suddenly flushed, her hair shimmering in the candlelight and her lips curved as if anticipating pleasure in a world which he'd found afforded little but pain.

He felt his body tighten. He wanted both to extinguish that ludicrous assurance and, conversely, protect and preserve it.

He shifted. 'You will have to,' he said more curtly. 'It cannot be honourable to keep something which by blood should go to him. I may not like it. I *don't* like it, but I still cannot see another choice.'

'There are always choices.'

'Not ones which I deem honourable.'

'Then expand your view. If you feel you have no right to it, don't keep it, but don't give it to him. Find someone else.'

*Find someone else? Good Lord, she made it sound as though he should give the land to the nearest beggar.*

'The Duke of Ayrebourne is the closest blood relative,' he said.

'Forget about blood. Surely there are other reasons that one can merit land!' She angled her body towards him and he found his gaze inexorably drawn to the soft swell of her breasts and the gleam of pale white skin above the black silk of her dress. Need stirred. He wanted her, this country girl morphed into a London lady.

He liked it.

And hated it.

'A gift from the Crown. Perhaps you have the ear of the Prince?'

'No.' She straightened, a sudden jolting, jerking motion. He recognised also the sudden intensity of her expression. He'd seen it before whenever she was possessed of a new idea. 'I have it! Give the land to the tenants.'

'What?'

'It is the perfect solution. They have lived at Graham Hill for generations. They have toiled and sweated. Give it to them. Or give them the money to buy it.'

She spoke with apparent sincerity, pressing her lips into a familiar straight line of determination.

'My God, you are serious?'

'Of course, I am. Never more so.'

'You do realise how outrageous such a suggestion is?'

'Outrageous is not the same as impossible,' she said, looking damned smug with the retort.

'It would set London on its ear.'

'Again, not necessarily a negative. And I thought you already behaved in a way which caused tongues to wag. Indeed, I rather thought you relished such behaviour,' she retorted, her chin angled in that firm, determined way he also recognised.

'But this is different.'

'You mean it is all right to cause comment by the acquisition of mistresses, but not by giving land to the people who have worked it for generations?'

'For goodness sake, stop talking about mistresses.' Anger flared. The woman seemed to delight in the mention of mistresses, taking every opportunity to bring them into the conversation. Surely any proper wife would be saddened or shocked or angered.

But then, of course, she was not a 'proper' wife and had no desire for the position.

'I merely meant that you do not seem to rule your life based on what is acceptable to others. Therefore, you should not dismiss this suggestion due to that reason alone.'

'And now you start to sound like an Oxford tutor,' he muttered.

But her words were both true and untrue. Certainly, he no longer received invitations to any respectable establishment, but was he really as unacceptable as he supposed? Indeed, his behaviour was even lauded within a certain quarter.

His skill at cards and pistols was known in every gentlemen's club. He was entirely cognisant that his very presence caused tension to rise whenever he entered the card room. He knew well the nervous movement and hurried removal of those less comfortable with high stakes. And that his wild recklessness was aped and admired.

'Anyhow, if you are going to shock society you might as well do so for a worthy cause. Indeed, the more I consider the idea, the more I think it has merit,' she said in irritatingly firm tones as though she had given the last word on the subject.

'And I think it's crazy.'

For the first act, Ren studied the orchestra with a single-minded purpose. He refused to look at this woman who was his wife and yet not his wife, this woman who wanted an annulment, mentioned his mistresses every second sentence, but also seemed under the erroneous impression that she should have input into the fate of his estate. Moreover, just because she lived her life in a way which was not typical of the disabled, she imagined it gave her leave to spout ludicrous ideas smacking too much of revolution.

Still, at some point, he found his tension ease as he relaxed into the seat. The music was pleasant and the ballet well staged. But, despite the perfect, precise movements of the dancers, he found his gaze drawn to Beth. It was her absolute involvement: the way she leaned forward, as though mesmerised, swaying to the music, her movements unselfconscious, rhythmic, instinctive, her eagerness palpable.

She would be that way about making love, he thought.

There might be restraint at first, but not for long.

He pushed the thought away.

He was illegitimate. He lived in London. His life was one of dissolution. Even now, she was the subject of gossip because of him. She might not see the glances, the sneers, the fancy ladies ducking behind their fans, but he did. And eventually she would become aware of them and hurt by them.

It angered him that she should be the subject of gossip, even more so that he should have put her in that position. Indeed, it angered him that he had come up with this ludicrous idea to go to the theatre. He should in actuality have insisted that she leave London with all possible dispatch. He was a fool.

He was a selfish fool.

He must stop such nonsense forthwith. Beth would be returned to Allington. He would give Graham Hill to the Duke and continue his path to hell.

*I think if you are going to shock society you might as well do so for a worthy cause.*

The words came so clearly that he glanced towards her to see if she had spoken, but Beth remained mesmerised and silent even as her words rotated in his mind like a child's chanting of a nursery rhyme:

*You might as well do so for a worthy cause,*
*You might as well do so for a worthy cause,*
*You might as well do so for a worthy cause.*

He remembered how he'd hated the Duke as a boy. He remembered the rumours about village girls and the way his gaze slid over Beth, lingering too long on her slim, girlish figure and the hint of breasts pushing against the bodice her dress.

'*I do like to acquire beautiful things,*' he'd said.

Everything had been simpler then. Black and white. Good and bad.

At school Ren had learned how to be a gentleman, to pay one's gambling debts before one's tailor, to know how to wear one's tie and value one's honour above all things.

But what was honour, when all was said and done?

The ballet was magic. From the moment the orchestra started, Beth was entranced. She forgot about the crowded foyer and her momentary panic. This, she realised, was what Ren had meant all those years ago by the *ache of beauty*. Could sighted people see music? It seemed they should, as though music was a physical entity.

For the first time, she could understand London's appeal. To hear something like this was remarkable. To have such a multitude of instruments—cellos, violins, flutes—singing together. Never before had she felt so enveloped by sound and sensation, so transported. Indeed, it seemed to her that her blindness did not matter. It was inconsequential compared to the sounds vibrating through and around her.

Once, she'd thought that she could never leave Allington, even for a short time. Now she realised it would be worth any discomfort to hear music like this or the opera. She had never heard the opera. Perhaps the opera was even more entrancing in its interplay of voice and instrument. This warm theatre had a magic so far removed from mud-splattered bogs and the long winter months when Allington's silence was uninterrupted.

The music ended, the last note fading into the thunder of applause. Beth remained still for long moments. She could not move. She could not shatter that moment.

'It was so beautiful that it hurt,' she whispered at last when she could speak and the applause had died.

'I remember—' Ren said, but broke off the words.

She turned towards him, wondering what he had been about to say. She wished she could see his expression or that she could explore the lines and contours of his face without attracting attention.

'Do you come here often? I suppose you must if you have your own box?' she said instead.

'No.'

'Why do you have a box?'

'It was Edmund's.'

'He used to like music. Mirabelle would play to us both,' she said.

'You spent a lot of time with them?'

'Yes, I enjoyed visiting. Jamie is not the best of company.'

Those had been happier times. Edmund would read to them while Mirabelle sewed and Beth sat listening to the rustle of thread through cloth. When Edmund was away, she and Mirabelle would keep each other company. They'd talked and planned. She had felt the tiny clothes that Mirabelle was making and Mirabelle had let her place her hands against the fabric of her dress over her abdomen so she could feel the baby's movements.

Except it had not survived. Mirabelle had not survived. In many ways, Edmund had not survived. He had changed, withdrawing into himself, a broken man.

'I should have come for Mirabelle's funeral,' Ren said, the words blunt and stark.

'Yes.'

'I saw Edmund in London but I should have been there for him and you.'

'Yes,' she said. 'But at least I understand now why you didn't come back.'

'I do not make the best husband, even for one married only for expedience.'

'You saved me from Ayrebourne which was the purpose of it.'

He was silent. She wished again she could discern his expression and almost reached forward.

With an abrupt movement, he stood. 'Shall we depart? I do not think it will be crowded now.'

The Duke stood at the base of the staircase. Ren stiffened. He had not noticed his presence in the theatre earlier and felt a confused shock, as though his preoccupation with the man had caused him to manifest in the flesh.

Looking at him, Ren felt that instant wave of dislike. There was a pale blandness to him.

He smiled, greeting his acquaintances in a way which was both obsequious and yet calculating.

'Ayrebourne is here,' he said into Beth's ear.

He felt her stiffen, her fingers tightening perceptibly against his arm.

Ayrebourne noted their approach. He stepped forward. 'Cousin,' he said, somehow giving the word a sarcastic twist.

Ren made his bow.

'And Lady Graham,' Ayrebourne said to Beth, again making his bow. 'I haven't seen you in London before... Cousin Rendell, you should not hide her away. Her beauty has only grown greater.'

Ren watched the Duke's gaze flicker over Beth. His eyes were blue, but an odd light blue which somehow added to his overall pallor.

'Indeed, dear Lady Graham, you should visit me at Ayrebourne,' the Duke continued in silky tones. 'I am still there on occasion for hunting weekends. Do you hunt, Lady Graham?'

'No.'

'Of course, you can't see. So sad. There is a beauty to the hunt. The noise of the hounds, their speed, their singularity of purpose.'

'It seems a rather cruel sport,' Beth said.

'There can be beauty in cruelty.'

'Not to me.' Beth's tone was sharp and she straightened her spine, that familiar determined expression flickering across her features. 'On the topic of cruelty, I went to your estate and found your people starving.'

'Are they? How unfortunate. Perhaps I will visit and you can show me.'

'I would imagine your manager could do that,' Ren said curtly. 'I do not think my wife needs to act as a guide to your own estate.'

The Duke's expression did not change. 'Indeed, although it appears Lady Graham might have some particular expertise.'

He enunciated the last word mockingly, playing with the syllables. Ren saw Beth's brows draw together. 'I can certainly make some practical suggestions. You should stop enclosing the farm land and asking them to pay rents they cannot afford.'

The Duke yawned. 'Good gracious, I must say, Rendell, you have acquired a spitfire.'

'My wife is a person, not an acquisition,' Ren said coldly.

Before the Duke could make any reply, Ren realised that his mother had sidled up to them.

'Ren, darling, how nice to see you and so unusual for you to be with your wife. Beth, I did not know you had come to London. Did you enjoy the evening?'

'Yes. The music is quite wonderful, except I was discussing the tenants with Lord Ayre—'

'Darling, not the time or place,' his mother said, almost sharply. 'Ren, you really will have to school Beth in social etiquette. You cannot have her rambling on about tenants every verse end. Now can I drop you anywhere? I have my carriage—'

'No,' Ren said. 'And I find my wife's discourse on tenants more fascinating than the simpering gossip of the *ton*.'

'How quaint,' the Duke said. 'I wonder if Celeste is aware of this sudden fondness for your wife's company. She will perhaps be inspired to develop new topics to better amuse you. Maybe she could adopt the plight of chimney sweeps.'

Fury flashed hot, molten and empowering. Ren stepped closer to the Duke so that he was only inches from the man's face. He could smell the sweet scent of the opium Ayrebourne too frequently consumed. He could see the pores in his pallid skin, the paleness broken only by the tiny red threads of broken blood vessels.

'I believe you forget yourself and what is considered appropriate to discuss in front of a lady. I suggest you keep it in mind,' Ren said.

For a moment, the Duke met his gaze. His pale blue eyes were fringed with sandy lashes and they blinked slowly, the movement almost furtive as though it served to prevent his expression from being discerned.

'Of course,' he said. 'I hope to spend *considerable* time in dear Lady Graham's company and would not want to offend.'

Ren heard Beth's exhalation and felt her fingers tighten on his arm.

'If you will excuse us,' Ren said. 'We must leave and we do not wish to monopolise your time.'

'Absolutely. Delightful to see you both again. Hopefully, the pleasure will be frequently repeated. Goodbye, dear Lady Graham.' The Duke made his bow and, accompanied by Ren's mother, stepped towards the exit.

# Chapter Eleven

'He really is quite vile,' Beth said, with a soft exhale.

By mutual consent, they waited for a few moments before walking through the warmth of the lobby and into the cooler air outside. She again felt that nervous apprehension, the uncertainty of a world not yet explored. Her fingers tightened on his sleeve as she attempted to differentiate the details within the onslaught of sound: horses' hooves, jangling reins, laughter, conversation, a newsboy shouting. She forced herself to breathe and to focus on a single sound. This kept her nervousness at bay, although she was still thankful when his carriage arrived, the door swinging open.

It felt safer within its confines. She liked the thought of being closeted from the world—from the Duke—with a warm brick at her feet and the reassurance of Ren's hand on her own under the thick travel blanket.

She exhaled, thankful as the carriage moved, the rhythm restful.

'I am sorry you had to encounter him,' Ren said. 'I didn't anticipate that he would be there.'

'He is nothing. I am foolish to let him distress me.'

Yet she was…uneasy. Tonight had again reminded her of the soft silkiness of his menace. It was worse than the noisy, rough boys who had scared her as a child or even the bull that had almost trampled over her when she fell into his paddock. Those threats had been loud, tangible, understandable—not this quiet, secret menace.

She shifted, squeezing Ren's hand. 'Let us forget him. We are much too serious for a holiday. If theatre is not your favourite pastime, what do you enjoy?'

'I—' He paused. 'It appears there is little I enjoy.'

'Or little you can speak about without shocking my sensibilities.'

He gave a low chuckle that was almost genuine.

'No, I rather doubt you are easily shocked. When you asked yesterday, that was my reasoning. Now it is not. It is just that I've realised I largely pursue activity for distraction as opposed to enjoyment.'

The words hung in the silent carriage.

'Perhaps you won't allow yourself to enjoy. It's as though you are punishing yourself. None of us asks to be born or can control the way we come into this world.'

She expected a quick biting retort, but he said nothing. Instead, his fingers tightened on her own. Without conscious decision, she leaned against him. She closed her eyes, the tension easing with the carriage's movement and the comforting thud of his heart.

She didn't know quite when the sense of comfort changed, but gradually solace morphed into tingling, growing awakening. She became aware of the hard, angular muscles of his chest. She felt the quickening of his breath and the movement of his thumb against her palm. He traced circles against her skin, his touch igniting a warm, growing, heated need. Sensation flickered and grew.

Gently, with his other hand, he tilted her chin upwards. She felt the tingling graze of his fingers and his movement so that he was no longer beside her but angled over her. Sensation built into eager anticipation. His lips touched her own. She heard herself gasp. The tingling heat grew into a raw, yearning need. She reached up for him. She traced the lines which bracketed his mouth, the scar on his chin and a tiny, puckered mark by his left eyebrow.

He groaned at her touch. His kiss deepened. She felt herself arch against him, the action instinctual. His body was hard, his chest and shoulders muscled under the fine cloth. His hands caressed her back. She felt the movement of his fingers pushing her gown off her shoulders. It slid down. The cool air touched her bare skin and she felt the instant pucker of her nipples.

And then the carriage stopped.

Beth jolted awake as if from a trance. Her dress had slipped so that one breast was almost exposed. Her breath came in hurried pants and a confused mix of emotion flooded and engulfed her.

Tugging at her gown, she shifted from him. Heat washed into her face. He caught her hand, stilling it. 'Beth,' he muttered. 'I've wanted—I've always wanted…stay with me tonight.'

*He'd always wanted…?* A joy, a need, a jubilation filled her, a pulsing happiness. *He'd always wanted…*

'Ren,' she whispered.

She had never expected this. She'd never known that she wanted it—him—so much.

His hands touched her cheeks, cupping her chin and sending a tingling, needy fire that started from his fingers and filled her.

He kissed her again. She allowed herself to melt into him and feel the muscled movement of his arms. She felt the thrust of his tongue between her lips—promising…

She pulled from him.

'I can't,' she said.

Ren stood in his dressing room. He poured himself a drink and swallowed. He stared into the darkness outside, punctuated only by the intermittent flicker of the gas lamps, their weak shimmer reflected on the puddles and damp cobblestones. Behind him, he could hear his valet as he folded his clothes, brushing away lint with his usual meticulous movements.

'May I enquire, my lord, as to your plans for tomorrow?' his man asked.

Ren took another sip. He had no plans. Beth's arrival had seemingly divided his life. Everything he had done previously now seemed unimportant, merely the filling of time.

Clouds passed over the moon like mist. For a brief moment, he'd indulged in childish fantasy, a life where he belonged, with a family...with Beth. His fingers tightened against the tumbler.

*I can't.*

What had he expected? She was pure and sweet and good. She had come here on behalf of the tenants, not to breathe life into a platonic marriage that had only ever been forged through necessity.

Of course she would not want him. She'd never had any interest in marriage. She'd made that clear enough even as a child. She valued independence, above all. She had married him out of duress. She'd married him to save the land and Jamie.

She'd married him because he was better than the Duke.

Except, if he forced himself on her or if he manipulated her or seduced her, he would be no better. He was a rake. He knew a thousand wiles to make a woman want him.

But not a single way to make a woman love him.

He would not seduce Beth. He was better than that. He had made a promise eighteen months earlier. Theirs was a marriage in name only and so it would remain. Good Lord, if he was not good enough on the day of their wedding, he was even less worthy now.

He could not offer her the life she deserved at Allington or Graham Hill. And what could London offer her? Occasional entertainment, maybe, but what was that in comparison to the loss of independence?

Outside, a carriage passed through a puddle. It was raining again, a heavy, drumming rain. It pattered against the window pane and dripped from the foliage outside. He could go, he supposed, to Celeste. He could bury himself in her and forget about this woman who was from his past, from another world, another life. Celeste would welcome him. She would treat him like a hero because he was rich and she liked trinkets. She would not argue about the rights of tenants. She would not tell him to go on wet picnics. She would not make his emotions surge like a boat tossed in deep waters.

She would not make him feel so wonderfully alive. Or fill him with this mix of joy and pain and lust and need all stirred together in a confused, complex muddle. With her, sex would be, as it had always been, an escape, a dulling of emotion.

Except he didn't want Celeste. He had no interest in Celeste. There was only Beth.

Allie would not stop asking questions. She wanted to know about the theatre. She wanted to know if Beth had met the Prince Regent, if she had had wine and if the dancers were well known. She wanted to know about the ballet's plot and with whom Beth had talked and whether she had heard any gossip.

Beth let the girl's words flow over her, hardly attending. Occasionally she answered. The music had been nice, she said. The orchestra was talented and, no, the Prince Regent had not been in attendance. All the while she felt a confused longing...

She wanted to be with Ren. She wanted it with every fibre of her being. She had always loved him, but now that love had matured. It was no longer childish affection. When she'd said that she didn't want marriage and all that it entailed, she did not know...she hadn't understood. She didn't realise that she would or could feel this deep, insatiable, painful yearning.

She didn't know that she could feel a desire which dwarfed all else to triviality. She wanted to press herself to him, to inhale his scent, to taste him, to feel the hard, sinewy movement of his muscles sliding under his skin and to run her fingers across his face. She wanted to discern his expressions, the twist of his lips and the strong line of his chin. She wanted to help him to laugh and to share his sorrow.

She wanted to be one with him, part of him, fused with him.

Her refusal to sleep with him was not due to any lack of desire or maidenly fear. It was not that he had married her and then hurried off to London. Or that he had mistresses. Or drank. Or gambled.

In that moment within the carriage, all of that had dwindled to unimportance.

Was still unimportant.

'Lord Graham is very handsome,' Allie said, interrupting Beth's thoughts as she took out the hair ribbons she had carefully tied earlier.

Beth nodded.

'Sorry,' Allie said. 'I forgot. I mean, I guess you wouldn't know.'

'I know,' Beth said. She might not be able to see, but she could feel—the contours of his chin, his cheekbones, his lips and his arms tightening about her.

Her hand went to her cheek, recalling the touch of his fingers and the way they made her feel goose pimples while also invoking a sizzling fire.

'I was, you know, um…wondering if you two might…um?'

Beth smiled wearily. 'Gracious Allie, you are not normally so tongue tied.'

She heard the rustle of cloth as her maid shrugged. Then she felt the brush on her scalp as Allie combed her hair. Her strokes were rhythmic.

'You know,' Allie said. 'Be like a real husband and wife.'

'You know why I can't.'

'You do not want anyone to have to look after you.'

Beth nodded. 'I will not be a burden.'

'You do realise you have been running Allington since your father's death and Graham Hill since Master Edmund left and don't you be saying as how Master Jamie is doing it because he is too busy with his seeds to do owt useful.'

'He helps. He reads things to me. Besides, I may move well enough around Allington, but that is because I have its layout memorised. Here I am less able. You know it is so.'

'And I also know human beings can learn.'

'And if I miscount the stairs before I have learned? I will not have anyone looking after me as my father had to do with my mother.'

'Except,' Allie said more gently with a final brush to Beth's hair, 'he *wanted* to look after her. Isn't that what love is all about?'

Beth made no answer but stood, carefully feeling her way to the bed and slipping under the covers.

'Goodnight,' she said.

She closed her eyes. Hopefully Allie would leave soon. Her head ached.

But Allie did not go. Instead, Beth heard the continued rustle of clothes and the clink of glassware. She tossed in her bed, squeezing her eyes more tightly as though that would stop her circling thoughts.

When had she known that she could not have a life as a wife and mother? When had she first worried that she could somehow transmit her own blindness? When had the fear begun? When she learned about her great-aunt? When Jamie had brought that bull from halfway across the county?

'You do realise that they have a perfectly adequate bull at Graham Hill,' she'd said.

'Mediocre at best. This one is remarkable. Besides, he is part of a scientific study. He will prove that strength begets strength, that a stronger animal sires a stronger animal.'

*Strength begat strength. Weakness begat weakness.*

A bottle dropped. Beth groaned. 'Allie, can't you do this in the morning?'

'Um, yes, I suppose,' her maid said, but Beth heard no footsteps towards the door. 'Um…you know, miss, I mean, my lady, that I—um… I hears all sorts in the servants' hall. Stuff which no proper lady should hear.'

'Yes, I am sure.' Beth did not want to be rude, but she was tired and had no desire to play true confessions. 'No one judges you for that.'

'I mean,' Allie continued as though Beth had not spoken, 'some of it is useful stuff like how to get out wine stains.'

'I got wine on my dress?'

'No, I— No, I was just wanting to give you an example of some of the information what I get in the servants' hall.'

'Thank you, but I am tired and I cannot even see stains so cannot possibly remove them.'

'No, my lady, I mean, I would always remove your stains only it's not only about stains, I mean that we talk.'

Beth allowed herself a smile. 'I am relieved. Otherwise I would worry about the dearth of entertainment or decent conversation in the ser-vants' quarters.'

'I…um… I also heard from Miss Pollard as how she used to work for a lady what didn't want any more children on account of her and her husband having half a dozen in round numbers. Apparently she said that at certain times of the monthly cycle, a woman can't get pregnant, plus she can't get pregnant on the first time neither. Not that the latter applied to the woman in question, of course.'

The final phrases were said in such a garbled rush that Beth required several seconds to make sense of the words. Then, once she had fully understood their meaning, they reverberated in her mind—distinct and with added clarity. Heat warmed her cheeks.

Perhaps in an excess of nervousness, her maid again knocked something off the counter. It clattered on to the floor, breaking and briefly silencing the flow of words.

'I'll—I'll just clean this up, like,' Allie said.

Beth heard her hurried movements and the grazing sound of a towel moving over the floor. Then, as if unable to bear the silence, Allie began a complex and convoluted narrative about dog breeds, only pausing for breath after a detailed description of a French poodle with digestive issues.

'Right,' Beth said into the sudden silence and

speaking with greater authority than was usual. 'Thank you for the edifying conversation. I will be certain to avoid obtaining a French poodle, but I am exhausted so I will bid you goodnight.'

'Yes, my lady. And let me know if you'll be needing anything.'

'I will,' Beth said, still firmly. 'Right now, all I need is peace and quiet.'

'Yes, my lady. And—um—his lordship is just across the hall. If there is any emergency.'

'An emergency?'

'Like—like a house fire or something.'

Beth gave a low chuckle, her good humour overcoming her irritation. Could the girl be any more obvious?

'I assure you there will no house fire. And, for goodness sake, do not play cards.'

Two hours later, Beth still lay awake. She could hear the house around her. She could hear the tapping of branches against the window, the whisper of wind, the steady drumming of rain and the smouldering sizzle from the fire dying in the hearth. The house must be old, she thought. Old houses resembled living entities, the creak of

floorboards like irregular breaths and the whistling draughts through ill-fitting window frames
but whispers. She shifted. The sheet rustled. It
was late. She should be able to sleep. She should
be exhausted.

Yet she could not calm her mind. She felt dis-
comforted. Images of Ren made her heart pound
faster, while memories of the Duke made her
blood run cold, as though on a seesaw. That brief,
seemingly innocuous meeting had upset her much
more than could be considered rational. It was
that sneering callous tone of his voice. It was the
way he had stepped too close and how she had
felt naked despite her black gown and petticoats.

It was the childhood memories he evoked, that
feeling of being watched on her own property,
the lingering wisps of that peculiar sweet smell
that seemed a part of his persona.

Then there had been that day he had followed
her into the woods between the two properties.

'I thought you might like some company,' he'd
said. 'A cane is little use on such a rugged path.'

'I am used to it.'

He'd taken her arm. Her sleeves had been short.

She'd felt his fingers, firm and clammy against her wrist. 'Let me help.'

She'd said nothing; it had been as though her words had been swallowed, disappearing into this balloon of fear which had grown huge within her gut.

'You have become quite beautiful. I think young girls of twelve or thirteen years have the greatest beauty. There is a purity that is lost as they age.' The hand that was not on her arm had reached up to touch her face.

She'd flinched at the touch. 'I—I really must go,' she'd stammered.

'Shhh.' His finger had touched her lips. She'd stepped back, stumbling, and he had released her arm so that she fell to the ground. She had landed heavily, the breath pushed from her body.

For a second, she hadn't been able to move. She heard him step closer. Panicked, she'd tried to scramble backwards. She'd heard him laugh, a low chuckle.

Then Arnold had come, his firm tread and booming country voice bringing with it sense and normalcy.

'Your mother sent me out to fetch you, miss.'

'Over here, my good man. Miss Elizabeth had a stumble and I am just helping her up,' the Duke had said.

Beth had gone home and wondered if she'd imagined a monster or been saved from the devil.

*The devil, she was certain now.*

Ren could not give his land to such a man. The reasons against it lined up in her mind like so many dominoes. She tossed to the other side of the bed.

But were her objections even about the tenants? Or was she a fraud? Was it more about her own abject fear than the tenants' suffering? She did not want him as their nearest neighbour.

The cold clamminess dissipated into sweaty heat. Beth sat up. She could not remain in bed. She could not toss and turn with this incessant circling of thoughts. She needed to move. She needed to breathe cool air. She needed to free herself from the sheets which swaddled her, impeding movement so that she was suffocating within her own bedclothes.

Perhaps she should tell Ren about those moments. Maybe that would deter him? But how could she ask him to do something that he saw as dishonourable to allay her own fears? Or had she already done so?

Swinging her feet on to the floor, she stood. The wood was cool against her bare toes. The sheets fell away. She stretched, enjoying the freedom of movement. Stooping, she picked up her cane, carefully stepping from the floorboards on to the thickness of the rug.

She crossed to the window and, with a whisper of relief, laid her hot forehead against the glass.

Her comfort was short lived and her need to get outside continued. Outside, she'd hear the sounds of life. There would be newsboys and milkmen and scullery maids. She would hear the clank of pails, shouts or maybe a lad's whistle, proof of the existence of life, however muted.

With the wall to guide her, she made her way to the door and then stepped out into the passage. The air felt chilled, the floor boards even colder under her feet. She stood, uncertain, trying to remember the balcony's location. Moving carefully, she swung her cane like a pendulum as she stepped along the passage.

A clock chimed from somewhere within the

building's interior. Simultaneously, a door opened. She felt the breeze of its movement.

She turned. 'Allie?'

'No,' Ren said.

# Chapter Twelve

A single wall sconce lit the narrow hallway, casting elongated shadows. Beth stood attired only in her nightgown. Her hair hung in a single braid down her back like a rope of molten gold. The white cotton of her gown was cut low, her nipples visible, dark circles pushing against the cloth. His gaze was drawn to the cleft between her full breasts, a darkly shadowed 'V.'

'Ren?' Her free hand reached forward, outstretched, as though to orientate herself in space.

He took her fingers. He felt their tremble. 'You are cold,' he said.

In that moment, he was aware of their isolation, of her uneven exhalations, the thinness of the fabric, the dark areolas pressing against the cloth. 'Are you unwell?'

'No.'

'You should go back to bed,' he said, aware that the words came out jerkily.

'I couldn't sleep. I was going to the balcony.'

She made no move and stood quite close. He still held her fingers and she did not pull them free. He could feel the cloth of her nightdress against his arm. Her hair touched his chin. It smelled of lemons.

'Ren, I think I may not have been entirely honest with myself or you. I thought I was worried for the tenants, but now I realise I do not want the Duke to have any reason to spend more time near to us.'

'I do not want that either.'

'I fear him,' she said. Her lashes lay against her cheek, casting long intriguing shadows, her features just discernible in the low light.

'I know.'

'I wanted to be honest,' she said.

Slowly, he bent towards her. With his free hand, he ran his fingers against her chin, angling it upwards.

'You are the most honest person I know.' He touched her lips with his own, gently. She didn't retreat. A slight rosiness touched her cheeks. Her lips parted, moist.

'Beth.' He caught her lips again, no longer tentative.

His hands went to her shoulders. Her nightgown was loose so that it fell off her shoulder, exposing her pale skin, gleaming in the lamplight.

'You are so beautiful, so perfect.' His thumb grazed her chin as his other hand slid down her spine. She stepped into his embrace.

His kiss hardened, his need grew. His hands tightened on her waist, pulling her against him. He wanted her to feel, to know.

His bedchamber door was ajar, opening inwards. He stepped backwards, opening it with his body and half-carrying her inwards. She held him tightly as the door shut. He could feel her warmth and the soft yielding of her body against his own. The room was dark, save for the amber glimmer from the fire. Very gently, he placed his fingers against her face, tracing her lips, her jaw line, the place at the base of her neck where her pulse beat.

'Is it dark?' she whispered.

'Yes.'

'You are seeing with your hands.'

He bent, his lips following his hands. He felt her tremble. 'Hmm… I think I'd like to see some more,' he muttered.

Scooping her into his arms, he laid her on the huge four-poster bed. Her hair had loosened from its braid. It tumbled in a wild blonde mass, just visible within the low light. The cloth of her nightgown had ridden up her legs so that he could see the gleam of her skin. He lay beside her. He kissed her neck, trailing his lips to the pale, soft skin of her chest and the nipples puckering under the cloth. He pushed under the lace at the neckline, feeling the cloth lower as his fingers cupped her breasts.

She groaned, arching up to him.

'You're so beautiful.'

His hand touched her knee, pushing her night-dress further up to reveal more of her long, slim legs.

She showed no embarrassment, no reluctance. Her hands reached under the cloth of his own nightclothes. Her fingers traced his muscles, his chest, back and shoulders.

He shifted. 'Beth,' his voice rasped, low and strained. 'You're sure?'

She smiled. Her hands traced the line of his ribs.

'Yes.'

Her touch was sensitive, inquisitive, but without artifice, and it made his blood roar. Need flared.

He wanted this. He wanted her more than he had ever wanted anyone. He needed her more than he had ever needed anyone.

Almost roughly he pushed the neckline of her nightgown lower so that the fabric ripped. The noise both shocked and excited him. He tried to be slow. He was a man who valued control and had made loving a woman into a tantalising art form.

Except with Beth it was different. His desire was too great. His restraint, his control slipped. It felt as though this need had been pent up in him for years.

No longer slow, but with an urgency greater than any he had experienced, he kissed her lips, her neck, her breasts, her nipples. Then he slipped between her thighs and, pushing against her, took her fully and completely.

* * *

Beth woke the next morning. For a confused moment, she felt disorientated, aware that the bed was not her own. Then she remembered.

She had slept with Ren.

As she moved, she felt his warm body at her spine. She had slept with Ren. Her lips twisted upwards. She had slept with Ren and it had been wonderful. Her body felt languid, sated.

She smiled, allowing her lids to close. Just for the moment, she wouldn't worry about what would happen next. She wouldn't concern herself with his mistresses. She wouldn't think about how she was not the type of wife he needed. Or that he might feel tied to her or obligated.

She wouldn't worry.

Ren stirred beside her. 'You look very beautiful in the morning,' he whispered. His breath felt warm and tickled her cheek.

She turned towards him, raising herself on to her elbow and placed her head on his chest so that she could better listen to his breath and the steady rhythmic thump of his heart.

Her world was one experienced through sound and touch, but she had never experienced something so intense as making love with Ren. She had never felt so overcome with sensation that sight or lack thereof was immaterial.

'Any regrets?' he asked.

She lifted her head.

'No,' she said.

She explored his face with her hands. His skin was rough. She could discern the prickle of stubble under her fingertips. He had always been freshly shaven in her presence and there was an intimacy to this early morning stubble.

Later, she might have regrets. Later, she'd force herself to deconstruct that small, irrational part of herself that was already building happy endings. They could not have a happy ending. Indeed, it would be even harder to turn from him after this physical experience and the depth of feeling it had engendered.

But to live without knowing such sensation existed...

She explored his face, the line of his chin, his lips and cheek. 'You're smiling. And the muscles in your cheeks are not tight. Nor is your expression grim. Do you know how unusual that is?'

'No,' he said. 'But I am quite certain that last

night's activities helped on both counts. Indeed, with a little more of such treatment, no doubt I shall be positively grinning and euphoric.'

She giggled as he raised himself, flopping her on to her back and shifting his body so that he was poised over her. She felt his weight. She felt his leg move between her own. He kissed her neck, her chin, her nose, the tips of her ears and her lips. A tingling, sizzling trail of sensation engulfed her.

'I... Ren— We...' she whispered as he lowered himself more fully on to her.

She wanted to say how this would be the second time and Miss Pollard had not said anything about the second time. She wanted to say that she could not risk being with child, she could not risk tying him to her, she could not risk...

But her thoughts and even her power of speech dissolved into heat and need.

Beth was still asleep when Ren woke again. He sat up, conscious that the stark light of day had brought with it harsh reality. He stared at the crumpled sheets and the petite woman with her blonde hair tumbling over the pillow. The grey morning light enhanced her beauty, emphasising her fragility, the fine bone structure and her skin, both pale and luminous. There was a perfection to her that was not entirely of this world.

Most men might feel some level of guilt after sleeping with a mistress. Few, he thought, would feel guilt after sleeping with a wife.

He pushed his hand through his hair and stood, moving with care and slipping into his dressing room so he would not wake her. He went to the window, placing his hands against the ledge and staring outwards into the dull London morning.

Beth was everything that was good and pure and trusting. He'd had no right to touch her, to seduce her and take her to his bed. She'd been vulnerable. She'd been distressed by her encounter with the Duke. Or perhaps she'd been over-excited by the late night and unfamiliar surroundings. He should have ordered her hot milk. Or given her a warm brick for her feet or summoned Allie. There were any number of suitable, caring and appropriate actions which did not involve taking her to his bed.

He'd married her to save her from the Duke who was a rake and a cad. But he was no better.

Good Lord, he still had Celeste in her apartment across town and prior to Celeste there'd been others. He drank too much. He gambled too much. He raced horses too much. He was illegitimate. He had no place or role in Allington or Graham Hill. He could not live there and she could not live here.

She'd wanted an annulment.

But now what was the honourable action? He could hardly take a woman's virginity and then send her back to the country as though nothing had happened. Yet for Beth to remain in London would expose her to snide comments, the taunts of the society, references to his mistresses and infidelities. Even more important than any of this, she was unfamiliar with this house. Her reliance on servants would be so much greater. She would not enjoy the same level of independence that was so dear to her.

But was he already sacrificing her independence for his honour? If he gave Graham Hill to the Duke, as was honourable, that man would be Beth's nearest neighbour. What if he chose to spend more time at the estate? Would she ever feel comfortable again, even in her own home?

He remembered her confession last night, the way her lips had trembled slightly: *I fear him.*

The Duke was a predator. London was rife with rumours. The Duke's mistresses were not sophisticated courtesans. He did not set them up in lavish apartments, as was typical of the *ton.* He went to brothels and chose the youngest prostitutes, girls who were little more than children.

No, it could not be honourable to give Graham Hill to this man. It could not be honourable to put Beth and the tenants into his orbit.

But neither could it be honourable to keep the land his father had driven him from.

With a muttered curse, Ren sent for his man. He would go riding. He would gallop until his thoughts cleared and calmed the awful restlessness which, all too often, took over his soul.

An hour later, Ren rode down Rotten Row. Tallon's hooves thundered across the turf as Ren hunkered low over the animal's back. He loved the wild, obliterating thunder of hooves. He loved the power and strength and speed which made his heart race. As with high-stakes gambling, fast riding served to block out his thoughts and to focus his entire attention on the animal's movement, the wild drumming of hooves and the cool damp breeze biting at his cheeks.

At last, reluctantly, he slowed them to a steady, rhythmic walk. Tallon was spent and needed rest. Bending forward, he stroked his hand over the animal's sweaty flank. Several other riders passed by, also exercising their horses. Most greeted him, touching their crops to their hats. He might not be welcome in their drawing rooms, but he had too much money to be long ignored.

That would change, he supposed, if he were to follow Beth's suggestion. Gambling and whoring were largely acceptable, but giving away land would seem foolish at best, revolutionary at worst.

For a brief moment, he remembered the schoolboy taunts. He remembered the water going up his nose and into his eyes as he was thrust under the water pump, unable to breathe or see. His hand went to his eyebrow, touching the tiny scar that still remained.

He turned Tallon towards the stable, his gaze roaming across the other riders. They were disparate: older gentlemen from the country, likely in town to please their wives, French roués reliving past glories and young bucks with their fashionably high collars and perfectly tailored jackets. For a moment, he allowed himself to study the different groups. He smiled grimly. The young bucks were watching him also with sly, sidewise glances.

Their mothers might despise him, but the sons did not.

So was he the rebel? Or was he, in fact, still currying favour with schoolboy bullies? Or compensating for his illegitimate birth by being a better gambler, a better drinker, a better whorer? And was he here at Rotten Row to enjoy the morning and the time spent with a fine animal or was his sole purpose to outrun his own thoughts?

Escaping was not living.

These last few days with Beth—now *that* had been living. His smile broadened as he remembered her tasting the strawberries, placing the ripe fruit between her lips and savouring each bite. And at the opera, he recalled the way she'd focused only on the music, leaning forward and swaying slightly. Then last night...his heart squeezed in his chest as he remembered how she had arched under him, wanton and eager.

A bubbling euphoria pulsed through him. He reached the stable and dismounted.

'Cool him off,' he directed, handing his reins to the groom.

'Yes, my lord.'

'And get my curricle. Today is a good day to change the world.'

# Chapter Thirteen

When Beth awoke, the bed was empty. She stretched tentatively, but the sheets were cold and she could hear no movement in the chamber. Outside, the birds were already loud so it must be morning and possibly late.

Sitting up abruptly, she tried to remember the layout of Ren's bedchamber. The cool morning air touched her bare skin. Rising, she fumbled through the blankets until she found her nightdress. She pulled it over her head, clutching nervously at the frayed edges of the torn neckline.

Grabbing her cane, she stepped towards the room's exit, striking her hip against the nightstand.

'Bother,' she muttered.

Moving with greater care, she crossed to her

own bedchamber, exhaling with some relief that she encountered no servants in the corridor.

'Good morning, my lady,' Allie said.

Beth jumped, jerking around. 'Allie?' Her voice squeaked in surprise, even though her maid had been greeting her in the exact same way for the last ten years.

'I—' A wave of heat washed over her face as she clutched her nightgown more tightly.

'Sorry to make you jump. You must not have heard me in the dressing room. Shall I give you your chocolate?' Allie asked, as she had also done every day for the last ten years.

'Yes, absolutely, um—thank you.'

'Did you want me to help you back to bed?'

'I—er—no. I just—um—I was up. I needed to stretch,' she said.

'Of course, my lady,' Allie said. 'I have your chocolate right here.'

Beth sat on her bed. Allie handed her the hot beverage and she sipped carefully.

Thankfully, Allie retreated back into the dressing room and Beth leaned back against her headboard, trying to make sense of her thoughts.

Last night had changed everything…and nothing. It had changed everything because now they were no longer eligible for an annulment. Indeed, she no longer wanted one. She wanted Ren.

It had changed nothing because the marriage must end.

She squeezed her eyelids shut. She would not have children if they were likely to be blind.

Besides, while last night had been momentous for her, it likely had meant little to Ren.

She rang the bell.

'Help me get dressed. We'll go for a walk. I cannot stay inside all day,' she told Allie, as soon as she heard her footsteps. 'You'll need to guide me, but no talk of ribbons or anything else for that matter.'

'Yes, my lady.'

It was a cool morning. The air felt damp and Beth was glad that they had dressed warmly. Placing her hand on Allie's arm, they stepped along the street and, obedient to direction, the girl remained quiet for once.

Beside her, Beth could hear the footsteps of other pedestrians, their brisk tap mixed with the whirring of pram wheels and the rattle of carriages. Occasionally, she heard other sounds: birds, a boy's whistle and a newsboy shouting.

Even the air smelled pleasant, as though the breeze had pushed away that city smell of coal and the Thames. She felt her step lighten and the stir of a small, hopeful, illogical part of her. *What ifs* circled her mind. What if she could live in London? What if Ren cared for her? What if he didn't want children? What if there was a chance for them?

'Beth!' She startled at Ren's voice as though her thoughts had conjured up his presence.

'Ren!' Her fingers tightened on Allie's arm.

She heard his firm footsteps and inhaled again the scent that seemed so unique to him.

'We need to talk. Leave us,' he said to Allie.

She heard Allie's murmured greeting and the rustle of her clothes as she bobbed a curtsy. 'You have now taken to dismissing my servants out of hand?' she asked.

'Yes,' he said. 'Beth, I need to tell you right away. You're right.'

'I am?'

'I cannot give it to the Duke.'

'Really?' She felt a bubble of hope. 'You'll keep it?'

'I can't. That remains the same. But there must be a better, an alternate, solution and I owe it to the tenants to explore every option. I am going to see if I can give the land to them. Why not give it to those who love it and will nurture it and who have farmed it for generations? What do I care if every earl and duke despises me across all of England?'

She reached for his hand, clasping it tightly. 'Really? I am so glad. It is the right thing to do. Indeed, if you could see his tenants, even Arnold's sister's child was naught but skin and bone and then there is Mrs Cridge and I do worry about Mr Sloan's toes.'

'His toes?' She heard laughter ripple through his voice.

'His whole foot actually.'

'His foot?'

'Yes, the toes are swollen and he cannot farm and I know that the Duke would kick him off the land.'

'On account of his foot?'

'And there are so many others like that. I mean,

Mr Brack has a sore back and Mrs Stow's son has fits and—'

'Enough, enough! I do not need a catalogue of all the tenants and their ailments. Come, shall we walk back into the house? I need to go to the solicitor and then later, you and I…we have so much to talk about.'

'We do?'

That irrational hope flared and flickered.

It was a confluence of sound: shouting, rattling, a whip's snap, a high-pitched whinny, hooves, a woman's scream.

'What? What's happening?' The noise surrounded her, coming at her so that she could not discern its cause or make sense of it. She stepped forward as though proximity might bring clarity.

'Beth!'

And then the air moved. It swirled, picking her up. She heard Ren's shout. She felt her cane fall as her arms flailed. She heard her own scream. A force propelled her, slamming her backwards until she was stopped by Ren's firm grasp. She felt his arms tighten about her as she was lifted, pressed against his chest, the thunder of his heart audible.

In the background, the wheels slowed to a rattle. Someone shouted. The horse whinnied again.

'Beth? Are you hurt?' Ren's voice was deep. She felt its vibration through his chest as she heard the words.

'I'm fine,' she said.

His arms felt strong and she wanted only to stay within the safety of his clasp. Now, in contrast to the earlier cacophony, the street seemed eerily quiet. Everything appeared to have stopped: the carriage wheels, the prams, the newsboys, even the birds. She heard only the horse's laboured breathing and the frantic beat of her own heart.

'Sorry about that, folks,' a masculine voice spoke, breaking into the hush. 'No one hurt? Nelson here is still learning the ropes.'

'Drive a little slower until he does,' Ren said. 'Or you will hurt someone.'

'Yes, sir.'

Then there seemed to be a return to normalcy. She heard the wheels move again with a clip-clop of hooves. A pram started to roll. The nannies chattered.

Ren released her. 'Fool of a driver. You're not hurt? You are certain?'

She shook her head. 'I am fine,' she repeated.

'Thank God. Why did you step towards them?' Ren asked.

'I—I heard the noise—' she stammered. 'I didn't know I was.'

She shivered. As a child, she'd dreamed that her world of blackness was filled with unseen dangers—the menace of the unknown. Later, she had tried to change these thoughts, imagining instead a world of wonder, of mint-green grass, of unimaginable delights. But sometimes...

'I'm sorry,' she said.

'It is not your fault. The drivers should not have been so foolhardy. I am just glad I caught you. I'm sorry, too. I should have looked after you better. Come, let us get you back into the house. We'll ask Allie to bring you a sustaining cup of tea.'

'Thank you.'

They climbed the six steps to the front door and entered the hall which smelled of lemon-scented floor wax. They crossed the floor. Beth stumbled at the bottom stair. She did not yet know dimensions of the hall.

'Twenty-one steps up,' Ren said as he took her to the second floor.

'Thank you.'

She felt oddly distanced from everything and everyone, as though she was collecting data for one of Jamie's experiments. Lemon floor wax, twenty-one steps to the second-storey landing, five steps to her bedchamber...

'Sit down until Allie brings the tea,' Ren said.

Beth complied. She sat on the armchair near the hearth within her bedchamber. She could still smell the lavender that Allie had spilled last night. The door opened and Beth heard the rattle of cups.

More data.

'Good gracious, you're white as a ghost. A good cup of tea will soon set you to rights. Probably the shock, most like. Now, my sainted mother would recommend sugar. Would you like sugar?'

'No, thank you.'

Sugar—did sugar help? Could one design an experiment on the beneficial impact of sugar?

'And Mr Robbins wanted me to find out if a doctor is required.'

'No,' Beth said.

She did not even have a scratch. She wondered why everyone insisted on fussing.

'You're quite certain?' Ren asked.

'Absolutely.'

She sipped her tea, pulling a face. Apparently, Allie had decided to heed her sainted mother's advice on the sugar.

'Truly, I am quite all right. Indeed, Ren, you do not need to stay here. Please go into town. I will be fine.'

'I don't need to go today.'

'But you do need to find out if your idea is even possible. I know you won't be able to think things through properly until you know this.'

'And you will be fine?'

'Absolutely. Besides, I am certain that Allie will ensure that my every need is met and then some.'

'Right,' he said. 'I will talk to my solicitor. I will leave you in your maid's excellent care and we will talk later.'

Ren strode towards his solicitor's office. The street was pleasantly busy. Ladies walked by, likely on their way to the dressmaker or to purchase a bonnet. Coffee from the coffee house on the corner scented the air and the weather had improved, the clouds punctured by weak rays of flickering sunshine.

Despite this, Ren felt apprehension. That moment in the street had happened so fast. Indeed, if he closed his eyes, he felt certain he would still see the carriage hurtling towards her. The image of horse and vehicle was imprinted on his mind. It clutched at his stomach and made his palms damp with sweat and his breathing quick.

Last night he had recognised that she was a vital aspect of his life.

Today he knew that she was more important than life itself.

And he knew also that they would make this marriage work. He loved Beth. They would stay married. Moreover, he would not give Graham Hill to the Duke. He would find another path to honour, both for Beth's sake and for Sloan and his toes or his fits or whatever it was. Sloan, Stow and Brack—they were names and people he had known his whole life. Honest folk. They had given him apples. They had rescued him when he got stuck in the upper limbs of an oak tree and had taught him how to ride and fish.

Over the years, Ren had schooled his thoughts

not to drift to Graham Hill. It hurt too much. He refused to pine over a past that was not his. Now, for the first time since that awful day, he allowed himself to remember childhood pleasures. There was the brook to the left of Graham Hill close to Mrs Cridge's cottage. They used to wade in its chill waters which flooded every spring, but dried to the merest trickle by August. Then there was the blacksmith, a kind giant of a man, his bulging forearms glistening with sweat as he struck the glowing molten metal. Ren had loved the forge. He'd loved the movement of the bellows wielded in the man's huge hams of hands, the way he would shaped the fiery metal, his forehead and torso streaked with dirt and perspiration. And the country smelled sweeter and seemed layered with colours; the different greens of vegetation, verdant and full of life.

The memories hurt, but it was not that crippling, searing, incapacitating pain. It was not that feeling of dislocation, that knowledge that everything he had known or loved or believed was a mirage.

Rather it was a duller ache, mixed with remembered pleasure.

'Ren!'

He turned, looking into the street towards his mother's rather ostentatious carriage and perfectly matched bays. She drew to a sudden stop in front of him.

The footman jumped from his post, swinging open the door.

'You are getting out?' Ren asked, after the usual salutations. He really did not desire his mother's company, but could hardly be uncivil. Since his father's death they had been polite, socialising when needs must. For Edmund's sake he had never wanted to fuel the rumours which were already rife.

'Yes, dear, I thought I would walk with you for a moment. Unless you would like to get in? We can drop you somewhere.'

'I am going to my solicitor and am almost there,' he said.

He waited as his mother descended from the carriage. As always, she was dressed in the height of fashion, bedecked with feathers and flowers so that he did not know if she aimed to imitate a bouquet or an aviary.

She placed her hand on his arm, straightening and angling her head in a way which she must have imagined flattering. That was the thing about his mother; one never felt that she was entirely focused on the conversation or activity. There always seemed a part of her evaluating whether she looked her best and how she might position herself to evoke the most admiration. There was a stiffness to her face, as though afraid to display emotion for fear of setting lines within her skin.

'So, darling, you are going to your solicitor. Does that mean you are doing it? Giving the estate to the Duke?'

'What?' he asked sharply. 'How did you know?'

'Beth told me. She came to me before I returned to London. She hoped I would convince you out of it.'

'And do you hope to dissuade me against the plan?' he asked.

'Not at all darling. I mean, if that is your wish.'

He raised a brow. She seemed quite quiescent and he wondered at it. 'It is not my wish, but I thought it honourable.'

'So that is what you are arranging now?' she

asked, raising a gloved hand in greeting to an acquaintance across the road.

'No, actually.'

Her face puckered into confusion before smoothing it into her usual expression. 'You have revised your plan?'

'I do not wish to willingly give the Duke such power over the people and land I grew up with,' he said.

He saw her brows contract momentarily, her expression perplexed before regaining control.

'Well, that is wonderful,' she said.

'Yes, isn't it?'

'So you will keep it. I am glad. You will assume the duties of lord of the manor. And, please, let me know if you wish to entertain, I mean once we are out of mourning. Edmund never was a great entertainer, but your father and I entertained frequently. I would be happy to help. Beth, of course, cannot.'

'My father and you?' he said snidely. 'Really, I did not know you and the painter entertained.'

She had the grace to blush.

'I am sure I do not know what you mean,' she said, dropping her gaze to study the beading on her reticule. 'But I am happy you are keeping the estate.'

'I'm not, actually,' he drawled.

Her eyebrows drew together slightly and she appeared to be studying several young gentlemen as they strolled past with their high, foolishly stiff collars and Hessian boots. He waited, knowing her well enough that her apparent abstraction was an attempt to better assess this new information.

'Darling,' she said at length. 'I am a little confused. Could you clarify?'

'Beth and I have come up with an innovative plan where I could return the land to the tenants. I have decided to explore that option with my solicitor.'

His mother gasped, for once not even bothering to hide her reaction. Her jaw dropped as she gripped his forearm with sudden fervour. 'You what...? That does not make sense.'

'It does, actually. It will enable me to avoid giving the estate to a man I cannot respect while also living in a manner I find honourable.'

'But...' She leaned into him, lowering her voice as though concerned she would be overheard even within the busy bustle of the street. 'I— We will be the laughing stock. And what will I live on?'

'I will ensure your income continues.'

'From trade!' Her nose wrinkled. 'And the talk it would cause. Good Lord, people will think we are revolutionaries. Or that you have taken leave of your senses. I don't know which is worse.'

'The former. So much more distasteful than mere insanity.'

Her frown deepened. 'I do not think it a laughing matter.'

'Indeed, no, although I think the Tower is more salubrious than Bedlam.'

His saw her jaw tighten and knew she was curbing her temper with difficulty. She inhaled, her hand further tightening on his arm. 'Darling, you must reconsider. I mean, your marriage was bad enough—marrying someone with neither title, money, nor social standing. And blind. But this cannot be endured.'

'Really, Mother. Such a talent for melodrama. You should take to the stage.'

'Please, be sensible. Our neighbours will be quite shocked and the Duke will be—'

'I did not know I had to take the Duke's feelings into consideration,' he said.

Her cheeks turned a mottled red. 'You might be wise to do so. Please, I will pray that you will abandon the plan.'

'Gracious, I did not know you were of a religious bent. Desperate times, I suppose. Shall I walk you back to your coach?'

'Jest if you must but, please, do not take any impulsive action. Think about it,' she urged, again nodding distractedly to a friend.

'I have been doing rather a lot of thinking recently,' he said, as they approached her well-sprung vehicle with its gilt trim and emblazoned coat of arms. 'I think perhaps now is the time for action.'

They had turned back and were at the coach. He saw her pause, a hand on her footman's gloved hand as he aided her into the plush interior.

'Please, reconsider. I— The *ton* does not like those who act as traitors.'

'A threat, Mother?'

'No. Whatever you think of me, please know I care for you.'

'Then you will be happy that I have made a decision that feels right,' he said. 'And might even make me happy.'

As the carriage rattled away Ren started again towards his solicitor's office. His mother's objections did not concern him. He had expected them and he knew well enough that she could take care of herself. She had seemed almost eager for Ayrebourne to have the place. Likely she had concocted a plan to curry favour. How odious.

Indeed, if Ayrebourne were to be become his 'stepfather' it would mark a new low in his rather dubious history of paternal figures. But then again, she was likely too old to be eligible for his attention.

At last Allie left. She had been hovering around Beth since the incident on the street. Beth could hear her distracted movements, punctuated by sighs and suggestions of additional tea, an extra blanket, hot brick or smelling salts.

In desperation, Beth had sent her for a wrap if only to gain a few moments of solitude.

That moment on the street had changed everything.

It had been a blast of reality. It had successfully decimated that small part of her intent on constructing fairy tales, castles in the sky and happy endings.

The marriage must end. Her own vulnerability had been cruelly hammered home. Good Lord, she could have been struck and become an invalid like her mother. Then Ren would have been saddled with her care, as though his life had not been difficult enough.

No, she must face the fact that despite a lifetime of trying, she was less able to look after herself, less able to avoid danger. And she refused to be a burden. Moreover, she would not risk bearing a child she could not look after. Or one who might also be blind, so that Ren would be burdened with the care of both of them.

*'I do not want your father here,'* her mother had once said shortly after her fall. *'I do not want your father tied to me, nursing me. If you love someone, you want what is best for them. You do not want to see their life crippled.'*

But could they even get an annulment after last night? Would he divorce her? Could he divorce her?

She heard Allie return. Beth replaced her cup

on the table and, as she did so, accidentally struck the table, spilling several droplets of lukewarm tea on to her hand. Surprisingly, she felt the smart of tears. She blinked. Couldn't she even do this simple task without error?

'My lady.' She heard Allie's hurried footsteps and the rustle of cloth as she dropped the wrap. 'Did you hurt yourself?'

'No, it isn't even hot. Apparently, I am unable to put down my cup without mishap.'

'It is just that you are in a strange place, my lady.'

'No, it is just that I am blind. An individual who is sighted can usually manage such a simple task.'

'Good gracious, not if you saw my brothers at meal time. Anyhow, that spill's easy enough to fix. Don't you be distressing yourself.' Allie came with the flannel. She pressed it against Beth's hand. Its cool dampness felt soothing against her skin. Somehow, its very comfort made the tears threaten more.

'I just—sometimes, I just wish...'

'What, my lady?'

Beth felt the tears spill down her cheeks. 'That I wasn't blind.'

Angrily, she wiped her tears away with the back of her hand.

'My lady, you never did let that stop you and I don't see as how you should be starting at this late date. Lud, I remember when you insisted on riding that horse and fishing. You went to the river and got the biggest fish of them all. Gracious, there's some young ladies who wouldn't go anywhere near a fish, sighted or otherwise.'

'Yes, and Ren or Jamie or Edmund had to lead me there and back or I wouldn't have been able to find the stream, never mind fish from it.'

'They never minded.'

'I know!' Her voice rose. 'But I did. I do. I wish—'

She let the phrase remain unfinished. She wished she could be Ren's wife. She wished she could risk the snide comments and mistresses and convince him that they could have a life together. She wished she was strong and that she could be his equal. She wished she could tell him that she loved him, had always loved him, would always love him. But if you love someone you want what is best for them.

'Everybody, sighted or not, needs help every

now and again. Did…um—' Allie hesitated before lunging forward in a rushed gabble of words. 'Did his lordship upset you or hurt you in some way last night? Because if he did, he'll have me to answer to and that you may tie to.'

Beth allowed herself a slight smile at the thought of her feisty little maid accosting Ren.

'No,' she said. 'You need not threaten him. He did not upset me.'

'Then 'tis the excitement of the city, no doubt. We are country folk and not used to its bustle and all this to-ing and fro-ing and ballet dancing and the like.'

'Yes,' Beth said. 'Yes, that is it. We will leave soon.'

'You want to leave?' Allie asked, her voice squeaking in surprise as though the concept was entirely new to her.

'Allie, you know that was always the plan,' Beth said softly.

'Yes, but I thought… When?'

'Soon. Today.'

'But you will wait for his lordship to return? You will talk to him?'

'I—' Part of her wanted to escape from the

complexity of her feelings while a part wanted to remain and throw herself in Ren's arms as though he might magic a solution.

'Yes,' she said. 'But you should start to pack anyway. All holidays must end.'

# Chapter Fourteen

Beth found time hanging heavily. She hated being in a strange environment. She hated having to tap out her movements and bang clumsily into furniture. She hated standing in a corridor and not knowing which way to turn or hearing a clock tick, but being uncertain as to where it came from or how it might guide her.

It all served to prove that her independence rested largely on a string of numbers, of steps and dimensions for Allington and Graham Hill. Wrenched from those environs, she was stumbling and uncertain.

And the memory of those chaotic moments still circled in her mind, that panicked, confused feeling of danger, mixed with the paralysis of not knowing how to react or which way to jump.

That paralysis—the knowledge of danger, but

the absence of any insight into how to avoid that danger—that was the worst.

She shivered, pulling her wrap more closely about her. Last night she had thrown caution aside, but this morning she wanted to pull it about her like a blanket and hide, as a child might in a winter storm.

*I should have looked after you better.*

Those had been Ren's words. They had also been her father's words after her mother's accident. Of course, it had not been her father's fault. His horse had cleared the jump. Her mother's had not. But he had felt burdened by guilt.

Beth did not want to be the burden her mother had been. Her mother had always thought that worry had led to her husband's gambling. Beth wanted a union where she was a strength and helpmate. And, as that was not possible, she would remain alone.

The doorbell sounded. Beth paid it little heed. Ren would not ring his own bell and she knew no one in London—except Mirabelle's aunt. She hoped it wasn't her. As she recalled, Lady Mortley had a vast interest in Egyptian relics which, while fascinating, became somewhat tiring as the sole topic of conversation.

'My lady?' Robbins said, entering the library.

'Yes?' Bother, it must be Lady Mortley after all.

'It is the Dowager Lady Graham,' he said.

'Her ladyship?' That would likely be worse than Egyptian relics. 'Did she want to see his lordship? Did you tell her that he is not about?'

'She asked for you, my lady, most specifically.'

'She did?' Beth sighed. 'I suppose you must show her in.'

'Yes, my lady.'

Her mother-in-law's arrival was heralded with the usual swish of skirts, and that unmistakable floral perfume which Beth always felt was more a cloying taste than a scent.

'My lady, it is kind of you to visit,' she said.

'Yes, dear. Roberts, do bring up tea,' her ladyship directed.

'Robbins,' Beth corrected, irritation flickered. If her mother-in-law was going to order about the servants she could at least remember their names. 'I hope you enjoyed the ballet?'

'Yes, yes, delightful, although some dialogue

would make it so much more comprehensible. But that is beside the point. I saw Ren.'

'Yes, I know,' Beth said. 'I was there.'

'No, I mean, I saw him today. In town.'

'I believe he is doing errands,' Beth said, cautiously.

'He has some ludicrous, revolutionary concept of giving the land to the tenants.'

Beth felt her lips curve into a happy smile. If Ren had told his mother, he must have decided to do it.

'And you may smile, but I do not think it is anything to rejoice about. He will be ostracised, you know,' her mother-in-law said.

'He said he already was.'

'Nonsense. Perhaps by a few fussy mamas and dowagers because he drinks and gambles and has any number of mistresses.'

For some reason, the words hurt. Of course Beth knew he had mistresses—but any number sounded so...so numerous.

'You didn't know?' her mother-in-law was asking, honing in on the weakness.

'I knew,' Beth said, schooling her features.

'I am not saying that he has them all at the

same time. It is Celeste Lapointe right now. Former opera singer, I believe. Limited talent. You
might have seen her last night?'

'I didn't,' Beth said. 'One benefit of being blind
is that one does not see one's husband's mistresses.'

It hurt, all the same, to have a name to roll
around her thoughts.

'Anyway, the *ton* forgives that sort of behaviour
from gentlemen. Particularly if the gentleman is
rich and with an estate and title, but giving away
of land to tenants—that is quite another thing
entirely.'

'It is acceptable to lose an estate at cards but
not to give it to people who have worked on the
land for generations?'

She heard her mother-in-law make a slight 'tsk,'
moving as if shifting or straightening in her chair.

'Darling, you are an idealist. The world is not
meant for idealists. Besides, Ren should not be
giving it to anyone, he should be keeping it. He
should be Lord Graham with all its inherent honour and responsibility and I intend to convince
him of it.'

'I believe that was my point when I came to

see you earlier and you said there was little you could do,' Beth said.

'That was prior to this ludicrous suggestion that he give the land to a bunch of peasants.'

'Farmers. You would prefer he give it to the Duke?'

Her ladyship leaned forward, her perfume becoming even stronger with her movement. 'Yes. It would be better than an idea which is tantamount to revolution. Besides, I have come up with another suggestion which I think will serve.' She paused as though to build suspense.

'Yes?' Beth asked.

'Darling, you know I am uncommonly fond of you and I do not say this to hurt you in any way.'

Beth swallowed. She felt a flicker of something; pain or fear, perhaps. She rubbed her palms against the fabric of her skirt. 'I imagine that statement is a precursor to something quite hurtful.'

'We all know that Ren married you out of—' Lady Graham paused. Beth could almost hear the word 'pity' echoing about the room. 'Kindness.'

Beth made no response and after a moment Lady Graham continued. 'But the need has passed. I hear that your father's unfortunate debts are paid and Allington is prosperous, at least sufficient for your needs. And, darling, really you are not suited to be his wife. I say this not to hurt you, only for your own good. A man like Ren needs someone to keep him entertained so that he does not stray, or at least not so much.'

'I am cognisant of that. I plan to return to the country today or tomorrow.'

Lady Graham took Beth's hand within her own. Her mother-in-law's hand was soft and smooth, but distasteful somehow, and Beth had to fight the desire to pull her fingers free. 'You see, my dear, the Duke has a relative. A cousin. Granted, she is not quite as close a relation to my late husband as the Duke, but there is kinship. Therefore, even if Rendell continues with this…his concerns about his own parentage, this marriage would allow him to feel that the estate was continuing within the Graham family and that his children have a right to the estate. Annabelle is also well versed in social etiquette and will be an asset to him. It is an admirable solution.'

'Except that I am married to him,' Beth said,

pulling her hand free. 'And England does not yet endorse polygamy.'

'Darling, I was thinking of a nice, quiet annulment.'

Heat washed into Beth's face. With an effort, she stiffened her spine, forcing herself to be coherent and practical.

'Lady Graham, that was my wish at one time. Indeed, I have spoken to Ren about it, but I do not believe we would qualify...any more... I mean. I will suggest a divorce, although I fear that would bring its own scandal.'

Despite the hurt, Beth felt wry amusement at her own words. *Qualify?* Good gracious, she sounded as though she were seeking to enter a horse race or a baking contest at the village fête.

'Darling, I suspected as much, but do not worry. There is another way to get your annulment. You were married when you had not yet reached the age of majority.'

Beth nodded. 'But that shouldn't matter. Young girls all over England are married while still under age.'

'With their father's consent,' her ladyship said, smoothly.

'He was dead. Jamie consented.'

'And Jamie was not yet twenty-one. No one was able to give consent which is grounds for an annulment.'

For a moment, Beth could not speak. It was a practical solution. Really, it was a perfect answer, particularly when one threw in Annabelle, the newly discovered relative.

'You must have been quite elated when you discovered that technicality,' Beth said in clipped hard tones which sounded foreign to her. 'As I recall, you have never liked me.'

There was a relief in saying the words.

'Darling, it is not that I do not like you. Your character is admirable. But you lack practicality and have some shockingly revolutionary ideas. As well you are limited by your disability. Ren would have to escort you everywhere or you would be blundering into things. And really, the *ton* does not admire clumsiness. You are not the sort of woman that Ren needs. Men like Ren have a very low threshold for boredom. There may be a novelty about you right now, but that will wear off with remarkable rapidity. And being nursemaid to one woman would only make him seek others to an even greater extent.'

There was almost a relief to hear the words, a confirmation of what she knew already.

'I know,' Beth said. The anger lessened, filled now with a heavy, hopeless leaden feeling. 'You are certain about the annulment.'

'Yes. I visited my own solicitor after seeing Ren.'

'You are thorough,' Beth said.

She heard her mother-in-law's movements. They almost sounded agitated and she reached her hands to the elder woman's face to better read her expression. She startled slightly, but acquiesced to Beth's touch.

'You are worried?' she said, fingering the slight furrows in the older woman's face.

'I—' Beth heard her mother-in-law swallow and heard her quickened inhalation. 'It might surprise you, but I love my son. I want him to be successful. I don't want him ostracised. Ever since that day when his father—Lord Graham—sent him away, he has been searching for where he belongs. This could be his chance. I don't want him to throw it away. I...'

Her mother-in-law did not finish the sentence, allowing her words to trail into silence, and Beth had the sense that there was something more, something left unsaid.

Beth dropped her hands and stood. 'I will talk to Ren.'

'Darling, one more thing—I really think it would be better if you were not to cohabit.'

'I will return to Allington,' Beth said dully.

'It will be too late to get to Allington today.'

Beth stiffened. 'But where else would I go?'

'Somewhere you can reach today so you don't need to spend another night here. Somewhere he cannot instantly find you. Men can be persuasive. I would suggest that you remove yourself. I know a place. It is not too far out of London and is on the way to Allington so will not necessitate additional travel which, as I recall, you do not like. It is quiet and small. You could arrange to go immediately.'

'I must talk to Ren.'

'You could,' her ladyship said, doubt threading through her voice.

'You don't think I should?'

'I do not wish to be indelicate.'

'This entire conversation has hardly been delicate,' Beth said wryly. 'No reason to censor yourself now.'

'Very well. As I said, men can be persuasive. And should you become with child, well, that—that would complicate the matter. As it is, I suppose we will have to wait a few weeks to be certain, but we do not wish to increase the likelihood.'

'I—I see,' Beth whispered.

Her ladyship's point was valid. Were she to sleep with him again... And she could not risk having children. She could not risk tying him to her or bearing children equally as disadvantaged as herself. She touched her sightless eyes.

'Very well,' she said. 'I will leave today. I will go to this place you have suggested. But I *will* talk to Ren first.'

'Darling, I really think it would be better—'

'No,' Beth said. 'On this my mind is decided. But be assured I recognise the need for an annulment, or a divorce if annulment is not possible, and I am not easily persuaded.'

There was a pause, then Beth heard movement as her mother-in-law rose. 'Very well,' she said.

'I will give your servants the address of the place I have in mind and make the arrangements. I can find my way out.'

Beth listened to her mother-in-law's retreating footsteps, the slight creak of hinges as she opened the door and then the muted voices within the hallway. Likely she was talking to Robbins or the groom. Finally, the outer door opened and closed.

Beth sat in the sudden solitude. She felt oddly removed and was conscious of a certain numbness. In many ways, she wished she could follow her mother-in-law's advice and leave immediately, but it seemed cowardly and cruel. Besides, it would worry Ren and hurt him. One could not share intimacies like they had the previous night and then slope off like a thief in the night. No, she needed to talk to him, explain to him, convince him.

The discussion with his solicitor had taken longer than Ren had anticipated so it was afternoon by the time he returned. Still, despite this delay, his earlier ebullience still lingered. Indeed, he even wished Robbins a pleasant afternoon, although this gentleman seemed lugubrious, nodding his head as though holding the sentiment in serious doubt. Maybe it was his ankles or feet, or some other part of his anatomy, aching due to an upcoming weather system or meteorite. This made him remember the picnic and felt himself smile, recognising a lightness in spirit he had not experienced in a long time.

'Her ladyship is waiting for you in the library.'

'Jolly good,' Ren said and then almost chuckled out loud.

Jolly good? *Jolly good?*

'Ren,' Beth said, the instant he entered the library. She sat in an upright chair close to the hearth. It was dim. The windows were small and narrow and the only other light was the flickering amber glow from the hearth.

He threw himself in the more comfortable seat opposite and pulled the bell for the lamps to be lit.

'It is possible,' he said. 'Indeed, there is not a single legal obstacle to prevent me from disposing of my land as I see fit. It is not encumbered or entailed.'

'You mean giving the estate to the tenants?' Beth said, her hands still clasped together.

'Of course. Naturally my solicitor disapproved

of the notion and looked as though he was suffering a sudden bout of dyspepsia, but there is nothing to prevent me from doing so, at least not legally, although he hated saying this.'

He grinned, remembering that gentleman's countenance. He had a dark moustache and he tended to purse his lips in disapproval, making the moustache twitch.

'And this is what you want? You will be ostracised, you know? Your peers will not like it,' Beth said, her expression surprisingly sombre and showing none of the elation he had hoped.

He leaned forward, taking her hands within his own. They were warm from the fire, but fragile. She seemed suddenly very slight and stiff within the tall, straight chair.

'Yes,' he said. Already, he could think of tenants who might be able to buy their farms outright. Others could perhaps rent with the intent to buy. 'You came with the suggestion. You advocated the plan.'

'I know.' She stood, freeing her hand and moving abruptly, banging into the side table so that the water glass fell. The tumbler shattered on floor. She stooped, her fingers sweeping the floor with quick, useless gestures.

'Don't. You'll hurt yourself.' He caught her hands, holding them. 'There's glass. Allie will clean it.'

'Beth?'

Tears shimmered in her sightless eyes. She again pulled her hands free and sat back on the chair, sitting awkwardly. 'You will be without any dishes at all at this rate. This is the second thing today.'

'It doesn't matter.'

He rang the bell and moments later Allie and another maid entered.

'Light the lamps as well,' he directed.

They did so and, while the maids cleaned, removing the glass and wiping up the water, Ren watched his wife.

Her usual calm had deserted her. There was a tension evident in the hunch of her shoulders, the angle of her neck and the way her hands clasped together. She had always hated it when her blindness caused mishap. She always hated any reminder that her disability made her less independent.

His gaze roamed the full shelves, their embossed titles glimmering gold in the lamplight. He had been busy today. He had planned a future, not only for the tenants, but for himself and Beth. He'd allowed his mind to fill with happy images: a proper marriage, children, a family.

He had somehow imagined they could spend time at Allington and here in London. He had decided that she would gain comfort and familiarity in this house. They'd go to the ballet or the opera. He'd read to her.

Yes, he'd designed all manner of pretty pictures.

At last the maids finished. They curtsied and left, the door closed behind them and he sat alone with his wife once more.

'Can we talk?' he asked.

'It seems we have that capability. Inhalation, movement of mouths.'

She always did that, joked when feeling vulnerable.

'As I said, I will not give the land to the Duke so you need not worry that he will gain influence within the neighbourhood. And I don't care if every stuffy peer in the House of Lords has a screaming fit.'

'That would be noisy.' She gave a wan smile, then paused. He saw her fingers pluck at a loose thread. 'I am thankful you will not give it to the Duke. Truly thankful, but before you give it to the tenants…um…please, look at all your—your choices in case there is something else, you know, another choice—'

'What do you mean? You were all in favour of giving the land to the farmers before. Have you thought of something?'

'I—' She seemed about to say something, but then shook her head. 'Ren, I need to tell you something. I will be leaving. This afternoon. Allie is already packing.'

'You are?'

A log crackled. The clock ticked.

'Yes.'

'You still want to end this marriage?' he asked.

She nodded.

It hurt again, slicing through him, the way it had hurt after Edmund's service when she had first suggested an annulment.

'I am not certain if an annulment is possible any more,' he said gently.

He saw her lips quirk slightly and felt a moment's reprieve in that shared humour which had always been at the foundation of their relationship.

For a moment that picture of home, purpose, belonging and love came back into focus.

Her face straightened, her expression serious, sad almost. 'An annulment is possible,' she said. 'I was not of age, nor Jamie, so there wasn't appropriate consent at the time of our marriage.'

As she spoke, her voice oddly flat and without expression, his vision of home and family shattered, just as the glass had shattered. She had thought about it. She must have researched this while still in Allington. She must have summoned the country solicitor, Mr Tyrell. He would have listened to her plight. He would have returned to his office and pulled out huge dusty tomes of law books. This was no momentary, nervous wobble. Her desire for an annulment had been well considered. Last night was the aberration.

He should not be surprised. Beth had never wanted marriage. Independence had always been her primary ambition.

The silence lengthened. He tried to find his

voice. His mouth was dry. He stood and poured himself a brandy, swallowing it in a single gulp.

'You have thought this through in great detail,' he said at last. 'It appears you are serious about this intent.'

'Yes,' she said.

He poured himself a second drink.

'I feel,' she said, still in that oddly flat voice, 'that it is best for all concerned if our marriage is concluded.'

# Chapter Fifteen

Concluded...finished...completed...done...
over...

The words thumped through her mind just as
Allie thumped through the room, her disapproval
evident. Beth sat quite still, listlessly aware of Allie's movement.

Those vague, unformed, unacknowledged
hopes lay in ruins about her. They could not be.

That night with Ren had been wonderful, momentous. She would hold it dear to her heart. She
would cherish it for ever.

But she would now do the right thing. She
would leave today and go to this cottage as Ren's
mother had suggested. Then she would return to
Allington. The marriage would be dissolved. She
would return to what had always been her life.
She would help the tenants. She would support

Jamie in his scientific pursuits. She would live for Sundays and Miss Plimco on the organ. She would be thankful that the Duke would not control Graham Hill and, in time, Ren would marry this Annabelle and she would be a good neighbour.

Except, she realised dully, that her contentment had been shattered.

She now wanted things she could not have. She had seen what life could offer. She had glimpsed the joys of partnership: shared goals, shared jokes, shared pleasure—

Allie banged something heavy on to the floor.

'I did not realise we were taking the bricks from our beds and choosing to drop them all into our cases,' Beth said irritably. 'I cannot believe it is possible to make quite so much noise while packing clothes.'

'And I did not realise that we are suddenly seeing her ladyship as an ally. Going off like this, if you ask me, it's a right rum do.'

'I didn't,' Beth said. 'Anyhow, I believe her ladyship wants what is best for her son and I want that, too.'

'Her ladyship wants and has always wanted what's best for her ladyship as far as I can tell.'

'Yes, well in this instance, I think she is right and that my immediate withdrawal is indeed best for his lordship.'

Allie thumped something else on the floor. 'And I'm thinking his lordship was looking quite happy this morning. Maybe you're what's best for him, if you don't mind my saying so.'

'Would it matter if I did?' Beth said. 'And, please, is it possible to pack with a little less noise?'

'I reckon it's possible, but not likely. A person needs to relieve their feelings.'

'And it appears you are determined to do so by throwing coal or bricks about our accommodation.'

'I am determined to make you see sense.'

'I cannot be the wife he needs. I cannot be independent. I cannot be fashionable. I—I cannot give him children,' Beth said. 'Those are unarguable facts.'

The bottles clinked as Allie moved them. 'None of them is in the least unarguable. Indeed, I am very able to argue on all counts and that you may tie to. Particularly this nonsense about children. I know I'm a maid and not to know these things, but the only thing what doesn't work is your eyes and I don't know as if they have much to do with making babies.'

'I couldn't look after a child.'

'And those fancy ladies do? You'd have servants. Me, for a start.'

Beth stood, walking to the window. She hadn't spoken to anyone about this, not even Jamie. Slowly, she rubbed her finger tip on the cool glass pane and spoke so low that she heard Allie step closer. 'There was an aunt in my family who was blind and also a great-aunt who could see very little.'

'Yes, I remember your mother mentioning that. But both are long gone.'

'But I worry—' The pad of her finger squeaked against the glass. 'You know how Master Jamie always goes and gets prize bulls and horses to make certain that the foals and calves are strong? I— What if faults or weaknesses can be passed from a parent to a child? If a strong bull creates a strong calf, could not a blind woman create a blind child?'

'Gracious, my lady, you have been spending too long with Master Jamie, is all I can say. I knew you worried that you could not properly look after a child—but this is not sensible. Indeed, Master Jamie, for all his good points, is not entirely sensible and well you know it.'

'Not sensible perhaps, but intelligent. And our livestock is some of the best in England.'

'That's as may be. I don't know much about cows. Personally, I've always favoured sense over intellect. Life doesn't come with guarantees whether you're blind or sighted. Babies are born healthy and take ill. They are born ill and recover. You takes your chances. We all do. I call thinking any different than that borrowing trouble.'

'And I call it being realistic.'

Ren blinked blearily. He handed his hat and coat to Robbins. It was only midnight. He had meant to stay out at his club but even the cards had not been able to hold his attention. In fact, he feared he would lose a considerable sum if he continued to play so distractedly.

'Did you wish a fire lit in the library or study, my lord?' Robbins asked.

'Neither. I'll go to bed.'

'Yes, my lord.'

'And send up a bottle of brandy.'

'Yes, my lord. Your mother called around this evening, my lord, following your departure.'

Ren frowned. He had been seeing entirely too much of his mother of late. 'What did she want?'

'I could not say, my lord. She said that she would call in early tomorrow.'

'Good lord, make that two bottles. One will not be sufficient.'

'Yes, my lord.'

'I am joking, Robbins.'

'Yes, my lord. I knew that.'

Ren walked up the stairs. The house felt very quiet. Ludicrous, he knew. Beth hardly made any noise and he had at least a score of servants.

Still, it felt silent with a hushed emptiness. He pushed open her bedchamber, staring inwards, like a child might pick at a wound. There was no fire in the grate. The nightstand had been cleared of any bottles. The hearth was fresh laid and the bed made.

It seemed as though every hint of her presence had been scoured clean, leaving no trace of her, as though she had never been. He had known she was leaving. She had said that clearly enough and yet, when faced with the stark reality of her absence, he felt hollow, the vacuum almost worse than pain.

From the hall landing, he heard Robbins's tread and he turned away going to his own room where Robbins had placed the cut-crystal decanter and glass.

'Thank you.' He took a sip from his glass. The fiery liquid burned.

After dismissing Robbins, he sat in the comfortable chair, staring into the flickering flames. He frowned, trying to discern his emotions. It was an unusual occupation as he generally tried to escape his emotions, not discern them. Indeed, by rights he should drain the decanter and order another.

But he wouldn't.

He felt that under the pain and hollow ache, Beth's visit had changed him. She might have left no lasting impression on his house, but she had on his heart. For the first time since he had been sent from Graham Hill, he felt he had a role to play.

Beth could not give him love, but she had helped

him to climb from the morass of drink and gambling.

She had given him his self-respect and purpose. He did not want to lose it again.

Lady Graham entered the next morning. Her hair was arranged in a mass of ringlets, somewhat youthful for her age, her gown was of the latest style and her hat bore some sort of fruit.

'Darling, you're back,' she said, seating herself close to the fire and looking about the study with an appraising glance.

'Your powers of observations astound. We are expecting a famine?'

'Pardon?'

'Your hat.'

'Don't be foolish,' she said, making a slight 'tsk.' 'I have determined the perfect solution.'

'To feed London's needy?'

'No.' She permitted her forehead to crinkle in irritation. 'To your dilemma.'

'I didn't know I had one,' he said.

'Yes, regarding the estate.' She spoke in low and confidential tones, somewhat ludicrous given that they were in his study.

He straightened. 'As I said yesterday, I have made a decision on that.'

'I know, darling, but may I be honest with you?' She leaned forward so that a bunch of grapes bobbed in a rather mesmerising fashion.

'That would be a novel experience.'

'I know you believe you have no right to the land because Lord Graham may not be your father. We have never really spoken openly about this and I am not proud of that episode in my life. However, I think I have come up with another suggestion which will solve any concerns you might have in keeping the estate.'

'Another suggestion?'

'Yes, I am hoping it will encourage you to…to reconsider this idea about giving the land to the tenants. You see, the Duke has a second cousin. A female.'

'The Duke?'

'Of Ayrebourne.'

'I am delighted for him. Perhaps she will encourage him to stop starving the tenants. Or we could always send your hat as emergency rations.'

'Really, I do wish you would be serious.'

'I am. I find starving a very serious matter,' he said.

'I am sure that is all greatly exaggerated. Both Beth and her brother have very modern ideas.'

'That people should not starve amidst plenty is indeed revolutionary. But pray enlighten me about your solution to the situation, if it does not involve your hat.'

'You can marry his cousin. Her name is Annabelle and she is also related Lord Graham and while the kinship might not be as close as the Duke's it would ensure that any children you have would be of the right lineage to inherit the estate. This would free you from your peculiar suggestion to give away the land. Indeed, you could keep the estate with a clean conscience.' She finished in firm tones and with a self-satisfied smile, unpleasantly reminiscent of a cat licking cream.

'You have obviously given this a great deal of thought. There is a problem. I have a wife.'

'But that's it. You can have the marriage annulled.'

'Indeed?' His eyes narrowed. 'And what exactly do you know about annulment?'

'That it is entirely possible in your case. You

see, neither Beth nor Jamie were of age so there was no proper consent.'

'How fascinating. Oddly, those were the exact words that Beth said to me. Is it possible that you spoke to her yesterday during my absence?'

Her hands moved as though a little nervous and he saw a slight pursing of her lips.

'It appears that you and my wife have some form of telepathy. Or you decided to share this information with my wife, which rather puts an entirely different light on her departure.'

'Yes, I spoke to Beth. She told me that she wants an annulment. Darling, it makes sense. I am certain she is ever so grateful that you married her and paid off her father's debts, but Allington is doing well now. Apparently, Jamie's schemes are actually prosperous. Anyhow, we had a lovely talk. We are quite of an accord. She was so understanding.'

'And what did she understand exactly?' he asked.

'That marriage to the Duke's cousin would solve everything. That she is really not able to be a suitable wife to someone in your position.'

He stood. He felt his hands ball into fists and

it took all his self-control to keep his tone calm and his voice civil.

'So your perfect solution is that I marry the Duke's cousin?'

'Exactly.'

'Except I do not want to marry the Duke's cousin. I do not want to marry anyone. I wish to remain married to my wife. I wish to give the land to people who love and respect it. I want to live with my wife in Allington or London or wherever she wants and I don't care if I am a social outcast from now until doomsday.'

'You don't care now, but—'

'No "buts", Mother. And no meddling. This my decision. You have hurt me many times. But not now. Not again.'

He rang the bell.

'You are throwing me out?' she asked, her jaw slackening.

'I hope that won't be necessary and that you will go of your own accord. But if needs must...'

She stood rather quickly as Robbins appeared. 'If you could see her ladyship out,' Ren directed.

He heard his mother's footsteps as she exited the building and felt his grin widen.

'Robbins!' He strode into the hall, as soon as he heard the front door close. 'I'm going to Allington.'

The best thing about the journey, Beth decided, was its conclusion. They had taken less than two hours, but she still felt a heavy exhaustion so that she could scarcely climb out of the vehicle. Her body ached and she felt bruised from the carriage's constant motion. She had little notion of their current location and felt too tired to properly assimilate sounds and other clues.

Instead, she followed Beth, taking her word that they were at a small house beside a pretty lake.

At least, she'd kept that feeling of panic at bay throughout the journey. Indeed, it almost seemed as though her exhaustion was so absolute that she lacked the energy to sustain an emotion of any intensity.

Instead, she felt numb, like when her fingers trailed too long within the brook's cold water during springtime.

Thankfully, Rosefield Cottage proved pleasant enough. True to her word, the Dowager Lady Graham had sent notice of their arrival and they were met by the caretaker, a local woman. She pulled them inside and soon had Beth sitting next to a roaring fire which crackled comfortingly within the hearth.

'I made some fresh stew, if you have a fancy,' the caretaker suggested. 'It is just simple country fare, but hearty.'

Beth agreed and soon held a fragrant bowl of stew which she ate close to the fire. Outside, the wind whistled and she could hear the lapping of water from the lake,. Somewhere upstairs she heard Allie's movements as she prepared her room. These noises were punctuated by the fire's crackle and the scrape of her own soup spoon against the bowl.

Quite a change from last night.

Beth pushed that thought away.

This was her future. It would do no good to look back to yesterday or she would become maudlin and feel sorry for herself. They would stay here at the cottage tomorrow and leave the following day. She did not think she could face the remaining journey so soon. Besides, she felt that this comforting numbness might persist as long as she remained in the peculiar limbo of travel.

Eventually there would be pain—just as there was pain when her fingers warmed after freezing in the brook. Once she got back to Allington and she was no longer so overwhelmed with the sounds and fears of travel, she would feel. It would hurt, but there would be life also. She had to hold on to that. She would let Jamie know that Ren would not give away Graham Hill. She would visit the tenants, ride Lil and continue the myriad small activities which had made her life pleasant.

And which would make her life pleasant again.

Six hours later, Ren stood in front of his brother-in-law's desk. Jamie, of course, was useless. He peered up at him through tiny gold-rimmed glasses. 'But I haven't seen her.'

'What do you mean? You must have.'

'I have not. If I had done, I would have explained about the experiment. She asked me to find all the information and I have done so.' Jamie tapped on a sheath of papers, sending up a tiny, visible cloud of dust. 'In fact, I think she said you were also interested.'

'What?'

'Here.' Jamie pushed forward the papers as

though expecting Ren to review them immediately. 'It appears that manure combined with gypsum caused greater growth than manure alone. Beth said you had a particular interest.'

'I— What?— No.' Ren silenced a muttered curse. 'I will look at them later. But please, could you focus on your sister's whereabouts for now. I mean, if you haven't seen her, where is she? Where else would she go except here? Do you know of other places she might be?'

'No,' Jamie said, then with a seeming lack of concern, he returned to his work, bending over a ledger, the nib of his pen scratching with irritating regularity.

'You are not worried?'

'No, she wrote, or rather Allie wrote, that she would be a few days before returning.' Jamie said, dipping his pen into the inkwell again and tapping off the excess liquid with care.

'She wrote? But you said you hadn't heard from her?'

'Said I hadn't seen her,' Jamie clarified.

Ren bit back a second oath. Frustration would not help. 'Where did she write from?'

'London.'

'Where in London? And where was she going?'

'The letter came from your house, but it did not include her destination.'

'Damn,' Ren swore. 'You will let me know if you see her or receive any more notes or any other form of communication for that matter?'

Jamie nodded, but seemed already abstracted.

Ren left Jamie's office. That, he supposed, answered that. It appeared Beth was actively avoiding him. He had again tricked himself, indulging in concocting a comforting fabrication. He had convinced himself that his mother had manipulated Beth, but he was giving his mother too much credit.

Beth was independent in her thoughts.

Her decision was not because of his mother. Beth had little enough reason to remain with him. She had never wanted marriage. She valued independence above all and marriage to any man limited a woman's autonomy. Moreover, he was a rake with a predilection for gambling, drink and duels. Given her father's debts, she had every reason to fear a gambler.

Grim-faced, he swung on to Tallon as another, more awful thought struck him. Was it possible that Beth had seduced him to dissuade him from giving the estate to the Duke? Good Lord, that would be the ultimate irony. He, the rake, the user of women, to have been used by his own wife! But Beth would not be the first woman to exploit her body. And she'd always said that individuals with disabilities were too frequently thought as innocent, as though a lack of sight served as proof of morality.

Damn.

That familiar need to ride and ride grew. He wanted to gallop so fast that he would outrun his thoughts. He longed to move with such speed that every ounce of his energy and concentration was focused on remaining astride the animal, rendering anything else superfluous. He wanted to flee that sense of dislocation and isolation that he'd had for ever, or at least since the return of the bloody portrait painter.

For a brief, fleeting moment, he had hoped... He still hoped...

He needed to find his wife. Or obliterate his thoughts with a wild, thundering, clattering of hooves. Or drink. There'd be plenty of brandy at Graham Hill, thank God. His fath—Lord Graham had always kept a good stock. Yes, he'd go to Graham Hill and drink until he didn't see that blonde hair and beautiful face. He'd drink until he'd forgotten that brief, momentary illusion. He'd drink until he obliterated those pretty pictures of hearth and home and Beth.

Tomorrow, maybe, he'd find that purpose again that he'd so recently discovered, the new and improved Lord Graham.

Tonight, he'd drink.

By habit, he slowed his horse while walking through the village. The road was quiet and unchanged. It was as it had been in his childhood. Most of the tenants were inside, perhaps eating supper. He could see smoke rising from the chimneys and the flicker of lamplight from windows. Likely they'd be out again before dusk turned to night to check on goats and chickens. Beside their homes, he saw the occasional milk cow, their bells clanking, and pigs at the troughs, their tiny, curvy tails twitching.

A faint tapping caught his attention. He angled towards the sound and saw that it came from his old nanny's house. Indeed, she'd pushed open the window, and was waving, a small white hanky visible against green shutters.

She had not attended the funeral. Indeed, he had not seen her for several years and had little desire to do so now, but he could not ignore her summons.

Dismounting, he tethered Tallon to the fence post. He walked the rutted path towards the cottage and entered a miniscule space scented with wood smoke, onions and a mix of other smells too tangled to discern, although arnica and some other tincture was among them.

Nanny sat at the window, her face a net of wrinkles fanning out from her blue eyes, still bright despite her years.

'I was hoping you'd pass this way,' she said as he bent down and kissed her cheek. It had the cool dryness of the elderly. 'I hear you're not intending to give the land away to the Duke now.'

He felt his jaw drop. 'How could you possibly know that?'

She didn't answer. 'Sit!' she instructed. 'I also know that you have some novel idea about giving it away to the tenants.'

'Yes, it was Beth's suggestion.'

'I know.'

'Is there anything you do not know?'

'Very little,' she said. 'The idea is unusual to say the least. I dare say even the tenants will find it highly irregular. People are often resistant to change even when they are the beneficiaries. As for the well-to-do and all those grand lords and ladies, well, you won't be making yourself popular.'

'I don't think I've ever tried.'

'No? What about that small lad that went to school?'

He allowed himself a smile. 'I think I aimed for survival, not popularity,' he said. 'Although recently, I have recognised that I also wanted their admiration.'

'To know one's self, that is the sign of intelligence or madness. I am uncertain which, now that I come to think of it. Anyhow, why are you still standing? You make my underpinnings hurt just looking at you. Sit!' she directed again.

He did so, choosing a chair opposite, and feeling huge in comparison to this tiny woman shrunken with her years.

For a moment, she said nothing, pressing her gnarled fingers together and studying him as though his expression might provide a clue or information.

'I haven't stolen anything from the pantry, honest, Nanny,' he quipped.

'You never did. That was always Edmund or Beth. Or maybe even Jamie, although that was likely only in pursuit of science.'

'He once took a slice of chocolate cake to see if the mould would grow a different colour from that on the vanilla cake he also purloined.'

'I could have told him the answer to that one without the bother. No, I think you have always searched for belonging. I think even before you knew the truth you recognised you were different. You always tried to be better than the others. Perfect.'

He smiled wryly. 'I made up for that in later life.'

'Like you needed to earn love,' she continued, ignoring his comment.

He glanced towards the window at the shadowy shapes of the trees visible through the panes. He had glamorised those years before the return of the portrait painter as a halcyon time. But was that accurate? Hadn't his brother and father always shared a greater bond?

'I could never understand why they liked hunting and fishing, Edmund and Lord Graham,' he said.

'He was proud of you, you know? Your father.'

'The painter?'

'No, Lord Graham. Before he knew about the painter, he was very proud of you. He didn't understand you, but he was proud of you and proud of your talent. Maybe that's why he reacted so badly. Anguish does awful things to a man. Not that I'm defending him. It's never right to whip a child.'

'Maybe.'

'And just so as you know, there's nought wrong with being different. Never did understand why people want to be sheep. They are not even intelligent animals. Can't even right themselves. You still paint?'

'No,' he said. 'I haven't in years.'

'Might be time to start.'

'I can't,' he said, remembering his last uncomfortable attempt.

'Seems as how you have the use of your hands

and eyes so I cannot see why you would not be able to.'

'It is not as easy as that.'

'Some people just can't be a sheep. And you can't make yourself into a sheep if you are not a sheep and never meant to be a sheep.'

'Pardon?' The whole interview was taking on a somewhat surreal flavour. He wondered if age was impairing her faculties.

'I am not mad,' she stated.

He smiled. 'Apparently not, or if you are it has not impaired your ability to read my thoughts.'

'You know there is only one person whose opinion and respect matters in life,' she said.

'Indeed, and I will talk to her. Once I find her.' He shifted, preparing to stand.

'I wasn't meaning Beth.'

'What? Then whom?' he asked.

'But you do need to talk to her.' She continued as though he had not spoken.

'Which I will do if I can locate the woman.'

'I know where she is.'

'You do?' he gaped.

'You underestimate me.' Her wrinkled face split into a grin that was almost devilish.

'You know where she is? Tell me.'

'Not tonight.'

'Pardon?'

'It is late. You have chased down from London. You are exhausted. You need to rest,' she said, as firmly as she had done when he was three and had wanted to stay up late or eat too many bonbons.

'That is ludicrous!' Ren stared at the small, frustrating woman. How was he able to negotiate and trade for thousands, win duels and boxing matches and yet be foiled by his elderly nanny?

'Not at all. I am certain any conversation with her ladyship would be more useful and rational after a good night's sleep.'

'I couldn't persuade you to let me find my wife first and then rest?' he asked.

'No. But she is quite safe.'

'She is? You are certain.'

'She has Allie with her. My great-niece or something like. She'll be fine. That girl would fight a tiger for her.'

'That much is true. You will tell me her address tomorrow?'

'Yes, and do eat and sleep. A much better use of

your time than imbibing brandy which was what you were planning.'

'Mind reading again,' he muttered.

'Not at all, but men are creatures of habit and it seems you have become somewhat habituated to the consumption of alcohol,' she retorted.

He felt his lips twitch. For a brief moment, he imagined telling Beth about this entire interview. He imagined her chuckle and wide, giving smile. In that instant, he suddenly felt certain that she would never have slept with him if she had not cared.

'Very well,' he said. 'I will get this prescribed rest and then you will tell me of my wife's whereabouts tomorrow. How do you even know anyway?'

'Ah.' She tapped gnarled finger to her nose. 'Now that would be telling. We have a deal?'

She thrust out her hand, the fingers swollen and twisted with arthritis.

'Yes,' he said, shaking the proffered hand gently, suddenly conscious of her age and fragility.

Ren neither rested nor did he spend the night drinking copious alcohol. Instead, he ordered a

light repast and then cleared the desk of everything except the two lamps. With care, he took
out the plans for the estate which he had found
rolled and tied with ribbons. He untied the strings,
carefully spreading the paper flat and placing two
books and a paperweight on each corner to better smooth the sheets. After moving the lights
closer, he bent over them, carefully studying the
routes, the waterways, the location of buildings
and fences.

Taking out the ledger, he cross-referenced them
to determine which farms appeared most profitable, the type of crops grown, the proximity to
water and other amenities. Then, taking out the
pen, he dipped it into the ink well and started
to write. He worked in a peaceful silence interrupted only by the scratch of his pen, the clock
and the occasional crackle from the fire. Every
so often he paused, drumming his fingers, as he
reviewed his notes.

There was, he realised, a reason that enclosure had become so popular during the last half-
century. Larger holdings, run by landlords, could
yield more crops with greater efficiency. Such

estates permitted the rotation of different crops, the provision of more fodder for animals and the utilisation of new tools.

But individual ownership did not mean that these things could not occur. Rather, it meant that there needed to be a process to ensure this co-operation and that the smaller holdings worked together as an entity. Someone was needed who had business acumen, literacy, agricultural and scientific knowledge. He could take that role. He could ensure that the farms remained up to date with new inventions and agricultural methods. Indeed, could not he and Jamie form a team? With Jamie ensuring the latest scientific method was employed, while he took over the business side of the estate and ensured that the crops and livestock were marketed with skill, so that each farm was its most profitable?

At last Ren rose. He was tired. He could not remember when he had last thought and planned with such intensity. He rubbed his temples, conscious of an ache behind the eyes.

Yet his weariness felt like a good type of tired,

the kind he used to feel after a long day painting outside.

He felt happier.

He felt less broken.

# *Chapter Sixteen*

Mrs Cridge sat at her window next morning.

'Lovely to see you, dear,' she said. 'And now would you be liking a cup of tea?'

'No,' he said firmly. 'I would not be liking a cup of tea. I would be liking my wife's address.'

'Yes,' she greed. 'Apparently, she is staying at Rosefield Cottage.'

'Rosefield? That is halfway between here and London. I remember going there as a child with my mother. Who owns it?'

'Mrs Holmes, an elderly, rather distant relative of the late Lord Graham.'

'But why? How does she even know this Mrs Holmes?'

'I don't know.'

'Really. Something you are not cognisant about. You are certain it is her?'

'Absolutely, I heard it from Miss Marks, who has just returned from Lichfield which is close to Rosefield Cottage. Anyhow, the servants there had to open up Rosefield Cottage and she heard tell that her ladyship was coming to the neighbourhood.'

'How did she know it was her?'

'I find that there aren't as many blind, beautiful, blonde young women around as you would think.'

He gave a sharp bark of laughter and then nodded, turning to leave.

But with his hand on the doorknob, he looked back at the small, wizened woman. 'You never do anything without good reason. Why didn't you tell me last night? It is close enough that I could have made it by nightfall.'

She smiled, her wrinkled cheeks bunching with an almost mischievous look. Then she took one gnarled forefinger and again touched the side of her nose, winking.

Ren chose not to take the carriage to Rosefield Cottage, but rode. Tallon was well rested and they would make good time. He worried that if he delayed she would have left again and he would be forever trailing after the woman.

Of course, the irony was that Beth had spent her entire life within a five-mile radius of her home and had now taken to traversing the countryside. It might have made more sense to simply wait for her return, but he could not.

He needed to find Beth. He needed to talk to her. He needed to determine why she had left and to explain his plans for the estate. Most importantly, he needed to tell her that he did not want to marry the Duke's relative or anyone else's relative, for that matter.

As he rode, he found himself taking in more details about the land than he had previously. He saw fields lying fallow which might well support turnips. He saw fences requiring repair and bogs in low-lying areas which should be drained.

His mind filled with ideas. For the first time since childhood, he did not feel the imposter. He had no right through birth, but he could and would earn a right through good management.

And Beth? All things felt possible now. He would convince her that he loved her. Yes, he was illegitimate. He gambled. He drank and, yes, he'd had mistresses. He could not change the past, but he could promise her fidelity in the future. He might not be worthy of her love, but he could be, he would be.

Shifting his body forward, Ren urged Tallon to a faster pace. He felt a growing eagerness as they cut across the green pastures. The animal's hooves drummed on the grass, earth flying up behind. They moved effortlessly, man and horse, and it struck Ren that for once he was riding in pursuit of something as opposed to riding away.

He slowed by the woods, carefully guiding Tallon along the uneven path. Rosefield Cottage was in a sheltered place, nestled beside a lake and backed by a small cluster of trees. As he approached, he saw the sun glimmering on the lake's rippled surface, its beams shining between puffy clouds—the type he used to describe to Beth as cotton batting.

It seemed that the very air felt different, energised and brighter. The sun was warmer, the hedgerows were a deeper green and the wildflowers had a more vibrant hue. Indeed, even a cow within the small enclosure by the house appeared more animated.

He grinned. Heavens, if he if he was mooning over animated cows, he was in a sad state.

The cottage was of Tudor origin, with stone and white plaster sandwiched between thick, dark beams. It had a steeply pitched roof and tall chimney.

He swung off his horse. A fir tree grew in front of the structure and the ground felt spongy and dense with needles. The stable yard seemed empty, except for a filled water trough. He called out, briefly wondering if he was on a fool's errand.

At that moment, Arnold strolled from the small stable, his round country face breaking into a grin. 'I thought you'd be here, my lord,' he said with the satisfaction of a skilled fortune teller. 'She's inside. Shall I look after your horse?'

'Thank you.' He handed the animal to him and then strode to the cottage door. Beth's little maid opened it almost immediately, ushering Ren into the interior. The ceiling was low and lined with heavy dark beams, making it seem even lower. Stooping, Ren stepped inside.

Beth sat at the window in the drawing room. Her hair was coiled at the base of her neck and shone in a shaft of sunlight which angled through diamond panes.

'Ren,' she said, the word a half-gasp which was not typical of her.

'My God, how do you do that?'

'Your smell: horse, hay, tobacco and your own scent,' she said.

'Likely quite unpleasant given that I have been chasing you across the country. Why did you come here anyway?'

'Your— I needed to break my journey and I needed time to think.'

'You couldn't do so at Allington?'

'No,' she said.

He sat in the chair opposite. His left side and his knees felt ludicrously high in the small chair. 'People in this place must be tiny.'

'I don't know. It belongs to Mrs Holmes. She is in London now.'

Beth spoke in quick, clipped sentences as though nervous.

'Yes, a friend of my mother's. Indeed, my mother appears entirely too much involved in this flight of yours. Apparently, she has filled your head with all manner of nonsense. First and foremost, I do not want to marry any cousin of the Duke's or anyone else. Secondly, no more mistresses. No more gambling and very moderate drinking. And I wish to stay married to you.'

Beth listened to his words. It felt as it did when he described something to her. She could see it. She could see herself living in Graham Hill. She could imagine evenings talking to Ren, laughing with Ren. And later, after the evenings by the fireside, she would spend her nights lying with Ren. She would feel that joy, that feeling which could not even be put into words.

Except—

'I can't,' she said. 'You know I never wanted to marry.'

'You didn't want to be forced into marriage like so many women are. Or forced to be dependent because of your sight, but, Beth, this is me.'

*It is me.*

She felt the smart of tears in her eyes. 'I know.'

'I've always wanted you to be independent. You know that,' he said. 'And I have determined that we can live at Graham Hill or Allington, whichever you would prefer. I mean, as long as Jamie doesn't mind. We can make this work.'

'Ren, I care for you but I don't— I can't—'

She could not finish the sentence. The lie stuck in her mouth.

'Love me?' He voice was husky.

She heard his anguish. It hurt her, a physical pain that seemed tight and vicelike, a squeezing, clenching pressure under her ribcage. He leaned closer to her. He placed his fingers against her face, framing her forehead as if to discern her thoughts.

She forced her expression to harden. 'Yes,' she said, pushing the word out.

There was a pause. She heard nothing, not even the clock's tick, as if time had stilled.

'You are certain?'

'Yes.'

'And the night we made love? What was that?'

She looked down. She balled her fists so tightly that her nails cut into her palms. 'A mistake.'

The words hung huge, heavy, hurtful. The tightening under her ribcage was so great she could not breathe.

'Yes,' he said.

His hands dropped from her face. She heard him stand, the movement quick, violent. The chair banged back against the wall.

'Ren—'

'Take heart, all is not lost. I am not giving the land to the Duke. I will not, so perhaps that night served its purpose.'

'What?' She stood also, reaching out to him, but finding only air. 'You can't think that.'

'No? It would be one explanation.'

She held on to the back of the chair, uncertain where to step in a house so unfamiliar to her. 'I am glad that you are not selling the land but my... my sleeping with you was not about land.'

'You once said that blindness does not ensure your good character.'

'But I didn't mean— You can't think that!' Her hand balled. She wanted to strike him or kiss him, but she couldn't take a step from the chair. Tears spilled.

'A nuisance being blind, isn't it? You can't even slap me!' he said in that snide tone she hated.

'Don't! Don't be like that. It makes you sound horrid.'

'Indeed, that was established by most members of society years ago.'

'Please, Ren. I don't— I never meant—'

'It would appear that an annulment would be suitable, given the circumstances. I will send you the necessary papers to sign. As for the tenants, I will do what I consider right by them. I am seldom influenced by a woman's wiles. Believe me, individuals with more skills than you have tried.'

He turned. She heard his sharp footsteps. She heard the firm click of the door as it opened and closed and then the retreating, more distant sound of his steps in the passage outside. The front door slammed with such force that the noise reverberated through the structure.

Beth flopped, limp as a rag doll. Her legs trembled. Her throat hurt. Her eyes hurt. That space deep under her breast bone hurt. Everything hurt.

# Chapter Seventeen

Ren rode away with a crazy recklessness. Twigs and branches snapped his face as he cut through the fields and down twisted roadways. He felt and heard the wild thunder of his horse's hooves as he hunched over, fusing himself to the animal's body. He should have known he was not good enough. He should have known she couldn't love him. He remembered the way his mother had looked at him, and then away, as though his presence caused her physical discomfort. He remembered the sting of Lord Graham's whip and the laughter of the boys as they'd chanted *painter's bastard, painter's bastard* over and over.

As though to match his mood, the cotton-batting clouds had turned grey, lowering so that their misty tentacles tangled through the trees and sat heavy upon the low hills. It started to rain, a dampening drizzle. He slowed, for Tallon's sake. He did not want him to slip on the wet grass. He would not cripple the animal.

He saw that he had come to a village, a small place with a cluster of cottages and an inn with a stone façade. It might be picturesque in summer, but now appeared drab, its hedgerows wet and the eaves of its thatched cottages brown and dripping. Still, he supposed it was as good a place to stop as any.

He entered a courtyard scented with straw and manure and swung off his horse. A stable boy was filling a water trough, pumping rhythmically. Two dogs circled, barking. Tallon whickered nervously. He was still young.

Tossing a coin to the boy, Ren told him to tie up the dogs and feed and water his horse. He went to the inn to order food and half-wondered if he should stay the night. Tomorrow he could head back to London. He need not return to Graham Hill. After all, he could initiate the paperwork and the transfer of title to the tenants through his solicitor in the City, likely with greater efficiency than if he were to use Mr Tyrell, a country solicitor with pedantic speech and a nose vastly too large for his face.

Ren sat in the taproom. The air was thick with pipe smoke, mixed not unpleasantly with the smell of ale and steak. Yes, London might be best. He didn't want to go into the ancestral home that wasn't his own. He didn't want to feel its emptiness without Edmund, or Mirabelle, or Beth.

The landlord came with beef stew, piping hot, its steam fragrant with beef and onions. He placed it before him. It tasted delicious, reminding him of Mrs Bridges's meals when his mother and Lord Graham had been away in London. Simple, honest country fare.

The room was not yet full as it was only mid-afternoon. An old fellow sat in a corner, smoking a pipe, wisps of blue haze wreathing his bald head. Every now and then he nodded and smiled, showing toothless gums.

Ren ate slowly and sipped his ale without haste. There was no need for speed. Tallon needed the rest and he had sufficient time whether he went to London or Graham Hill. Besides, the weather seemed changeable as was typical in an English spring. He noted through the tavern's steamy windows that the sky had cleared and a shaft of late-afternoon sun lit the dark wood tables, glinting off the pewter tankards.

He did not recognise many of his fellow punters, but he had been away so long that they might well be from Graham Hill, Allington or, more likely, a closer property. He watched as they bought their drinks, sitting down to swap yarns. There was a strength, a resiliency about these folks. They belonged, not through land, title or politics, but simply because they had been born here.

With his ale emptied, Ren stood, paying the innkeeper. He walked out, signalling for the boy to bring around his horse.

He would not go to London. He would return to Graham Hill tonight. Last night he had felt something akin to purpose. This morning he had felt optimism. He'd wanted to talk to the tenants, to determine crops and drain ditches.

He'd been himself again.

Signing documents in a solicitor's office in London was not the same as working with the tenants to ensure that each farm gained independence and prosperity in the best way possible.

He could not make Beth love him. Nor could

he change the circumstances of his birth. But he could choose to ensure that this transfer of property was done in the right way.

He could behave in a way that was deserving of a woman's respect.

Or perhaps more importantly, his own.

Riding Tallon again, he set off at a sensible pace. The sun now hung low on the horizon. The clearing skies had brought with them a chill wind and cool temperatures as afternoon warmth gave way to dusk.

By now the surroundings were familiar, the pasture land and fields of boyhood jaunts. As the sun disappeared, the faint outline of a crescent moon appeared visible against the dusky violet of the twilight sky and surrounded by stars, shimmering like diamonds.

Flicking the reins to the left, he took the shortcut through the woods. It would skirt close to Allington and he could then cross the fields to Graham Hill. Above him the branches rustled and a night owl hooted. Occasionally, he heard Tallon swish his tail against the midges. The animal's gait was good, solid and regular, although he still required training.

Every now and then, a mosquito whined close to his ear or their passage would spark an angry chattering of squirrels. The air smelled cool and earthy with a touch of damp. He could hear the tinkling of the stream running beside the path. Above him, peeking through the canopy of branches, he could see the silver sliver of moon and the stars' sparkle.

Would he have been aware of these sights and the myriad tiny noises and scents a week ago? It seemed that he had been oblivious. In this last week, he had seen and heard and felt more than he had for a decade.

He passed the halfway mark, the solid oak they used to hide behind as children. It was then that he felt that first prickle of apprehension. The sensation was a nebulous queasiness, that uneasy, illogical impression of being watched. Foolishness, he told himself. Perhaps he had had one too many ales. Or it was naught but a fox or other woodland animals whose glistening eyes he sometimes saw, luminous in the dark bushes lining the trail.

Still, he tensed, urging Tallon into a quicker trot.

For a second, he didn't see them, hearing only the branches and twigs. Even when he saw their looming shadows, he thought briefly that his eyes deceived him. Three tall, darkly clad figures approached on foot. One held a torch which illuminated their tall, cloaked figures by its flickering yellow light.

As they disengaged themselves from the forest, moving with sudden stealth, he instinctively pushed Tallon to move faster, hoping to skirt by them. Then he saw the dark shape of an arm raised, outlined within the flickering torchlight. Metal glinted.

A pistol fired, a single blast of sound. Tallon reared and bucked. Ren swore, controlling his animal, and again urging him forward with greater speed and urgency.

A second blast rang out. Pain shot through his shoulder. A red haze obscured his vision. The pain, combined with the horse's crazed movement, unseated him.

He fell.

The air was pushed from his lungs. He'd fallen on his other arm and he felt another flare of pain. Tallon's dark form bolted, galloping through the undergrowth in a wild, chaotic fury of jangling reins and breaking branches.

For a moment, after the crashing thunder of the horses' hooves, it seemed that they all briefly waited in sudden, eerie silence.

Ren pulled himself to a seated position. His whip had fallen. He grabbed it. The pain invoked by the movement made his senses swim into that red haze so that he feared he would swoon.

A man ran forward, laughing. 'What yer gonna do with that?' He slurred his words together, aiming his foot at Ren and kicking so that he fell forward again.

More desperate now, Ren struggled up. This time, he swung the whip, catching the man with a glancing blow. It nipped his face, a dark line of blood slicing across his cheek.

The man swore. Ren swung again, hitting him more squarely. This time the man staggered. Then the third figure emerged. The light flickered, making the men and trees tall undulating shadows. They wore masks so that he could not see their faces.

'You want money? Here!' Ren pulled out his

purse with the hand not clutching at the whip, throwing it to the men.

One of the figures bent down. He opened it, pulling out the coins. He rubbed them between his thumb and forefinger. The gold shone dully.

'We still gotta kill him,' one said.

'Just take his gold and run. Why stick our necks out?'

'We'll get more. He said. A lot more.'

'Or the hangman's noose. Gold's not much good to a dead man.'

Taking advantage of their abstraction, Ren again swung the whip. The lash struck the lantern. It rocked, its beam making a yellow arch. He swung again. The whip snapped. The lantern clattered. Briefly, light flared before flickering out in the damp soil.

After that flash of light, the woods seemed all the darker. Ren heard their curses. Another shot rang out. It struck a tree with a splintering of wood.

He heard the movement of the pistol being reloaded, the click of metal.

It was now or never. Doubled over in pain, Ren scrambled in a half-run, half-crawl. He pushed through bushes and undergrowth, determined only to put as much distance between himself and these men as possible. Twigs and leaves scratched at his face. He heard another shot. It came close. He heard the whistle of air as it passed his ear.

Mindless of the pain, he made a final effort before tumbling into the low ditch. He flattened himself to the ground. He smelled dirt. He felt its grit. He heard the wood's silence and the hard, rhythmic thump of his heart. Even with his eyes closed he saw the sparkle of a thousand lights.

When he next lifted his head, the silence remained profound and absolute as though even the woodland creatures were themselves hushed. Had the men given up the chase? Had they gone away, satisfied with their fistful of gold?

He felt his eyelids stretch as he looked about, as though by making his eyes wider he could see better. His gaze darted across the shadowy woodland shapes. A branch moved. He startled. His hand tightened reflexively on the whip. He dared not breathe.

He wondered if they were even yet moving stealthily, stepping quietly, encircling him. He lay very still and it seemed that this absence of movement was not a choice but a necessity. His limbs felt solidified, numb and heavy as rocks. His heart slowed, his eyes lids closed and the chill grew, deadening the pain.

He didn't know how long he lay semi-conscious, but suddenly, almost as if told by an external source, he knew he must move.

He must move or die.

With gritted teeth, he forced himself on to his hands and knees. He put his hand on to a tree stump. Strangely, his palm slid off it as though wet. He sat back on his heels, staring at the dark liquid dripping down his palm and forearm with disbelieving surprise. He touched his shoulder. He felt a warm wetness. His jacket was sodden.

Blood.

The bullet must have struck his shoulder. Odd that it hurt less than his other arm. He thought this in an almost detached manner, as though with academic curiosity. His thoughts seemed slow and pedestrian like the treacle Mrs Bridges used to give them.

He shivered. He felt very cold, but was also aware of the beads of perspiration on his forehead and under his armpits. Gripping on to the stump, he struggled to stand. The trees, the silver crescent moon and stars swayed.

He whistled for Tallon, but he was long gone. The woods remained heavily quiet.

As the shock lessened, the pain increased. It winded him, but also seemed to bring with it new clarity and determination. He'd walk to Allington. It was closer than Graham Hill—two miles at most. He could walk two miles.

Except walking was not easy. His wound bled. He tried to stem the flow, but this made the other arm hurt, an excruciating pain worse than the bullet.

Every movement jarred. He clenched his teeth, forcing himself to move forward, focusing on each step, left, right, left, right, as a soldier might march. The beads of sweat became huge, rolling down his forehead, stinging his eyes.

At last he exited the woods. Stepping into the clearing, he felt a peculiar mix of fear and relief. Help was more accessible here. He was on the road. Someone might pass, a farmer or late-night reveller. Yet he also felt vulnerable and exposed. Again, he felt his gaze dart from side to side, *what ifs* circling in his mind.

A few trees lined the road. They cast dim, eerie shadows in the faint light of the crescent moon. It seemed odd that the crescent moon remained so unchanged. But then the moon never changed. It had seen war and death and didn't change.

On occasion, he heard the rustling scurry of a woodland creature. He remembered how he had liked to paint foxes and squirrels.

It seemed, he thought, that if he died here tonight, he might regret not painting. He would also regret that he had not told Beth that he loved her. She might not love him, but he loved her. He would have liked her to know that.

His arm was bleeding less now. It was just a scratch—the merest trifle. The searing pain from the other arm was worse. It made him long to lie down on the road, to close his eyes, to sleep. The sweat made his hair stick in clammy strands to his forehead and neck. But still so cold. So cold he was shaking. Odd to be sweating while his teeth chattered. Their movement made the road, the trees, the bushes, the bright eyes of the animals, the crescent moon and the stars blur. It was as though he walked in a dream. Sometimes he remembered the dark figures of his attackers. At other times, he wondered how he had got hurt. Once, he decided that he had fought with Edmund and that Nanny would be cross. Nanny did not approve of fisticuffs.

Perhaps he should rest. He was so very tired— except he had something important to do. He frowned, trying to remember what he needed to do and where he was going. The chattering of his own teeth was so loud. Surely the whole world should hear it.

Allington.

Yes, that was it. He needed to get to Allington. He needed to get to Allington because he needed to see Beth. He needed to tell Beth that he loved her. He needed her to know that and also that he hadn't meant any of those harsh things. Suddenly he saw her clearly, almost as clearly as the trees and shrubs and the moon.

At last, the dim outline of the stable at Allington loomed from the shadows. For a moment he wondered if it was real. Then he found the rail that Beth's father had constructed. He held it, glad of the firm wood under his hand.

Turning, he saw the house. It looked huge and dark, with lights visible only in the two uppermost windows. The thought of traversing the courtyard seemed suddenly impossible. Perhaps Jamie would be in the stable. Jamie was always in the small office, reading or recording measurements or some such.

Ren stepped forward, meaning to go to the stable, but his legs buckled. Instinctively, he extended his arms to break his fall, but collapsed as pain twisted through his arm, searing and excruciating.

He lay quite still, squeezing his eyes shut. The pain eased a little. His body felt limp, spent. The grass and moss was damp but not unpleasant. He could stay here and rest—just for a little while. The air smelled of spring. He liked spring.

To one side, just over the stable's shadowy shape, he saw the crescent moon. And then his eyes closed and blackness descended.

Beth and Allie did not speak as the carriage took the rutted country road to Allington. The journey was short but unpleasant. Beth still hated the rolling movement as they were pulled through space she could not see or feel. She hated the uneasiness in her stomach and the aching bruised feeling in her spine and bottom.

Allie did not talk or attempt to distract her as she had done on the trip to London. Instead, the silence felt heavy with disapproval.

Her maid was equally annoyed that there had been no happy reconciliation at Rosefield Cottage, nor had Beth determined to chase Ren to London, but instead had ordered their immediate departure for Allington.

'It is entirely possible that he might return to talk this out some more and he can hardly do that if you keep on haring off like a frightened rabbit,' Allie said.

'I think we will only hurt each other more if we talk. Besides, the decision is made. It is the right decision. Love is about wanting what is best for the other person and not the pursuit of one's own needs.'

Allie had merely sniffed, again making the packing of Beth's few items a noisy affair.

At last the carriage slowed, and took a sharp turn. Beth straightened, recognising the twist and pressing her fingers against the cool glass pane. 'Are we there?'

'Indeed, although it's dark as coal dust. They have no lanterns lit. They must not have got our message about arriving earlier than was scheduled.'

The carriage rattled to a stop.

'I hope someone hears us,' Allie added. 'Mr Munson is deaf as a post and Mr Jamie is like as not conducting some experiment.'

'Then he might be in the stable,' Beth said.

'That's dark, too. Not to worry. I am certain if Arnold hammers hard enough on the back door, someone will hear us eventually. This is what happens when one is unpredictable in one's travel plans.'

Allie finished this last sentence with another sniff of disapproval and Beth heard the rustle of her clothes as she leaned forward to open the door so that the cool night air spilled inwards.

'You stay there, my lady. We don't want you walking about in the dark. Arnold and I will get things lit and the house woke up.'

'Thank you,' Beth said with a wry grin. Light or lack thereof made little difference to her and her legs and arms were numb with travel.

Therefore, within moments of Allie's departure she clambered out, determined to stretch her legs and roll her shoulders to work out the kinks which knotted her back and made her head ache.

It was the smell that caught her attention. She gasped as memory hit her, quick and painful. The smell had an earthiness, a sharp mineral tang, half-sweet and half-pungent. She remembered that smell. It had been everywhere, heavy and sickening, the day they'd brought her mother home.

Blood.

'My lady, I've sent Arnold to hammer on the back.'

'Shhh,' Beth replied as though silence would help her better follow the scent. 'Do you see anything? Anyone?'

'What? No, it is still very dark. You should wait—'

'Get a lantern and look. Someone is hurt. And where is my cane?'

'Here, my lady,' Allie said, getting it from the interior of the carriage.

'Go for a lantern and get Arnold as well.'

As Allie departed, Beth stepped forward. Fear

clutched her heart. What if Jamie had been injured?

'Hallo?' she called. 'Jamie?'

She heard a groan. She stepped towards the sound. Her cane struck something or someone. She heard a second muffled cry. Letting her cane fall, she dropped to the ground. Kneeling, she felt a man's jacket. It was a fine cloth, not the fabric of a labourer.

'Jamie?'

Her hands urgently explored. She felt a face. She recognised the contours, the firm chin and cheeks.

It was not Jamie.

Fear, pain and panicked bewilderment squeezed her gut as her hands frantically roamed over the cloth of his shirt to find his injury.

'Allie! Arnold! Help!' she shouted.

Her hands touched his chest, his face, and then his shoulders where she felt the warm, wet stickiness of blood.

'Here, my lady. What is it?' Allie's quick footsteps came up behind her, accompanied by the clank of the lantern.

'It's Ren. We need to get him indoors and get a doctor. Now!'

'I'll—I'll tell Arnold.'

'Beth.' Ren's voice was weak and husky.

She leaned over him. 'Ren, we will look after you. We'll get you inside. You're going to be fine, I promise.'

'You're real?'

'Yes! Yes!'

'I… Tell…' He started to speak, but his words dwindled into a rasp of breath, followed by a gasping, whistling exhalation.

The next few days were a blur. The doctor came. He smelled of medicine and tinctures. He removed the bullet and stitched up the wound while Allie held up a light. Then, when Allie left to retch, Beth took over the job. She stood, as directed, her arm raised as she listened to Ren's muted groans and the rasp of needle through skin.

The arm was not broken, but rather the shoulder socket and blade were out of alignment and not moving properly. The doctor was able to shift both back into place. The wound would heal, provided Ren was able to fight the infection.

'It appears,' he explained, in his low, guttural tones, 'that an infection entered the wound with the bullet. For this reason, he has a temperature and there is considerable inflammation. We will need to keep him cool and the wound cleansed. He has also lost considerable blood. The next few days are critical.'

*Critical.* The word sounded like a death warrant. Beth wrapped her arms tightly about herself, feeling as though she might split into a thousand shards.

Morning brought Jamie's return. He had been conducting a science experiment which apparently could only be done at night. He came into the sick room. He smelled slightly of manure which mixed unpleasantly with the mustard plaster that the doctor had ordered.

'But what happened?' he asked.

'I don't know. He was attacked. He hasn't been conscious,' Beth said.

'But we've never had anyone attacked at Allington.'

Beth almost smiled. Jamie sounded so personally offended, she thought, with the tiny part of her brain which still functioned. Odd the way this minute portion of her mind still assimilated unimportant details while the rest of her was paralysed in awful, soul-destroying agony.

'His purse had been taken,' she said.

'That is evidence.'

'Yes,' she said. 'A random robbery, I suppose.'

Jamie grunted, but she had the sense that he disagreed. She could ask, she supposed, but it seemed too hard to structure her sentences.

'Let me know if he wakes up.'

She nodded.

'Can I do anything?' he added more gently.

'No.'

'Look after yourself.'

For long hours, Beth sat beside Ren. She heard his agitated movement, punctuated by groans as his pain and restlessness increased. His temperature rose. Even before she touched his forehead she could feel the heat from it, radiating like a brick hot from the fire.

Sometimes he would toss. At moments he

shouted, addressing someone or something not in the room. Allie or Mrs Ross, the housekeeper, would come in. They would change his linens, give him water or feed him small portions of soup.

Unable to help with this, Beth cooled him with wet cloths. She'd touch his forehead with the flannel. It seemed that this soothed him and, for a moment, secured him some peace.

At times Beth rested fitfully, falling asleep in the chair only to jerk awake. Often those first moments of consciousness brought with them panicked fear when she thought she could not hear his breathing and reached desperately for his arm, needing to feel concrete evidence of life.

When the doctor or Allie sent her to bed, she lay, unable to sleep, in the small antechamber connected to the bedchamber. It seemed that everything and everyone waited. Even the tick of the clock sounded as though it were merely ticking down long seconds, waiting.

Now that she knew that she might lose him, Ren's existence felt as vital to her as her own beating heart. He needed to be in the world. She needed him to be in the world. Even if they could not be husband and wife, she needed him to be in the world.

At times, Jamie would come in. He would stand, tall and shuffling behind her, uncomfortable in a sick room.

'Has he said anything?' he'd usually ask.

'Nothing sensible,' she'd say.

The doctor came daily and changed the dressing. Beth wanted to ask him if Ren would be fine, but couldn't find the words. Besides, she knew the answer: maybe.

Maybe. She hated *maybe*. It kept her suspended in this no-man's land between despair and hope. It filled her mind with what ifs. What if he died...? What if...? What if...? What if...?

Sometime during the third night, she woke with a start, aware of a peculiar stillness. She could not hear Ren's harsh breathing, or the thrashing of feet and arms. She stumbled forward, an urgent, uncoordinated movement of limbs. Something crashed, shattering.

'Allie!' she shouted. 'Mrs Ross!'

She found his wrist. It felt cool to her touch, but

she could not find his pulse. Instead, she heard only the thumping of her own heart.

'For goodness sake, stop crashing into things. You've already spilled the water,' Allie said, bustling into the room.

'Allie. How is he? He—seems different. Allie… is he…? I couldn't bear it—'

Allie pushed passed her. Time stopped, suspended.

'Don't fret yourself, my lady. His fever has broke, as my sainted mother would say. I think he is sleeping soundly.'

Beth breathed again, huge gulping breaths. She felt the tears spill, tracking down her cheeks.

'I'll get the doctor to make certain of it. But my mother took me to enough sick beds that I know when the fever's broke and that you may tie to,' Allie said.

'Thank you.'

'I'll come back and clear away the glass. You sit down before you hurt yourself. There's glass and water everywhere.'

Relief filled her. Beth sank on the bed. She had no choice, her legs were wobbly as a newborn calf. Tears tracked unchecked down her face. Her throat was clogged, sore as though swollen.

Reaching forward, she rested her hand against his forehead. Yes, it felt good. It was no longer burning hot or sticky with sweat, but instead felt smooth and dry.

When the doctor arrived, bringing with him that scent of ointment and tinctures, he confirmed Allie's diagnosis.

'He's out of the woods,' he intoned like a wise man with a prophesy. 'A lucky man. Lucky you came along when you did. Plus he has a strong constitution. It was touch and go for a while there, I'd say. Touch and go.'

'Thank you,' Beth said.

Again, she felt tears, hot burning tears, brimming over and trickling down her cheeks. Good Lord, she was becoming a regular fountain.

'There, there,' he said, patting her shoulders in a paternal manner. 'He'll be fine. The power of love does miracles. The power of love does miracles.'

'Yes,' she said.

Because she loved him. She could no longer pretend or hide from this truth. Nor did she want to pretend or hide from it. Love, however impossible, was love.

She loved him with her heart and with her soul and with her body.

Ren woke. His head hurt like some mammoth creature had jumped on it, was still jumping on it. He squinted. The blinds were drawn, but even the narrow cracks of light running each side of the cloth were too bright. His shoulder hurt. Both shoulders hurt. His back hurt. Everything hurt.

Still half-squinting, he looked to the chair at the left of the bed. It was empty. The pillow, likely embroidered by some long-dead seamstress, was indented as though occupied not quite recently.

But whoever had been there had gone.

Was it Beth? Or had he imagined her? He'd felt sure she had leaned over him, stroking his forehead. Her fingers had felt cool and her touch gentle. Sometimes her hair had brushed against his cheek. She'd smelled of lemon.

'Good, you're coming round,' Mrs Ross said, stepping up to the bed from some part of the room out of his line of sight. She was the housekeeper, a sturdy woman somewhat resembling a ship in full sail.

She did not smell of lemons.

'Mothballs,' he muttered.

'Pardon, my lord?'

He shook his head. He had not realised he had spoken out loud. The movement hurt his head.

'Now, you rest and I'll bring up some chicken broth. And would you be liking a sip of water?'

The water was cool. It dribbled down his chin. He tried to wipe it away, but winced.

'There, there, my lord,' she said, dabbing at his chin with a cloth.

Good God, he was not a child. 'Where am I?' he asked.

'Allington, my lord.' She was still fussing around with the damned napkin. 'You were attacked, but you're on the mend now.'

'Beth? She was here?'

'Yes. Her ladyship was here.'

He smiled. He had not imagined her presence.

'In fact, she found you. Very lucky you were, too. Goodness knows what happened, but likely the constabulary will want to talk to you.'

'She found me?'

'You had collapsed. You don't remember?'

He shook his head, again wincing. He remembered the report of the gun and pain and the bolting of his horse. And walking. And the moon.

'It's lucky that she did. And you've had us that worried, I can tell you. The doctor came several times and he wasn't looking none too happy, although he doesn't seem a particularly sanguine gentleman at the best of times. Anyway, you're out of the woods now.'

'And... Beth? Where is she?' he managed to say, his voice hoarse.

'I think she was going to come in later.'

'Now!' He pulled himself upright. The movement made his shoulder and arm hurt, a jabbing, searing pain. Pinpoints of light danced before his eyes so that he feared he'd faint.

'Your lordship—stay still, for goodness sake. The doctor did not say you should be moving around. In fact, he said quite the opposite. He said you are to lie still. He's had to put a stitch or two into that there shoulder and doesn't want you to do further harm.'

'I don't care if I broke every bone,' he muttered,

gritting his teeth as he struggled to swing his legs over the edge of the bed. 'I need to see Beth.'

'Good gracious, I cannot see anything that is so urgent that you would need to jeopardise your health. The doctor—'

'Is a bloody quack. Are you going to help me or must I do this myself?'

'I will get her ladyship, if you are so determined,' Mrs Ross said. 'I certainly will not allow you to reopen your wound.'

'Fine,' he said, any desire to argue squashed by the searing pain in his shoulder and a peculiar lightheaded feeling.

He leaned back against the pillows and allowed Mrs Ross to bolster them. 'But if she won't come, tell her I'm out of this bed and I will find her.'

'Yes, my lord.'

Beth entered his room. It had the stuffiness of a sick room, warm but with the lingering scents of mustard, arnica and other tinctures.

She stepped to the bed, carefully finding the chair and reaching to touch his hand. His skin felt cool, no longer sweaty.

He grasped her fingers. His grip was wonderfully firm. 'Beth, thank you. They said you found me?'

'Yes. What do you remember?'

'Not much,' he said. 'They took my money and my horse bolted. Badly trained beast.' His voice was husky, but had surprising strength.

'We have him. He is fine.'

'How did you find me?'

'You made it to Allington. Goodness knows how. When we arrived back Allie and Arnold went to rouse the household. I got out from the carriage and I smelled blood.'

'Smelled?'

'Yes, it has a distinctive odour.'

'So it really was you who found me? Not Arnold or Allie.'

'It was me.'

'Thank you.' His grip tightened. She felt that sizzling, scorching tingle at his touch. It moved through her, igniting something at her core.

'I feel you shiver. You *do* care,' he whispered.

She shifted, shaking her head and pulling her hand away. 'I care? Of course, I care. I want to be your wife and…and share your life, but I can't.'

'Why? After this, you're still saying no? I love you.'

'You do?' Joy grew, burgeoning, blossoming.

'Yes, unequivocally, yes. After I was shot, I knew I had to tell you. I love you. And you care for me, too, I know you do.'

'Yes, I love you,' she said quite simply. 'But love isn't enough.'

She remembered her mother's words. *'If you love someone you want what is best for them.'*

'Yes, it is,' he said. 'It is enough. It is everything.'

She shook her heard.

'Beth, what is it? What do you fear? That you will be a burden to me? Like your mother?'

'In part,' she admitted.

'But no one needs to look after you. You are not an invalid. You may lack your sight, but you are independent. You are self-sufficient. Good Lord, you're a life saver. You saved my life.'

'And if I fall? If I miscount my steps? If I do not see a carriage approaching, like in London?'

'You may get injured. Just like I got injured.

Just like anyone can get injured. Would you not want to be with me if I were hurt?'

Her eyes stung. She would want to look after him while she still had breath in her body. She would look after him to her very last breath—to the grave and beyond. She heard his movement and felt the graze of his fingers as he reached up to catch a tear as it brimmed over, trickling down her cheek.

'I have my answer,' he said gently. 'I do not fear looking after you. We will look after each other.'

'Ren, it is not just that. I cannot—I *will* not have children,' she said, the words bursting from her as though too long contained.

'What?'

'You need an heir. I want you to have an heir. I don't want the house or the title to fall to the Duke. And you want, you *need* a family, your own family. You've sought all your life to belong.'

'But why can't you have children? How do you know?'

She stood, and paced the seven steps to the window. 'My great-aunt was blind. And my aunt. I am blind.'

'So?'

'Years ago, Jamie made Father get this fine bull that he thought would make the herd stronger. He did this because he believed that the bull could transmit his strength to the calves. I fear that I may transmit my blindness to any children and I can't—I won't do that.'

'Beth—'

'No.' She turned. 'My mind is made up. I love you. I love you so much, but I cannot be enough for you. You need children. You need a family and I cannot give you children. Eventually you will resent me. I am sorry, but I will seek an annulment. I must.'

# Chapter Eighteen

Ren felt the words leave him. He saw the certainty in her face.

'I am so sorry,' she whispered. Tears shimmered.

He lay quite still. Physical and emotional pain twisted together so that he was unsure where one began and the other ended.

He wanted her. He wanted a family with her.

Wordless, he watched, unable to stop her, as she quietly exited the room.

Over the next few days, Ren started to heal. Physical pain lessened. His mobility increased. Thankfully, his right arm now seemed fully mobile, although the incision still hurt on his left.

Beth went to Graham Hill to meet with the manager. However, a sudden deluge of rain led to spring flooding which delayed her prompt return.

Mrs Ross relayed these details in crisp tones. He supposed Beth could hardly control the weather, but wondered whether she was glad of the reprieve. Perhaps he was, too. He needed to think, but her presence made thinking impossible. Knowing she was even in the building seemed to put him on a seesaw of hopelessness and love and need...

Time hung heavy. A constable came and asked questions. Jamie joined them and they went to the library and sat around the hearth. The constable was young and looked nervous, a twitch flickering across his clean-shaven cheek.

'Right, sir. I...um...just wanted to get a few of the details about the attack,' the constable said.

Unwillingly, Ren made himself remember that night. He described the public house. He described his ride and how he had taken the shortcut through the wood. He forced himself to recall the three men with their covered faces, their guttural voices, the glint of the metal, the flash as it fired and the acrid scent of its smoke.

The constable and Jamie made notes.

'Likely a robbery,' the constable said, nodding. 'A most unfortunate but random event.'

'Yes, most unfortunate,' Ren said, wryly.

'You said the voice was guttural. Do you remember what he said?'

'No, it's like a blur,' Ren said. 'Sounds…but I can't discern or make sense of them. I'm not giving you much to go on.'

'No,' the constable agreed. 'But I will ask around, see if anyone knows anything. Thank you for the descriptions. I will let you know if I learn anything.'

'Thank you,' Ren said.

The constable stood. Ren rang the bell and Mrs Ross showed him out.

'He won't discover anything,' Jamie said after the door closed. 'He doesn't have the mind for it.'

Ren shrugged and then winced. He was much improved, but some movements still hurt.

Jamie stood, as though to leave.

'You could review that gypsum experiment with me?' Ren suggested, suddenly not wanting to be alone with his own circling thoughts.

'I would like to do so, but I have something more pertinent and pressing to accomplish now.'

'More pertinent than gypsum?'

'Indeed,' Jamie said, walking briskly to the door.

So Ren sat alone again. He had certainly come to a sorry pass when he had actually requested information about bloody gypsum only to be rejected.

He wished he was well enough to ride.

Nagging thoughts circled his brain. Ideas for Graham Hill, thoughts of Beth, memories of his night with her, memories of that night in the woods, Beth's words, Mrs Cridge's words: *There is only one person whose opinion and respect matters in life.* Words, thoughts, ideas jumbled into a mad chaos so that he felt his head must explode.

He tried to read but gave up, laying down the book and leaning back so that he stared up at the ceiling. It had a crack resembling either the boot of Italy or a dog's hind leg. And now he was seeing random limbs.

As a child, his thoughts had sometimes felt this way; ideas and concepts spinning out of control, the very eagerness of his ideas rendering them incomprehensible.

Painting had helped.

He hadn't painted since that one failed attempt. But he remembered now how he had wanted to paint as he had stumbled through that blackened night. The regret had been huge, the feeling of a life wasted.

So what stopped him now? He certainly had nothing better to do. After a moment of indecision, he stood stiffly, aware of an awakening... an eagerness.

On exiting the library, he ran into Mrs Ross in the hallway.

'Don't you be hurting yourself now,' she said, her round face crinkling with worry. 'The doctor said you were to sit still.'

'Yes, and I'm seeing dogs and boots. Besides, I am not intending to do cartwheels down the hallway.'

'I am glad of that, but I doubt that seeing things will encourage the doctor.'

'Then the doctor will have to remain dispirited.'

Ren took the familiar back staircase to the nursery where he'd played as a child when visiting Allington. He stepped inside. It was dim with all the draperies drawn and had the stillness of a room long disused. He opened the curtains. Dust motes shimmered and danced within the shaft of morning sunlight.

He went to the cupboard where the paints and brushes had always been kept. He inhaled. It smelled wonderful, rich with the familiar scents of paint and turpentine. He pulled out brushes, charcoal, his old artist's palette. He had loved that palette. It had fit so perfectly into his childish hand.

Taking out each item, he laid them carefully on the table. He touched the brushes. He felt the heft of the smooth wooden handles in his hands and the prickle of the bristles against his fingertips. He touched the circles of dried paint, dusty polka dots on the palette and then eyed the white, blank potential of the empty page.

And then he felt it—that urge, that need to paint. It was almost visceral, like salivation at the sight of food.

The relief, the joy surprised him with its intensity. It was physical. His whole body relaxed as though he had been bracing himself either to feel nothing or to resist and now, now his breath came deeper, his shoulders felt looser and his fingers eager.

He grabbed the paper and charcoal, taking both to the low table beside the window. He'd sketch, he decided, smoothing out the paper with his good arm. He could not wait to bring out the easel or mix paints.

Pulling the paper forward, he ran a tentative, grey line across its width. That single line was enough. All hesitation left as he sketched with the hunger of a starving man. He sketched the horse standing in the far corner of the field. He sketched the stable. He sketched the large oak tree and the small wizened silver birch. He did not stop. It seemed he did not breathe. It felt like it did when he rode and rode and rode—as though he was immersing himself into something that was bigger than he was, dwarfing his pain and his emptiness.

The knock startled him. He felt as though he was being awakened from a long sleep. Everything seemed different and he found himself looking around the room as though it were an unfamiliar landscape.

'Did you desire luncheon, my lord?' Munson intoned.

'Luncheon?' he said blankly. 'No, I don't have time.'

'You are not eating, my lord?' Disapproval laced his tone.

'No.'

'Should I bring something up, my lord?'

'What? Yes, I suppose so,' he directed.

'Yes, my lord. What?'

'I don't know. Ham or cheese. And I need oil paints.'

'We have some, my lord.'

'They must be a decade old.' Ren said.

'No, my lord, Mrs Cridge sent a note both here and to Graham Hill instructing us to get some. She thought they might be needed, although I will admit to being puzzled. Anyhow, they are here.'

Munson went to another cupboard, producing the paints.

'Thank you,' Ren said. 'And I will have to thank Mrs Cridge. Oh, and bring flowers as well.'

'Flowers?'

'Yes.'

'Any particular type of flowers?'

'Colourful ones.'

'Yes, my lord, colourful flowers.'

Ren started to mix the paints. Even though his left arm hurt with the movement, he could not stop. The smell of turpentine scented the room. He loved the smell, he thought, as he pulled out his old easel, the movement both ungainly and painful.

With the easel set up and the paints ready, he rang the bell impatiently.

'Where are the flowers?' he demanded upon Munson's reappearance.

'I did not know the flowers were urgent. I just sent out one of the maids.'

'Of course they are. How am I going to paint them, if they are not here? Tell the girl to hurry up,' he said irritably.

'Yes, my lord. I will bring them immediately.'

Munson brought daffodils, bright yellow blooms, with leaves glistening with water droplets.

Edmund had liked daffodils. With care, Ren placed the vase on the table, before rummaging through the storage cupboard to pull out the atlas he and Edmund had used.

He ran his fingers over the soft leather and

then opened it. It smelled dusty. Ren smiled. He remembered how they would look at a random page, studying the contours of the land, the sea and the rivers, long winding, zig-zagging snakes. They'd pretend they were adventurers. Together, they had scaled high mountain peaks and taken tiny boats across open oceans.

Carefully, he placed the atlas beside the vase and then with equal care he mixed the colours. He needed just the right shade, a golden, sunshiny yellow that would create a wonderful contrast with the muted grey of the atlas cover.

He picked up the paintbrush. He dabbed the bristles into the paint. The bright yellow was vibrant against the tips of his brush as he ran it over the canvas in a slash of brilliant colour. The smell of the paint, the feel of the brush in his hand, the rustle of the bristles against the canvas sent a bolt of joy through him. He did not care that painting reminded him of his parentage.

He needed this. He needed to paint. It was a deep, all-consuming, abiding need.

When he had finished the daffodils, he looked through the window at the garden. In summer, it used to be so beautiful. It had been a fragrant place, resplendent with colour and filled with blooms: hydrangeas, roses, pansies, geraniums, petunias...

A thought struck him. He turned from the window. Nanny had always kept a looking glass on the chest of drawers. The top was empty, but he found it soon enough, stored in the top drawer. He picked it up and set it on a table. Then, slowly and with care, he stood before it, studying the image of his own face. He looked, he thought, older than his years. Lines bracketed his mouth. His chin was still bruised and purple from the attack and his expression remained guarded, slightly hostile and with an unwillingness to allow the expression of random emotion.

A tiny scar marked his chin where the boys at school had tripped him so that he had fallen down the stairs. The shadows under his eyes had doubtless begun all those years ago when they'd short-sheeted his bed or in the mornings when they had hidden his clothes and he had been flogged by the masters for being late.

Eventually, he'd taken up boxing.

But he'd lost himself.

Carefully, he mixed the paints again. He added reds, yellows and whites, dabbing and combining to create the right skin tone, slightly swarthy. Then, with equal care, he started to outline his facial features, his eyes, the aquiline nose which as a child had seemed too big for his face, but which he had now grown into. He added also straight dark brows, the angular cheekbones and the dark sweep of hair, stark against his skin.

The face in the mirror was that of a hard man, but the image he was creating also showed more: a conglomeration of the child, the artist, the adolescent and the survivor.

He had lost one identify, but this did not mean that he could not forge another.

Even after he had finished the brush work, he sat for long moments, studying the painting. Finally, he stood and washed out his brushes.

Ren rode with care. The roads were still muddy and he had no desire to exhaust or injure himself or his mount. Indeed, he felt somewhat like a fugitive having escaped the premises and the well-meaning care of Munson and Mrs Ross.

He went directly to Graham Hill where he was

met by Arnold at the stable. He dismounted cautiously, anxious not to reopen the wound, and then headed from the stable across Graham Hill's well-manicured park.

The size of the house always struck him in comparison to Allington. The latter offered more comfort. Graham Hill was larger, with its impressive front entrance, vaulted ceilings and marble floor.

'Her ladyship is in the study,' Dobson explained, as Ren entered.

'Thank you.'

He strode forward, pushing open the door.

'Beth, we need to talk—'

He pulled short. She was not alone. Jamie sat on the other side of the fireplace. He looked tired and appeared dirty. He had a scratch on his cheek and his trousers were splattered with mud.

'Jamie, are you well?' Ren asked.

'Yes, I haven't had as much as a cold for eighteen months. I would like to more closely examine this and determine if any foods might protect one against minor illnesses.'

'No, I meant—I wanted—I need to talk to my wife.'

Beth angled herself to him. He noted a conflicting mix of emotions flicker across her countenance. 'Hello, Ren,' she said.

'Excellent,' Jamie said. 'In fact, I am glad you are both here.'

'No, I meant—I would like to talk to Beth.'

'We have established that. As you can see, Beth is present, allowing you to converse. However, I need to also talk to you and this opportunity to talk to you together will save me time.'

'Right,' Ren said. He sat. He had no desire to learn about gypsum, manure or even the breeding qualities of cattle, but it seemed that he would speak to Beth privately more promptly if he listened.

'I have investigated your assault. Indeed, the perpetrators are being questioned by the constabulary.'

'You what?'

Ren gaped. If Jamie had said that he had taken up ballroom dancing, he could not have been more surprised.

'It was the Duke, of course.'

'It was? How do you know that? Isn't he in London?' Ren said.

'Deduction and the scientific method.'

'Please, Jamie,' Beth intervened. 'You are going to have to explain things better. I am as flummoxed as Ren. I had no idea you were even investigating. I mean, you usually only study agriculture.'

'Agriculture is preferable. However, I realised that our village constable lacked the mental capacity to properly investigate the attack.'

'So you chose to do so?'

'Yes, the conjecture that your husband was attacked as part of a random robbery was not sensible. Relatively few people go through those woods. During the last four days, an average of only three per day have traversed that route.'

'You counted them?' Beth asked.

Jamie frowned, an expression of irritation flickering across his features. 'No, Beth, that is not a sensible comment. You know I have been here some of the time. I organised a roster of village boys.'

Ren saw Beth's jaw drop slightly.

'Therefore, it did not seem reasonable that highway men would come from elsewhere to target an area so remote on the off chance of finding a vulnerable traveller.'

'No, I suppose not,' Beth said.

'Could they have been local people, desperate opportunists without any clear plan?' Ren asked, leaning forward, his interest piqued. 'The Duke's people are starving.'

'Their faces were hidden by masks. This indicates some level of preparation. I also interviewed people at the public house and they reported seeing at least one stranger to these parts.'

'You interviewed people? But you don't even like talking to strangers,' Beth gasped.

'The constable helped.'

At some later time, Ren would remember Beth's expression and laugh. She looked dumbfounded, as though her favourite dog had grown two heads.

He pushed this thought away.

'I still don't see how the Duke could have been involved,' he said. 'Isn't he in London?'

'He was, although he is at his estate now. Obviously, he was not the attacker. He merely organised the attack and paid the men to perpetrate the assault.'

As Jamie spoke, Ren suddenly remembered that

moment in the woods. He saw the cloaked figure with the masked face. He heard the low, guttural voice.

*'We still gotta kill him....'*

Before it had been as though he could hear only a dim distant echo, the sounds so indistinct as to be incomprehensible. Now the words became clear.

'The men, they said that they would be paid. They would get more money if they killed me,' Ren said. 'I remember now.'

'Exactly.' Jamie rubbed his hands together with an almost gleeful satisfaction.

'You think that the Duke would have paid them? That he wanted me dead?'

'That is my hypothesis.'

'You didn't accost the Duke, did you?' Beth asked, worry lacing her tones.

'No. He might have hurt me, if only to gain my silence. I felt it was better to remain unharmed so I could procure additional evidence.'

'So—' Beth began to say.

'I really feel that this would go faster if you would stop interrupting.'

Ren saw Beth grin and felt his own answering humour. 'Of course,' she said.

'As I mentioned, the constable and I went to the Three Bells Tavern. We spoke to several individuals about the stranger they had seen. Unfortunately, their descriptions were not helpful. People are remarkably unobservant. I really feel that schools and such should train individuals in the scientific method—'

'Please Jamie.'

'Right.' Jamie glanced at his sister. 'Anyway, the serving girl stated that there had been several thefts from the pantry.'

'Which must have been the men!' Beth said as though unable to contain herself. 'Maybe Ren had injured them and they had to hide until they regained strength so they stole food.'

'Precisely,' Jamie said. 'The constable seemed better equipped at locating them than analysing the complexity and motivation behind the original assault. Therefore, I was able to let him take over that part of the investigation.'

'And he found them?' Beth asked.

'Yes.'

She shivered, reaching for her brother's hand. 'Where are they now?'

'The constable made contact with Bow Street. I believe the men were going to be escorted to London for further questioning.'

'Thank you. Thank you for this.'

There was a pause. Jamie released her hand, reaching forward to poke the fire. She heard it crackle.

'But what about the Duke?' she asked.

'He is still at large.'

Ren saw her shiver. 'You really think he is complicit in this. Did the men say so?'

'I do not know. They are only just now being interrogated. However, there is evidence that they were being paid by someone. The Duke seems the most likely culprit, although this is more in the nature of a hypothesis as opposed to scientific fact.'

'I think he might be, too,' she whispered as she pulled a thread loose from her dress, wrapping it about her finger. 'There is an evil about him. It seems greater than mere violence.'

Ren reached forward, touching her hand and

stilling her restless movement. 'He will be stopped.'

'I worry that he is too clever. There will be no proof that he is behind the attack. It will remain a—a hypothesis.'

'In the event there is no evidence to connect him to this current assault, it would be illogical for him plan a second attack and hope to avoid detection,' Jamie said.

'I am not certain if the Duke is logical,' Beth said.

Her face had drained again of colour. He remembered how on that night that they had spent together, she had admitted her fear. He saw it again, in her quickened breath and the nervous movements of her hands.

'Don't worry. I will be fine. He won't jeopardise his own neck,' Ren said.

'I believe Ren is correct. The Duke will seek self-preservation above greed. I presume he hoped to inherit, in the event of your demise.'

'My guess is that his addiction to opium is impacting his solvency,' Ren said.

'Is that the sweet smell that is always about him?' Beth asked.

'Yes.'

Jamie stood, his movements as always brisk and businesslike. 'Now, I need to measure some seedlings. I have tried to increase the amount of nitrates and hope to ascertain the optimum levels.'

Beth nodded. 'Thank you, Jamie. This could not have been easy for you.'

'I find criminal investigation similar to science, although I don't think I would like to do it on an ongoing basis.'

'Let us hope that there is no need for you to do so,' Beth said.

'Talking about science, I could discuss the science experiment that I was pursuing with Edmund regarding gypsum and manure, prior to measuring the seedlings. I believe you had an interest in it.'

'Perhaps later,' Ren said and Beth heard that familiar ripple of mirth. 'But thank you. It is appreciated.'

'Yes,' Beth said. 'Thank you.'

After Jamie had left, Ren took Beth's hand again. 'We need to talk,' he said. 'We are going to talk. But I need to do something first. Stay here. I am coming back.'

\* \* \*

Ren dismounted and, after tethering his horse, walked up to the front door of the Duke's house. The bell was answered by a servant in a dirty livery. He seemed surprised by Ren's presence, stepping backwards and giving no opposition when Ren walked inside.

'His Grace is in the library,' he offered.

'Thank you.'

The residence had the size and proportions of Graham Hill, but there was a sense of neglect and sadness about it. The floor had not been polished. The banister rail was splintered, the brass doorknob tarnished and dust hung heavy in the air.

On entering the library, the feeling of neglect intensified. No fire warmed the hearth and long cobwebs were visible from the chandelier. The threadbare furnishings were sparse as though chairs and tables had been removed. The walls were vast and empty, rectangles of faded paint remaining as the only evidence of paintings removed and sold.

The Duke sat beside the dark hole of the hearth. The empty room made him seem smaller.

'Lord Graham,' the servant said.

'Still got use of my eyes,' the Duke said, by way of greeting.

He looked thinner and paler even compared to the night at the ballet. His necktie and collar appeared loose and his skin resembled that of a plucked chicken. His hands shook and Ren noted a sheen of perspiration across his flaccid cheeks.

'Ayrebourne.'

'To what do I owe this honour?' the Duke asked, casting his pallid blue gaze in Ren's direction.

'I thought you might wish to get dressed. I believe you may soon be getting a visit from the Bow Street Runners.'

The Duke's pallid eyes remained expressionless and he gave an imperceptible shrug. 'I may be getting visits from many individuals. On the whole, the Bow Street Runners might not be the most unpleasant.'

Ren walked further into the room. He sat on the only other piece of furnishing, a straight-backed chair to the right of the hearth. 'I suppose people who sell opium like to be paid promptly and become unpleasant when they are not. Really much better to make your tailor wait than the provider of one's opium.'

The Duke made no comment.

'I have heard also that one starts to shake if one does not get the dose of opium required. I had wondered if that were true. It would explain your desperation and your fast deterioration,' Ren said dispassionately.

Ayrebourne clutched the arm of his chair as though to prevent the shudders which seemed to rack him. 'You sound like your crazy brother-in-law.'

'Jamie is actually remarkably intelligent. You have been selling your furniture and paintings. Is your London house similarly denuded?'

'Why don't you and your pretty wife visit me and find out?' Ayrebourne spat out.

Ren stood. With one swift step he was beside the Duke. He leaned over him. 'Because my wife is not going to go anywhere near you ever again. And if I find that you have been within a hundred feet of her, I will not wait for the opium dealers to do their work. I will kill you myself.'

He saw Ayrebourne's hand shake and watched him swallow, the Adam's apple bobbing in his throat.

'For God's sake, man. Doubt I'll see her. Likely have to sell this place anyway.'

'Good.' Ren stepped away, returning to sit in the chair opposite. 'Now that we have established your immediate demise if you so much as think about my wife, we can discuss your estate. I will buy it.'

'The estate?'

'Yes.' Slowly, Ren pulled out the money order, holding it between his thumb and forefinger.

'You plan to buy it?' the Duke repeated, confusion flickering.

'Yes. I will buy this place. I will even offer you a fair price, given its dilapidated state. I have an advance here. It will enable you to settle your debts and keep your innards in one piece for the time being. You might even be able to purchase some more of your opium.'

The Duke licked his lips, his hand darting forward eagerly.

Ren smiled. 'Not quite so fast. There are conditions. First, you will provide me with a written confession that you were involved in my attack.'

Ayrebourne's hand retreated. He licked his lips

again. Sweat now formed in glistening beads across his brow. 'And if I do not provide this?'

Ren shrugged. 'I presume either the constabulary or your creditors will come soon.'

The Duke shifted. Instinctively, his gaze moved to the windows and doors as if he expected his immediate arrest. 'What will you do with the confession?'

'I will keep it. I will keep it to myself unless you come close to me, my wife, my mother or the tenants or any other innocent girl. If I hear that you have broken this agreement, I will give it immediately to the law.'

'Why should I trust you? You could go straight to the constable now.'

'I could,' Ren agreed affably, still holding the money order between his thumb and forefinger as though it was an object of great fascination. Very slowly, he shifted it between his fingers so that the paper crackled. He watched the man's pale blue eye follow the movement.

'I am afraid, Ayrebourne, you will simply have to trust me. It would seem that you are somewhat desperate for cash.'

'Fine,' the Duke said. 'I will sign your damn confession.'

'Good. Who knows, you might be able to settle your debts prior to your interview with the Bow Street Runners. I am certain you would create a better impression if you were less shaky and, um, sweaty.'

'What do you even want with this place?'

'Only to get you out of it. You must have thought all your birthdays had come at once when you learned I might give you Graham Hill. I presume my mother shared that titbit of information. And then you must have been quite desperate when I changed my mind and later survived your plot, staying alive so very inconveniently. Now where is your paper and ink? Or will you ring for some?'

'There.' He nodded towards a desk pushed to the wall and cluttered with books, papers and several dirty tumblers.

'By the way, you will vacate the premises by the end of the week.'

'By tomorrow, if you like.' The duke spoke in angry tones.

'Entirely satisfactory,' Ren said.

\* \* \*

Ren paused on the threshold of the library at Graham Hill. Beth sat in the chair beside the fire. The lamps had not been lit yet and the amber glow of the fire light cast delightful shadows.

His heart beat fast. He felt both an eagerness to talk to her, but also apprehension. If she didn't listen this time—

She turned as he entered. 'Ren?'

'The Duke won't be bothering us any more. I have convinced him that remaining in our neighbourhood is not conducive for his health.'

'He's going to leave?'

'Yes, I am certain the Bow Street Runners will be escorting him to London. However, even if he is released, he will not be returning here. I'll explain it to you later, but right now we need to talk.'

'No, Ren, you know—'

'I will not agree to an annulment. I will not agree to an annulment because I want to stay married to you. I love you.'

'I know, but—'

'No, I have listened.' He sat on a low footstool in front of her, taking her hands in his own. 'I need you to listen. I won't agree to an annulment because I love you and I love being married to you. I love everything about you. I love your spirit. I love your independence. I love your moments of anxiety and the strength it takes you to overcome those moments. I love that you think about things differently. And what you told me the other day was nonsense!'

Her mouth dropped. 'It's not.'

'When you were a child, you always said that you would not let your blindness stop you and that you were as good as the next person. It seems you no longer believe that.'

'But I do,' she said, stiffening in her chair and freeing her hands. Her brows pulled into a frown.

'So why don't you think you're as good as countless women who have sight but not an ounce of your strength and your spirit? You have worked all your life to prove that you are equal to any man or woman, sighted or otherwise. There seems to be only one person you still have to convince.'

'I cannot help it if you—'

'Not me. I knew you were my equal the moment you hit Edmund with that fish and don't tell me you didn't intend to do so. *You're* the only person you still have to convince.'

'I—am convinced. I travelled to London. I manage this estate and Allington. I found you. I helped to nurse you—'

'And you think that our child would be less equal if he or she were blind? You think you would be less of a mother and less of a wife because you are blind? You still think you are broken. You're not. People like the Duke are broken. You are whole and strong and I love you.'

Her frown deepened. She shoved one hand through her blonde hair so that it stood up, haystack-like.

'Beth, you gave me sight. For a decade I saw only ugliness and you gave me back beauty. None of us is perfect. Jamie is both brilliant and a fool. You see the world differently because you are blind and whether you know it or not that is a strength.'

'But—' Her lips opened. He saw her catch her breath.

'No, no buts. I love you.' He took her hands again, feeling their tremor. 'I was a man in hiding. Everything hurt and I didn't like myself. I tried to make myself into something I wasn't, something I couldn't like and I couldn't respect.'

'And now?' she whispered.

'Now I like myself. I respect myself. Whatever you decide, I will still respect myself and
my choices but, if you stay with me, if you love
me, I think we could give each other joy. We can
work together and make this place something important. We can be happy.'

Joy and hope filled her. She reached up to him,
cupping his face with both hands, running her
fingers across his jaw and gently outlining the
shape of his lips. 'I love you, but—'

'Then that is the only certainty we need.'

'And if our child is blind?'

'Beth, we do not have to have children. You are
enough for me. You will always be enough for
me. But, if we choose to have children, I do not
fear blindness. Our children will have strengths
and they will have weaknesses because they are
human. Our job will be to help them make the
most of their strengths and to overcome their
weakness. You can help them do that. You would
be a wonderful mother.'

'But I can't keep them safe. What if there are
steps...?'

'No one can guarantee a child will be safe. But I will do everything possible. Allie will help and we will hire as many servants as you want to keep them safe. There are always people to point out the dangers. But whether our child is blind or sighted, someone needs to point out beauty and to teach him or her to be strong and kind. You can do that. You can do that better than anyone.'

'I almost think it could work. I always thought that I could never be a wife or a mother.'

'You can.'

'You really do love me,' she whispered, the wonder of it striking her anew.

He leaned forward, cupping her face with his hands. 'Of course I do. It just took me a while to realise it.'

She smiled. 'And I have loved you, too. You taught me how to see the world.'

'And you taught me how to see beauty in the world again and, of the two, the latter is the more remarkable.'

He kissed her, exploring the intricate, delicate crevasses of her mouth, the soft, yielding lips.

'Ren, I never thought—I didn't think we could have a happy ending.'

Again he framed her face with his hands, his touch warm. 'But don't you know this is only a happy beginning?'

She smiled. 'And we can have everything.'

'Everything,' he said, running a row of kisses along the smooth line of her chin. 'In fact, I wouldn't mind having everything now.'

'You mean here? In the library?'

'Indeed, there is something about tossing books and papers aside—'

'It sounds very—spontaneous,' she whispered.

And then their lips met again. His arms encircled her and she knew. She wanted everything. She always had.

# *Epilogue*

The whistle of autumn winds blew outside the windows of the London house. Beth and Ren had travelled up two days previously and Beth was gaining more familiarity with its dimensions. They had spent only a short while there over the summer as the transfer of land to the tenants had taken most of their time.

The memories of those busy months gave Beth quick, happy pulse of joy. It hadn't all been smooth, but it was working. The tenants were happy. Jamie was being somewhat dictatorial about crops. He had a fondness for turnips, but Ren was working things out wonderfully. Indeed, the estates appeared to be more prosperous than ever.

Just then, the door opened outside. It would be Jamie. He had come up also and had gone to a meeting of the Royal Society. Apparently, his research in the area of gypsum and manure had warranted a presentation to the society which he would give the next day. She and Ren hoped to attend. Jamie had even written a paper, dedicating it to Edmund.

Dobson came in with the tea tray, closely followed by Ren and Jamie. Ren sat beside her. He took her hand right away, seeming eager to touch her. His was still cool from the temperature outside and she felt as always that immediate surge of comfort, joy and awareness. He pressed a quick kiss to her cheek, and her heart soared.

'All the legal formalities are almost finished. I am delighted to say that I hardly own any of Graham Hill, other than the house itself,' he said, accepting the cup of tea presented by Dobson.

'And society?'

'I had a few odd looks, but I think I shall recover. How about your day, Jamie?'

'Very interesting, I must say. I am fascinated with the different scientific areas which appeal to people. Indeed, I never fully realised the fascination of the stars.'

'Are you planning to expand your scientific interests?' Beth asked with some surprise.

'I will be building an observatory.'

'An observatory? Such an investment would indicate that you are quite serious about this science,' Ren said, his voice also echoing her surprise.

'Not particularly, but I think Miss Cox will enjoy it when she visits.'

Beth gulped, spluttering on her tea. She replaced the cup hurriedly on the tea table. 'Miss Cox?'

'Yes, I was actually going to suggest that you invite her to Graham Hill?'

'I—absolutely—I mean, once I meet her. Who is she?'

'I met her at the Royal Society, a sister of one of the Fellows there. I believe she will be at the presentation regarding gypsum. She has varied interests and found the scientific process I employed fascinating.'

'Then,' Beth said, 'I can only presume that she would be even more delighted to have the opportunity to actually see your lab and the site of the study.'

'Yes,' Jamie said. He stood. She heard his movement and the rattle as he replaced his tea cup. 'Well, you can invite her tomorrow. I'll just review my notes for the presentation.'

Beth listened to her brother's quick footsteps as he exited the room. 'Ren, is it possible that Jamie has a romantic interest in Miss Cox?'

'It is something which I always thought highly unlikely, but I've never heard him mention even a planet previously.'

'Indeed, no. Nor an asteroid,' she added. 'Although I don't know if it would be quite the thing for me to invite her immediately upon making her acquaintance.'

Ren laughed, bending to kiss her. 'Since when did either you or Jamie worry about whether something is the thing or not? Invite Miss Cox. It will make things interesting.'

'Ah,' Beth said. She took a breath, feeling the smile already on her face. 'I believe our lives may already be getting quite interesting in about nine months.'

She felt Ren turn to her, giving a sharp inhale of breath. He cupped her face tenderly. 'Really?' he whispered.

'Really,' she said, her smile even wider now, her heart fit to burst. 'I love you, Ren. Sometimes fairy tales do come true.'

\* \* \* \* \*

# LET'S TALK

# *Romance*

For exclusive extracts, competitions and special offers, find us online:

f facebook.com/millsandboon

📷 @millsandboonuk

🐦 @millsandboon

Or get in touch on 0844 844 1351*

For all the latest titles coming soon, visit millsandboon.co.uk/nextmonth

*Calls cost 7p per minute plus your phone company's price per minute access charge